For Andy
With ...

London's Gravity
A Novel

R.N.Lentell

First published in 2021 by:
R. N. Lentell

© Copyright 2021
R. N. Lentell

Cover Design by Tim Slade
ISBN: 978-1-5272-8761-7

Printed and bound in Great Britain by:
Book Printing UK Remus House, Coltsfoot Drive,
Woodston,
Peterborough PE2 9BF

For Gill and Nat

'One's first impression is of a heavy city, a place of aching heads. The very name London has tonnage in it.'

VS Pritchett (1974) *London Perceived*, pp 4-5, London: Chatto and Windus

Jack

Thornhill Square
1913

If Mr Gaisberg had been there with his recording equipment I wouldn't have to be writing this down, wouldn't have to be scribbling out my own account at the dark end of the year. But he wasn't there, and I doubt that he's ever even set foot in a piano factory. We have few visitors to the Kentish Town yard of the Brinsmead Piano Company, where I work, and he's not been one of them. Other people heard it, that monstrous music, but they didn't seem to take it in. Somehow they avoided properly hearing it, like I wished that I could too. All the wickedness underneath, that's what it screamed out, and even now I can't fathom why I was the one it spoke to.

It was late March. Mr Reynolds and I watched as Young George and Half-hand loaded another fine set of pianos onto the company's new lorry. Knowing we were looking on, George took his time to light a cigarette, before clambering up into the driver's seat. The pianos were part of a consignment bound for India, and it was good to see them leave on their journey to the docks. Mr Reynolds was the Master Finisher, and he went back to an upright piano he'd been working on.

But I hadn't got an instrument to finish. I should have had, but it was still up on the third floor. I said something like this to him:

'Where are they? I should have had that Style Thirty-Four by now.'

'Best go see,' he said, not looking up from the dampers.

Out in the yard I saw it pushed onto the hoist, but there was no sign of the men who knew how to move pianos. There was a couple of young lads.

One of them shouted out, 'Don't worry, Jack, we know how to do it.' Insolent little so-and-so. I should have been 'Mr Scrivener' to him. And they didn't, of course. They didn't know how to do it.

As I come to write this down, I've become aware of something else. I don't think I've imagined it. I've had a feeling that I had ... foreknowledge. It's niggling at me, this inkling that I'd been warned years ago, if only I could remember it.

Early on the Sunday after it happened, I left our house, squeezing past the battered baby carriage Priscilla's old employer had passed onto us when Alfred, our first, had arrived. On trips out, his place in it was now taken by the baby, Robert Ernest, just a couple of months old then. Those little ones were too much work for Priscilla to go to church, so I went for both of us, though to tell the truth it meant more to her than it did to me. We'd been married for four years, and had taken rooms in Brecknock Road, about a mile from Brinsmeads.

I walked down to Barnsbury, enjoying the stroll along Caledonian Road. It was a day of rest, so there was little traffic. It felt good to be without the noise and fumes of cars or vans. I cut through the gardens in Thornhill Square, hardly sparing a glance for a figure, more like a shadow than a man, in an old coat, crouched into one of the benches there. No doubt the respectable folk who live in the Square would get him moved on sharpish. St. Andrews stands on the northern side. It was my local church when I lived down that way. Mother and my sister, Alice, were still in our old rooms on Hemingford Road and I looked for them in the congregation, but they weren't there.

No, it's not our nearest church now, but we've formed a bond with it. Priscilla first saw it in 1907 when I'd taken her to Hemingford Road to meet Mother and Alice.

'It looks so much like dear old All Saints Church back in my village. We should get married here!' she'd said.

'All Saints is the real thing, Prilly. Seven hundred years old, isn't it? I won't say this one's a fake, but it's got less than

3

a century behind it.'

'They chose well then! Why go for a new look when you've got something tried and tested?'

'You're right,' I'd said, knowing it was useless to argue about it. 'Let's call it settled and it's one less decision for us to take.'

'Jack, I do wish we could tie the knot soon.'

'I know. I'm doing all I can, but it'll be a couple of years till I can afford it.'

She'd threaded her arm through mine. 'We can still look after each other, even though it's a long engagement, Jack dear.'

'Indeed we can,' I'd agreed.

So that's how it became 'our' church. Our wedding place, and where we held the christenings for Alfred and Robert Ernest. From that day to this: six years, more or less. And now, at the end of these short days, I find myself thinking again of the Grand Piano being rolled onto the hoist on the third floor of the factory. It was a special order, one of those smaller Grands – the Boudoir Iron Grand they called it, Style Thirty-Four, in an American Walnut case with wonderful inlays in a floral pattern. Such a beautiful thing. And even though I listened – had to, of course – I wonder now if even I really heard it and understood all the menace it released.

4

After the church service, I headed from the gate towards Hemingford Road. The shadow on the bench stood and moved towards me. Vagrants are a lazy lot, often as not responsible for their own misfortunes, but I still didn't know what to do when they asked me for money. Usually I ignored them, I mean wasn't I supporting a wife and two small children at the same time as saving every farthing left over?

'Hello, Jack,' said the shadow, 'I thought it was yer going into church.'

'How do you know …' I began as I stared into his face. It took me a second to realise who it was, since he was much thinner and much reduced from when I last saw him.

'It's Bert, Jack.'

Bert used to look after the dray horses, before the company went motorised. 'I see that now,' I said. 'I didn't realise you lived in this neck of the woods.'

'I'm roamin', Jack, roamin' on.'

'So what are you up to these days?'

'Trying to get in somewhere with 'orses. 'Orses is all I know. When I was your age I thought people would always need 'orses. And the men who look after 'em. But now … now it's all engines. Lots of blokes looking for positions and fewer than ever of them around. Went behind on me rent and got turfed out. I'm still looking. So I'm betwixt and between

5

right now – sort of.'

'That sounds rough, Bert. Good luck with the search.' I was embarrassed, hoping to bring our encounter to an end.

'Oh, I'll do stable boy, mucking out, groom, anything round 'orses. So in time I'll get in somewhere. Got taken into the sick ward, that one on 'olmes Road. They looked after me, got me back on my feet. But they wanted to send me down to St. Pancras, down to King's Road.'

'No! Not the workhouse?'

'The same. And I couldn't have that, see? I thought I'd be better roaming free. Though yer don't get yer 'ot meals on the road.'

I felt the question in the air, though I guessed he was too proud to ask it. I was going to pretend that it wasn't there, but an image came to me of Bert, powerful, high on the Brinsmead dray, clicking his tongue at the two mares. I fished in my pocket and found a silver threepenny bit.

'Thanks, Jack. Very civil of yer.'

'It's all right. Though I'll have to tell my missus where that quarter-shilling went.'

I greeted Alice and she put the kettle on, but Mother just nodded at me, as if her mind was somewhere else.

'She's somewhat vague today,' Alice told me. 'Not one of her best days, so I thought we should stay here and not go to

6

church.'

'I see what you mean,' I said. 'I'd no idea she'd got this bad. Is this how it is all the time?'

'Oh no, she has better days but then she may wander. So I have Irene from upstairs keep an eye on her when I'm out.'

'Anything I can do to help? Are you alright for money?' I wished I hadn't given the coin to Bert.

'You've done your bit, Jack. You've got a family now, and I've got some cash flowing in with … with one thing and another.' She smiled and nodded in the direction of the Singer sewing machine standing in the corner. 'Plenty of work coming in on the ties, and the hats – they can't seem to get enough of them.'

'Well, let me know if that changes.'

She's a year older than me, Alice, and we're close. She started working with Mother, sewing, just about as soon as I can remember. She always argued for me having piano lessons, although I never had very many until I got the apprenticeship at Brinsmeads, and then only because Alice told Mum that I needed to hold on to those pennies and not put them into the housekeeping jar. Yet, I knew that Prilly had never approved of Alice. We only spoke about it once, after I overheard her tell one of her women friends that Alice was 'no better than she ought to be'. I said nothing there and then, but when we were on our own I told her that I wouldn't have her gossip against my sister. I didn't often lay down the law to her like that, and she nodded, knowing that she'd overstepped the mark. Whenever they met, the two women were always polite, rather unnaturally so, but Prilly's censure hung in the air: in the reaches of my mind, I sensed that one day it might crash to ground, like a piano slipping off a hoist.

'So what are you going to call him then, Robert or Ernest?'

'If you ask me, then I'd say Ernest for sure. After Mr Reynolds, he's an Ernest. But Prilly's set on Robert so I expect that's what he'll answer to.'

'Mum and baby still doing well?'

'Very well, I think, Alice. Prilly's so tired, but she's wanted her own kids all these years. Yes, that's it I think: exhausted, proud, happy.'

'I'm making Alf a sailor suit, but it's not finished yet. Oh, before I forget, Jack, I've something for you. Would you like that scarf over there? I made one too many. No, not that one, that's for Frank.'

'Frank? You don't mean Priscilla's brother?'

'Yes. Do you remember at your wedding he asked me to run him up a tie?'

I hadn't remembered it. My memory went back to our

church on Thornhill Square, Alice, thirty-two then and still turning heads in a frock she'd made herself. I'd been pleased, our families getting on.

'Well, he liked that tie, and every now and then asks me to make him something else.'

I hadn't realised the two of them met sometimes, and I didn't wish to enquire further. 'And I like my scarf too,' I said, wrapping it around my neck. The mention of Frank Arnsby had introduced an awkwardness. Perhaps to get around it, she asked me about my job.

'How's things at the factory? Plenty of work on?'

'Not too bad. There's lots of competition but the order books seem fuller than a couple of years ago. It was grim after that German piano scandal business.' It had been in all the papers: the Guildhall School of Music hadn't renewed their contract with my firm. Their pianos would now be supplied by our main competitor. Brinsmeads had protested about the lack of patriotism in preferring a German company over us, but still our reputation had suffered.

'You should go and see your Mr Ronald and tell him he ought to order the Guildhall School's pianos from Brinsmeads again. He's in charge there, isn't he? He could wave his conductor's wand and it'd be done.'

'Hang on, Alice! The bosses won't want me poking my

nose into the business side. And he's hardly "my" Mr Ronald! I only met him the once. Anyway, it was his decision to take the work from us and give it to the Germans in the first place. I think we're stuck with it.'

A voice from across the room said: 'Bechstein'. It was the only word I heard Mother speak that day.

As I walked back up the Caledonian Road, I thought about Frank. He was handsome, charming, and unlike her other brothers, Ben and Edward, Prilly had Frank down as unreliable, feckless even. She was pleased when he'd got married to Lilly. 'Perhaps she'll settle him; I do hope so,' she'd said. The situation made me uneasy. There are times in music when the composer intrudes minor chords on a bass clef. It was like that: unsettling. I decided to put the whole thing out of my mind, and when I got home I forgot to mention Frank's scarf.

There was little enough time to dwell on family things. Brinsmeads consumed me. I didn't mind: it was endlessly fascinating. Most of my work concerned the fit of the mechanism that communicates the action from the pressed key to the hammer that strikes the piano wire. But not only that: Mr Reynolds taught me to listen to the instrument as a whole, querying the tone and playing feel of every piano that came my way.

Different smells wafted over the factory: aromatic resins given off by the timber as it was sawn and planed, shellac and linseed oil, coal smoke from the boiler room, which was fired up irrespective of the season. The steam it generated flowed through the huge cupboards in which timber bent to our design, and it supplied the gentle heat that caused the vats of glue to bubble. Although we used animal glues, their scent was faint and not at all unpleasant, once you're used to it. The Germans were using man-made glues, but we stuck to what we knew. Old Mr Brinsmead, the firm's founder, had known a lot about adhesives. In the last century he'd experimented with wooden joints and glues to see how much tension they could take. In a corner of a storeroom you could still see the rigs, some of them collapsed and crumpled where the strain of the piano wire had been too great. In the end he concluded that there was no alternative to using iron frames. They're heavy, but they can stand the forces racked upon them.

Over the next couple of months, Prilly said she felt her vitality coming back. 'Two's not twice the work of one, not at all,' she told me. 'I suppose I'm being spoiled; there never was an easier, happier baby than Robert.'

'He's always chortling when I see him nowadays,' I said.

'I thought Alf might be jealous but he loves to see that grin, just like me and you.'

'I'm going to put Alf in his sailor suit and Robert in the new baby clothes for next week's Mothers' Union bazaar. There'll be a photographer there. If the picture's any good I'll get a frame and make room on the mantelpiece.'

I snorted as I suppose I do when I want to say something but know not to. There was so much clutter on the mantelpiece already: our wedding photos, Alf and Robert Ernest as newborns, a strange piece of pottery shaped like a lighthouse that said 'Greetings from Herne Bay', and the cup without a handle in which we kept the pennies for the Prudential man. It was best not to interfere in my wife's domain, so I just said:

'Get two, dear. We'll give one to Alice. She'd love to see Alf in his suit.'

So the photograph stood in the centre, over the fireplace. Prilly and the other Mothers' Union ladies all holding their babies as they laugh at the photographer's joke; Alfred trying to say 'cheese'; pride of place was little beaming butterball Robert Ernest, gurgling in joy because the world was so perfect. I used to look with pleasure on the happy faces, and irritation that nothing had actually been removed in order to make space for the frame. But it's not there now, that photograph. Such a short time before it was packed away inside an old leather suitcase under our bed.

The Grand Piano was loaded onto the hoist on the third floor of the Grafton Road works. It was a special order, the Boudoir Iron Grand. It had a beautiful American Walnut case. I was looking up at it from across the yard, anxious to get the chance to work on it. It turned out the lads on the hoist had never worked with Grands, just with Uprights; they said they knew how to do it. But they didn't. Style Thirty-Four, a lovely thing. I could see what was going to happen as if time had slowed down. I wanted to shout out, but I suppose even if I'd been able to, it wouldn't have made any difference.

In November we'd begun to turn up all the gaslights at work so that we could see what we were doing in the early mornings and late afternoons. I was sighing in annoyance over a defective piano mechanism, when I noticed Mrs Evans come in from the office.

'Mr Scrivener, I've got a Mrs Smithson in the office. She says she's a neighbour of yours. Please would you come with me to talk with her.'

'Mrs Smithson? Yes, of course. Is everything all right at home?'

'Your wife has had to take the baby to the Infirmary, but let your neighbour explain it to you. Well, I suggest you leave your tools, I'll ask Mr Reynolds to take care of them later.'

I took up my coat and cap, the sudden tension in my insides making me feel I was going to vomit. Walking across the factory courtyard, I was trying to remember what Prilly had said this morning. Alfred growing out of his shoes, Robert Ernest looking a bit off-colour, some Mothers' Union friends coming over for a cup of tea: all the things from her realm that I rarely had to bother my head with.

I got the details from Mrs Smithson and then from Priscilla. Robert Ernest started crying, then he was screaming and hot. The women rushed their babies away. It wasn't our usual doctor who called, but a gruff Scotsman wearing a long coat. He examined the child in a skeptical way, until he looked into Robert Ernest's throat. He bundled him up and hurried him out of the house, pausing only to tell Prilly that she was to get herself to the Infirmary on Highgate Hill as soon as she'd arranged for a woman to care for 'the other bairn'. The diphtheria took our beaming boy three days later.

The Prudential paid out. That's how we were back, in pitch-dark style, at St. Andrews, Thornhill Square, on a gloomy November weekday. We walked through airs that smelt of soot alongside a carriage that conveyed Robert

Ernest's tiny coffin. The single black-plumed horse was restive and I wished Bert had been there to calm it. Alice held on to Mother, who thought it was someone else who'd died. Priscilla clasped me on one side and Ben on the other. She was crumpled up like one of old Mr Brinsmead's test rigs. Me? I had to be the man, which is to say, the cast-iron frame, hard and cold to the touch, standing the strain and making the world believe I didn't feel it.

The next month brought a slate grey Sunday. I was digging the square of earth that counts as a garden in Brecknock Road. Digging to make myself perspire, to make myself numb. Looking down, I found I'd turned over a couple of pennies someone had dropped there. I'd lost a child and found tuppence. With my thumb, I rubbed off the verdigris from one of the coins. It wasn't very old. It carried the head of Edward VII, and underneath Britannia was the year, 1906. I stood there, my face feeling the dampness in the air mingling with my own sweat. That's when it came to me, who it was who tried to put me on my guard: Mireli. I was gripped by the wish to hear again her exact words, to call them back as well as I could. More than that: I wanted to revisit those days before I was married, to build them up again from the fragments I'd recorded in my diary.

The piano was Style Thirty-Four, the Boudoir Iron Grand with an American Walnut case. I could almost believe that it was going to drift like a Zeppelin, though reason told me it couldn't. It glided off the hoist and seemed to float down three floors of space to the loading bay. But when it hit, that's when time suddenly ran fast again and the noise crashed in, the deafening bang, followed by ripping, splintering, and every note, every single one, sounded at once. It left an ominous minor chord in E flat hanging in the air. Threat and peril: I can still hear it, somewhere at the back of my skull. It hasn't finished with me. An omen: was it for me, for Priscilla, or for little Robert Ernest? For me, I suppose, but not only that. It was a warning to my entire world, for this whole stink-filled town.

City Road
1904

'I need a piano to go down to City Road. Today. Right away. And it's got to be perfect.' Horace Brinsmead had an upper crust English accent but his years in Australia had left him with an abruptness of speech.

'Yes, Mr Brinsmead,' said Mr Reynolds, wiping his hands on a cloth, even though they weren't dirty.

'And not a Grand, an Upright will do very well. What about one of those?' Mr Brinsmead was pointing to a batch of half a dozen Uprights in gleaming black that we'd just finished for the Guildhall School of Music.

Mr Reynolds stopped to think. I'd been working with him for eight years and I knew how his mind worked. It seemed wrong to take one of the school's pianos for another customer. Guildhall were regular buyers and we replaced a third of their stock every year. So he said something like: 'maybe they'll never be quite top-notch, sir, those Style X pianos. Oh, they're fine, strong, excellent for students to practise on, and most any other company would be more than content with 'em, but for us not quite tip-top. Is it not possible to take an X3 from the showroom, Mr Brinsmead?'

A flicker of irritation passed over Mr Horace's face. 'I'd

thought of that, but it won't do. We need to find one from the factory.'

'There's always George Grossmith's instrument,' said Ernest, nodding towards a Style Seventeen in the corner. 'That one's tip-top.'

'Good Lord! You mean I have to disappoint Mr Grossmith of all people in order to have the lady accompanied on one of our pianos?'

Ernest fell silent and I could feel his embarrassment. He didn't want to correct the boss again, having realised that Mr Horace was too new in the job to have picked up all the works jargon.

I said, 'it's just a figure of speech amongst the company hands, sir. We always call any finished, but unassigned, instrument "George Grossmith's piano". It's a joke that goes back some years.' He was looking at me blankly. So I said: 'I'm Jack Scrivener. I work under Mr Reynolds to regulate and finish the pianos.'

'Ah yes, Scrivener.' He went over to the piano, lifted the lid, and, still standing, played "A Wandering Minstrel, I" from The Mikado. Then, pulling a stool into position, he sat and played "Blue Danube" right through. He seemed to relax and when he spoke his manner reminded me of his father, old Mr Brinsmead.

'Good. Thank you, gentlemen. I'll ensure it's crated and sent down this morning. If you please, Mr Reynolds, speak with Mrs Evans. You will need to see to it today that the piano is properly set up.'

As soon as he'd said that I knew Ernest would send me. Neither of us relished working outside the factory, and he wanted to get back to the Grand intended for the White Star Line. 'Lord love a duck, Mr Reynolds! What's all that about?'

A little later I was in the office speaking with Mrs Evans. 'Mr Reynolds thought it best that I go. We're wondering, of course. What's it's all to do with?'

'You will see when you read the letter I shall give you, Mr Scrivener. Why it should all be so urgent ... well, that Mr Horace has not confided.'

She took a sheet of John Brinsmead & Sons headed paper, placed it together with the carbon paper, blank sheet and backing card and rolled them into the typewriter. Looking at her notepad, she typed out:

Frederick Gaisberg Esq.
The London Gramophone and Typewriter Company
21 City Road
London EC

19th October 1904

Dear Mr Gaisberg,

Following our conversation yesterday, I am pleased to say that you should by now have received delivery of a John Brinsmead & Sons Upright Pianoforte. The Style No. Seventeen that we have selected for you is of a highly robust construction, yet possesses a refined tone of a very superior quality. I feel sure that you will agree that the performance of this all-British piano far exceeds that of our various German competitors.

The bearer of this letter, Mr Scrivener, will ensure that the instrument is in perfect working order for your forthcoming recording session.

Yours sincerely,

Horace Brinsmead

Director

(Dictated by Horace Brinsmead Esq. and signed in his absence by Mrs Maude Evans)

Back in the 'Chamber of Horrors', which was our name for the spacious room in which we finished the pianos, I repacked my tool bag.

'It's the Gramophone Company, Mr Reynolds, they're the ones who're having the Grossmith.'

'Shame it's not the Columbia people.'

'Why's that?'

'Because they use the phonograph, what Edison dreamt up. He's got to be the best inventor there is: you know, electric light and everything. They say those machines give a better quality sound as compared to the gramophone. You should come down the Temperance Hall, Jack, we have one there sometimes. I'll never forget that night after the coronation when they played marching band songs. God save the King and all that.'

'Oh yes, I remember you saying.'

'They had some American songs playing the other night. Astonishing clarity and surprisingly loud, from that small cylinder thing. Made me wonder where such progress will take us all. Not that such contrivances can ever replace the piano, any more than the pianola has.'

'Do you remember who was singing?'

'Well, I'm not sure they said. You mustn't let big names and what have you get in the way of the sound.'

'But I'd still like to know who was singing. I mean otherwise it's like ... like a photograph in which you don't know any of the people. It doesn't hold my attention for long. But if you know who the people are, don't you look at it for quite a while?'

'Ha! The ladies do at least, as you'll find out when you get married, Jack! Last week Mrs Reynolds got the photographs of our niece's wedding. "Oh, look, Ernest," she says, "there she is, it was such a nice dress, don't you think? Doesn't the groom look like that man from the draper's shop? Do you think my hat was alright?" And on like that for a full fifteen minutes.'

'Then maybe I won't get married!' I said. 'Anyway, I've not met a girl I'd want to put the question to, and besides, I can't afford it, with what I pay to keep a roof above Mother, Alice and me.'

'That Annie you've mentioned, she's not the one then?'

I was always circumspect with him when speaking of girls, he being a teetotal man of strong religious views. 'We're just friends, Mr Reynolds, we're not courting or anything. She knows she can aim higher than me.'

'Just as long as she doesn't think you'll be leading her up the aisle when in fact you're taking her down the garden path.'

Two hours after that I found myself in a fog that smelt of tar, a couple of miles or so from the Brinsmead factory, from Kentish Town. I was on the top of a bus heading down City Road, squashed in between a man smoking a pipe and a woman who'd put on too much scent. I clutched my tool case and wrapped myself in my thoughts. I wondered what it would be like to hear my voice on the phonograph or to see myself walking along as if I was in one of Mr Muybridge's motion studies. It might be like a haunting, like seeing my own ghost. But it would be wonderful to listen on a gramophone to Paderewski, Rubinstein or one of the other greats of the piano. Of course, it wasn't likely they'd submit to the indignity of recording, or let their art jostle with the crackles that types like Harry Lauder and George Robey were happy to put up with.

Recording! This century is going to be like no other before it. Future generations will be able to hear it. They'll be able to see it as it really was, moving to the clatter of the film projector. It'll be the first century that will live on, forever and ever. Musicians, singers, people of prominence, they'll be immortal, like the Egyptian pharaohs tried to be. Immortality: isn't that why the toffs spend fortunes on getting their portrait painted, and why everyone – well, everyone who can rub a few pennies together – pays to get themselves photographed? It was a way of cheating death, wasn't it?

It'd been an easy run for the horses as they clip-clopped downhill towards the City. But now they were working to check our speed as the traffic had built up near the crossroads with Old Street. I clambered down at the stop opposite Bunhill Fields.

At the building, beyond the front door, there was a desk with a large doorman in a suit too small for him. He hardly glanced at the envelope I showed him.

'Mr Gaisberg? Top floor.'

As I crossed the hall he called over to me. 'Oi! Don't use the lift – it's just been cleaned – use the stairs instead.'

So I tramped up three flights passing two cleaning ladies on their knees scrubbing the landing hard and complaining to each other. 'The nerve of it, making us clean everything again! Who's they expecting then, bloomin' royalty?'

A sign read 'Studio: Silence' and I walked through the door into a large room. The first thing that drew my eye was a piano raised up on a square of portable staging. The stage was smaller than the width of the piano so the edges overlapped the sides. I saw at once that the instrument wasn't one of ours: it was a Bechstein. Nearby was a brass horn, a bit like the ones you see on gramophones, but mounted on a stand so that it was at head height. A tube connected the horn to a small but complicated machine, which I supposed was a recording appliance. The rest of the room held an odd arrangement of furniture: chairs on top of sturdy tables, high chairs like what you see against a pub bar, music stands, some of which were suspended from the ceiling on hooks. Cabinets held recording devices and gramophones, bookcases contained records in paper sleeves.

One side of the studio had been partitioned off to form an office. Through the window I could see someone inside and knocked on the door.

'Come in,' said an American voice.

'Mr Gaisberg?' I said, handing him the letter. 'How do you do? Jack Scrivener ... I've been sent by Mr Brinsmead.'

The young man in front of me stroked his chin as he read the note. 'As you can see, it ain't arrived yet.'

'I'm not sure why that should be,' I said, 'but if it's all the same to you, I'll wait until the men come with it.'

'Sure ... I'm pleased to see Mr Brinsmead is willing to trust a young man with this job. Very American of him, I should say. So, a piano for Madame Melba's recording tomorrow ...'

'What, Nellie Melba? Here? Tomorrow?' I blurted out, thinking that the charlady had been right about royalty. As near to royal as you could get without blue blood. Higher even: what was written about her in the music pages made you believe a voice like hers must have come straight from God.

'Yep. I see that he'd not mentioned it to you. That's good.

Perhaps you could keep it to yourself. If the word gets out, it'll spread like wildfire and crowds of admirers will lay siege to our offices ...'

'Of course.'

'In fact, I'm still guessing how Mr Brinsmead found out, except that he said there's an Australian connection between Madame Melba and his family. He's difficult to say "no" to, your Mr Brinsmead, don't you think, Mr Scrivener? He came over to tell me that she should be accompanied on a British piano. He was most insistent about it.' He turned back to the ledger he'd been examining and I realised he wanted our conversation over.

'Might I ask, Mr Gaisberg, if you would like the men to lift the Bechstein off the stage and to put the Brinsmead there instead?' It pained me to think of our Grossmith so ill-placed, but I'd wondered if the other piano had been lifted up to get it closer to the recording horn.

'Ah, that's a good thought ... but no, best leave it as is.' He must have noticed my surprise as he added, 'we vary the positioning of instruments according to ... several factors, and this time it might be best to have the piano on the floor.'

I went to the window overlooking City Road. There was little enough to see in the fog, but below me heavy traffic started, stopped, and started again. There were countless numbers of road wheels in this town, pulled along by how many horses? Tens of thousands? Perhaps a hundred thousand, all with people or loads to move. London, the centre of the entire world, and I'd been born into it! Not in the fashionable streets, of course, but in grimy Barnsbury. Yet here I was, on the fringes of the 'square mile', near the heart of all money and trade. I felt exhilarated: immortal Melba would sing to a piano of mine, or a least one that I'd worked on.

I enjoyed the feeling of self-confidence for a minute before I heard it, a muted growl like far-off thunder that lasted twenty seconds or more. I looked out the window, but there was no sign of the greater darkness that might presage a storm. Puzzled, I thought about the notes within that strange grumble. They'd been really low, forming minor chords that offered none of the prospect of release I felt when I heard thunder. There was something sinister about it, and, without being cold, I shivered. I stood there, gazing out the window at the parade ground opposite for another quarter hour before I heard it again.

'You hear it too, don't you, Mr Scrivener?' Mr Gaisberg was by my side. 'Not everyone does but to those that do, it's an unsettlin' sound, ain't it?'

'What is it? What causes that?'

'Progress causes it! It's the underground railway.'

'Of course! The City & South London, running up to Angel.'

'No, I don't think so. We have the Great Northern & City Line now. If I'd realised about it, the Company would have chosen a different home. Luckily, our mechanism don't pick up the rumble. Hope you don't have to wait too long for your piano.' He had his hat in his hand, and, placing it at a tilt on his head, left the studio.

Sitting on a chair, I took my tin from the tool bag and munched on a sandwich Alice had made for me. Even now, somewhere underground, men were hollowing out the city, eating up the London mud with spades and shovels. Progress. And with it, if you attune your ear, menacing sounds.

It was nearly three o'clock when I heard Bert and Half-hand struggling with our Style Seventeen, forcing it up stair by stair. I knew about piano lifting: the way gravity seemed to add to the load with each step up you take. I stood in the studio with folded arms.

'Hello, Jack, what are you doing here?'

'I'm here on Mr Horace's instructions to set up that piano, Half-hand. So kind of you to bring it to me before teatime. What kept you?'

'Traffic ...' he began.

'... 'orses.' said Bert. 'You lot never think of the 'orses. They've got to be fed and watered.'

'Looks like you're the ones that have been watered! How long were you in the Mother Red Cap?'

'Don't be like that, Jack ...'

'I'm the one that'll be here till late! Just put it down over there.'

But I wasn't there till late. At five, the doorman came in, with only half the tuning done.

'You there! Time you left. I've been told to shut up shop till the morning.'

He wouldn't budge when I explained the situation to him. 'Orders is orders. Off you go now.' So I had to arrange to be back at eight in the morning. Deciding to spare myself the fare, I began to trudge back up City Road. I was about to cross Shepherdess Walk when horses pulled out of The Eagle's front yard.

'Hey Jack! Wanna ride?' It was Bert and Half-hand on the company dray, even more well-watered than before.

'No, thank you.'

Bert took his pipe from his mouth. 'Let him go in and get his pint.'

'It's all he'll get nowadays,' said Half-hand, 'not like the old place before the Sally Army stuck its oar in. Then you really could get to ... pop yer weasel!' He gave an unpleasant laugh as Bert shook the reins and they moved out into the street with Half-hand singing in a boozer's slurred voice:

'Up and down the City Road

In and out The Eagle...'

Bah! I had no time for those two. Add up their ages, and they'd have a hundred years between them. They'd spent the time carelessly. They hadn't bothered to learn any sort of skill, unless you count growing muscle and getting on with horses as skills. No, they were last-century men. How would they survive in this one? They'd have no place in Mr Edison's world of machines and electricity. Mr Gaisberg would, and so would I. The pianoforte had drawn me in, and if I kept going, it would provide for me in return. New century or not, wouldn't people still want pianos?

As the road became an uphill one, I mean one that you'd notice, I sorted out what I wanted my work as a piano man to bring me. First would be my own home: nothing grand, but nothing poky either. Not too far from the factory, so that I could walk to work and not bother with omnibuses, trains and what have you. My house would have a drawing room. My own drawing room! Eventually I'd have my own piano in it. That was my second ambition then. Not for one of those cobbled together instruments you can get for twelve guineas; not one of those pianettes with the Whiteley name on it that people with no ear get for twenty pounds or so on the never-never. No, one day I'll have my own top-notch Brinsmead Upright. I'll invite Mother and Alice round and play Arthur Sullivan songs. Then they can see how far I've risen, all respectable, all by my own effort. And I'll have a gramophone, and a bookcase full of records. Whenever we want, Nellie Melba will sing for us. Ambition number three: the house will need a wife to go in it, and, God willing, a baby or two for us to fuss over. As they grow, the boys will have music lessons. If they've got talent, they could make music their profession. Otherwise, learn a craft – carpentry would be good – so they'd follow me into the piano trade.

So those were the daydreams I took back to Barnsbury. We have three rooms there. Mother shares a bedroom with my sister, Alice, and I have my own. We've only a couple of gas mantles, so tend to turn in early. I blew out my candle, settled back in bed and fell asleep in a minute.

As I stopped the morning alarm, I remembered that at night I'd been back at the Gramophone Company staring out at City Road, but it was bright sunlight. I'd opened the window and flown out over the cemetery at Bunhill Fields,

31

high above the pristine Guildhall and on to St. Paul's Cathedral. Then northwards to the great railway stations where the locomotives belched out an enveloping black smoke. I'd sat on top of Euston Arch, exhilarated. The city was all mine.

I'd only gone a few paces in the murky dawn, tool bag in hand, when I nearly bumped into someone going the other direction along Hemingford Road.

'Mornin', Jack, ain't ya going the wrong way?'

'Hello, Tom. No, I'm working down near Finsbury Square today. The job's overrun. Could you let Mr Reynolds know that I won't be in till later on?'

'You ain't heard then? I've been let go. The order book don't look too good – there's some others that'll be fetching their cards. We're being Bechsteined, I reckon. I'm off up to Collards to see if I can get in there.'

Tom's news had caught me on the wrong foot but still I managed to say something. 'I'm sorry to hear that, Tom, we'll all miss you. Good luck at Collards.' Worries about the future dropped into my head all that morning. At the new Angel Station, right at the top of City Road, I bought a ticket, stepped into the lift and fell deep under London. Even this early, the platform was getting crowded. That was the first time I'd been into the all-electric realm of the City & South

London Line and perhaps it affected my mind as we rattled along the same route that I'd taken yesterday by omnibus, though this time I must have been fifty yards under City Road. I wondered if Tom was right and we were losing out to the Germans. Bechstein pianos were very good, and sometimes they sold them for a price below that of our British equivalents. How did they do it? In my head I replayed the conversation with Frederick Gaisberg. He'd not actually said that he would use our Grossmith. In fact he'd avoided saying what he would do, but in my excitement at his mentioning Melba, I hadn't heard him. Did he think that German pianos were better? I arrived at Old Street Station, and, stepping out of the sardine-box carriage, my mood was as sombre as the faces of my fellow passengers.

I was early and the Gramophone Company building was locked shut. I walked up and down in the fog until the doorman opened up at exactly eight o'clock. I walked through the lobby and pulled on the lift gate handle.

'I told yer not to use the lift!' he called out, but I ignored him, operating the lever and rising up before he could do anything. Once more beside my piano, I opened my tool case, picked out the Brinsmead wrest pin tool, and restarted work.

Later on, Mr Gaisberg and a formally dressed gentleman came in and went straight to the office. Another hour and my work was done, so I took the stool from the Bechstein and played 'The old folks at home' on the Style Seventeen. Satisfied, I was wiping it down to get rid of dust and finger marks, when the formally dressed man came over. He peered into my tool case.

'Ah, you have a set of tuning forks, but observing you from the office I didn't see you make use of them.'

I wanted to say something like: 'those ruddy forks are as much use to me as a lantern on a sunny day' but instead I said: 'I have no need of them, sir. I sometimes make use of them for reassurance. Occasionally my own, but usually the customer's.'

'We have something in common then: absolute pitch. My name's Ronald.' He had a genial smile as he held out his hand. I was confused for a moment by what seemed to be an introduction lacking in propriety. But from a subterranean place of my memory I dragged up a name, Landon Ronald, the prodigious pianist and conductor. He must be Madame Melba's accompanist.

'How do you do, Mr Ronald.'

'I'd like to take your Brinsmead out for a canter,' he said sitting down, 'and I'll let you know what I think.'

After a few scales he told me that Edward Elgar was the greatest living composer, and launched into a piece I now know was the 'Enigma Variations'. I was awestruck. At first my ears told me that there were two or three pairs of hands, playing on two or three Style Seventeens. The emotion of it went straight through my chest and gripped my heart. I'd worked for ten years for Brinsmeads, because I'd spent two years in the soundboard workshop before training with Ernest, yet I'd never heard a maestro play. My own slight efforts, and those of any other pianist I'd heard, were nothing in comparison.

'I like this instrument,' he said. 'A light touch and a good tone for an Upright. You should be pleased with your work.'

'Thank you, sir. I hope it will play well for Madame Melba's recording today.'

'The most important thing for the accompanist is knowing what to leave out.' For a moment I thought he meant which piano to leave out, and later I wondered again, even though he said, 'it's the vocalist who must shine; excuse my voice.' He began 'Oh, lovely night!' softly singing and humming the soprano's part, three octaves below what would be expected of Nellie Melba.

My tool bag was heavy in my hand as I stood waiting for the bus up to Camden Town. I looked back towards the Gramophone Company's building opposite: there was a gulf as wide as City Road between me and Landon Ronald. We were two men who held the pianoforte close to our hearts, but next to him I was as unrefined as Bert and Half-hand were to me. Mind you, he seemed to appreciate the workmanship that went into making an apparatus to which only someone like him could do full justice. That's what I've found at Brinsmeads: craft and hard work earn the gentleman's respect.

In the days that followed the production of the Melba records, the papers were full of praise. At first I thought that any day now, Mr Brinsmead would tell us that Melba had sung to our Grossmith, and we should be acclaimed along with her. Or perhaps I'd be called into the office to explain why the Bechstein had been chosen. If he'd bought the record, perhaps Mr Brinsmead couldn't tell which instrument was immortalised there, maybe nobody could. Ernest said that the gramophone people don't just sell their discs here and in America. There were gramophones on the continent too. He thought they'd keep quiet about which piano they used.

'Think on it Jack, they want the Germans to buy the records too.'

Sometimes I woke at night, imagining that a black dog was growling by my bed. Then bad thoughts came to me: 'If you'd done a better job on that Style Seventeen, Jack Scrivener, they definitely would have used it to accompany Nellie Melba. Mr

Horace would have announced it and advertised it too. Whenever people thought of her they'd know she'd sung to one of our pianos.' But nobody else seemed to have questioned my work, and, if anything, my stock within the firm had risen. I know that from what happened a few months after, when we were getting up in daylight again.

'Thank you for dropping by the office Mr Scrivener,' said Mrs Evans. 'Mr Brinsmead wishes you to carry out a home visit.'

She must have seen from my face that it was not a very welcome wish.

'Well, you may come to think of it as something of an honour. Mr Duffield, he's a highly significant man in the world of commerce, apparently, he has one of our Grand pianos. He's hosting a soiree next week. Landon Ronald himself will play. So Mr Duffield asked us to ensure the instrument is in tip-top order and it was immediately thought that you were the man for the job.'

It was a Holland Park address. The piano had been little played. I took off the lid and set out my tools behind me. I heard a woman's footstep in the room. I didn't look up and started to feel behind my back for the wrest pin key. The implement was lightly placed onto my hand. Turning round, I saw there was a housemaid in the lounge. It was she who had picked it up and given it to me.

'Seemed to me that it were that thing you were feeling for.' She had a country accent.

'You were quite correct,' I said.

'Miss Sutton asked me to see if you would like a cup of tea.'

'Miss Sutton?'

'She's cook in this house.'

'Well, yes, I should like that. Two sugars please.'

'We always provide a sugar bowl.'

A few minutes later she returned with a tray. 'Is this how you earn a crust then, tuning pianers?'

'No, not exactly. I finish pianos in the Brinsmead works and there's a lot more to it than tuning them. It's rare that I make a home call such as this.'

'Is that a responsible job then?'

'I suppose in some ways it is. A great man such as Mr Ronald, well, he should only be asked to play upon a perfectly adjusted instrument. Will you have a chance to listen when he plays here?'

'I don't suppose so, there'll be work to do.'

'If the lady of the house is kindly disposed to you, then you should ask if you could. I happen to have heard Mr Ronald play, and I can assure you he won't disappoint.'

I drank my tea and found a white lie crossing my lips. 'You know, sometimes the intensity of a maestro's playing can send a piano out again. It might be a good idea if I come back after the performance. If I agree to do that, you must agree to bring me a cup of tea again. My given name's John but everybody calls me Jack, Jack Scrivener.'

'Everyone here knows me as Priscilla. You may call me Miss Arnsby.'

By the time I'd finished with the Grand piano, there was hardly enough time left in the day to go back to the factory. I walked through Hyde Park to Soho to buy a sheet or two of music. It was something I liked to do when I felt I could spare a shilling or two. I would join the small company of men who leafed through the slim volumes in the music shops, though I always had the nagging concern that I might be mistaken for one of those who had less elevated reasons for visiting that part of town. In Bowerman's on Poland Street I found a copy of 'The Egyptian Patrol'. It was in poor condition and they sold it me at half price. Metzler's was round the corner in Great Marlborough Street. I hadn't been inside before because they sold their own pianos and I didn't want to support our competitors. But their window displayed an open book of gramophone records, the mauve labels catching my eye. They were the ones Melba had made for the Gramophone Company that day at City Road. I opened the door, and pushed past the Metzler Uprights and some small American pump organs. In the gramophone section I gazed at the Melba recordings. If I ever did get to listen to them, I wondered if my ear would be able to tell which piano had been used. But each record cost a whole guinea. Who could afford that? It was half a week's wages for a man like me. So I progressed to the sheet music counter and bought a copy of songs for piano taken from Gilbert and Sullivan's 'The Sorcerer'.

A finely dressed young lady had come into the shop. I thought she was pretty, and her smile as she returned my glance was so charged that I must have blushed. I saw her amusement, realising that she was no more high-born than I was. Her confidence lit a fire. On my way back home a fresh determination seized me: I would take charge of my life. After all, I'd set up two pianos now for Mr Ronald, and that must count for something. Somehow, one day, I'd be able to afford to buy a new piano, and a gramophone, even if it was second-hand. It might be imprudent to write this down, but interspersed between these noble resolutions were baser things: memories of Annie kissing me as she stepped from her tin bath. And my imagination ran to another girl undressing: falling to the floor was the housemaid's uniform that Priscilla Arnsby so pleasantly filled out.

Wigmore Street

1906

I hurried across Regent's Park, my bag of piano tools in my hand. I saw them from a little way off and found my feet slowing out of curiosity. Three young women, brightly dressed in the gypsy fashion, were sitting crosslegged on the grass, using shawls against the morning dew. They were taking heathers from a bag and winding wire around the stems. I supposed they'd been to Covent Garden flower market early in the morning and were now making these offerings for buttonholes and hats.

'Fancy a lucky heather, Mister piano man?' said one. Her accent was strange to me: Irish, but there was something else as well, that I couldn't place. She was one of the younger two, who looked liked twins. They fluttered their eyes at me, but their ages were hard to guess. Perhaps they were still children, just on the cusp of womanhood. I stopped.

'I'm late.'

'Tommy piano man late to get to work.'

The other twin was studying my face. 'He's not a Tommy, he's a Johnny,' she said.

Then the older girl spoke. 'He's a Jack.'

This young woman seemed more than pretty to me, dark

and with deep green eyes. I was torn between my wish to look at her and my anxiety at being late for work. I nodded that her guess was true.

'Mireli's got it! He's a Jack!' said the first twin.

'Not a Tommy, or a Johnny but a Jack!' called out the twins together. 'Off to your work in Oxford Street, Piano Jack.'

The older girl laughed as she said: 'Not Oxford Street, Wigmore Street. Run away to your showrooms in Wigmore Street, Piano Jack,' she said. 'Maybe I'll find you when your work is done!'

As I walked away I heard them call after me: 'Not a Tommy, or a Johnny, but a Jack, Jack, Jack!'

There was something uncanny about how those girls had come to know things I'd not told them. There must be an explanation, and I tried to work out how they'd done it. It was easy for them to guess how I made my living, thinking about how I was dressed today, and the characteristic leather tool bag I carried. And I supposed they tried out the most common names on me first of all. I thought I'd remained impassive, but something I did must have given out that the twins' name guesses were wrong, and that the second guess was better than the first. And I reasoned that once the older girl had sensed that Oxford Street wasn't my destination, then

Wigmore Street was the best bet, because that's where the big piano firms were. Our premises, at numbers eighteen to twenty-two, were a couple of doors down from Kemmlers. Opposite, Maxwell and Whelpdale sold their Blüthner pianos. But the biggest company there nowadays was Bechstein, a few doors away from us on the other side of Wimpole Street. Over the course of my irregular visits to our showrooms, I'd watched them build their Bechstein Hall, and walked past the posters that announced the succession of luminaries performing there.

Perhaps I'd thought it through, but I still felt unnerved by that morning's encounter. Or should I say, even more unnerved? I'd been woken in the small hours by gaslight and voices seeping in from the living room. Coming out in my pyjamas, there was Mother, still in her nightdress, sitting at the sewing machine. She was talking to Alice.

'I promised John I'd let out the waistband of his trousers.'

'No, you didn't.'

'You're not him. You're not John. John's my husband.' My sister and I exchanged worried looks. Our father had been dead for twenty-five years.

'I think she's sleep-walking,' she said. 'Come on, Mum, I'll take you back to bed.'

But Mother wouldn't go. In the end I put the kettle on and

made her a cocoa drink, and at last she allowed Alice to take her back to their bedroom.

'I don't think that was sleep-walking, Alice, I think something's happened.' Mother was still confused in the morning, but I couldn't stay to help. Although the showrooms started work an hour later than the factory did, it was a longer walk, so I still rose at half past five.

'Drat! I've left those felts at Grafton Road. I'll have to pick them up first,' I'd said, rushing out of the house with only a slice of bread as breakfast.

For all the times I'd worked at our showrooms, it was only the second time I'd walked there from the factory, since I usually went straight from home. That first time I'd walked with Ernest and old Mr Brinsmead. When I'd then strode down Wigmore Street with them, I was a lad of twenty and it'd seemed impossibly grand to me. There were fine shops catering for ladies whose carriages would wait whilst they were inside making their purchases. Even in our showrooms I'd felt like an impostor, fearing that someone would cry out that I was posing as a salon citizen, when in fact I came from a street in grubby Barnsbury. Wigmore Street had always struck me as perfect: mainly shops and a few expensive residences. Yet someone must have decreed that the street was an unfinished work, since builders were rarely absent from one or other of its properties. They tore down the pride of previous generations, and laboured to build anew to suit the taste of their current masters. Even today, workmen were shouting out as they struggled to complete a huge new shop for Debenham and Freebody. I couldn't remember any more what had been there just a year or so before.

'Not like you to be late, Jack,' Ernest said as I put my tool bag down.

I told him of my troubled start to the day. 'Mr Reynolds, I wonder if you've ever bought one of those lucky heathers the gypsy women sell? There were some of them in the Park, making up the sprigs. I always wonder what to do when I'm asked for money. If I give it, I feel a fool; if I don't, I feel hard-hearted.'

'So they're still doing that, are they? Lucky or unlucky, that's got nothing to do with it. But yes, sometimes I've bought one. When I thought that possibly the woman needed the ha'penny more than I did.'

The Brinsmead Hall was at the back of the showrooms, nicely set out in a semi-basement with daylight coming through leaded windows. It had been built as a practice and performance space, with ample room for an audience of more than a hundred people. Of course, it couldn't compare with the Bechstein Hall, which must have been four times the size.

Since I'd been coming to Wigmore Street, our firm had never held a public performance, and one of the older shopmen told me they didn't have a licence like Bechstein did. At lunchtime Ernest and I headed to the Hall. It tended to be used as an unofficial storage space, and we usually ate our sandwiches amidst an assortment of boxes and pianos. I was surprised to see that it was now spotless and free of clutter. New chairs had been acquired, ready to be set out in rows.

'Looks like Mr Horace is planning a show or something,' I said to Ernest.

'He is. Saturday week. It's by invitation only. I understand it's by way of thanking our dealers, and what not. There'll be some newspaper men there too, so we should get a mention in print.'

'Do you know who's playing?'

'In fact I do. It's George Grossmith. He's quite a draw, though like all of us, he's not getting any younger. So it will be good to hear him before he gives it up.' Ernest looked awkward at this point. 'The fact is Jack, I've been invited, along with my missus, and a few of the most senior craftsmen.'

'Oh, I do hope you both go, it'll be a wonderful evening. I'm green with envy. I'll be thinking of you over supper with Mother and Alice!'

'We're going, alright! Umm, I took the liberty of asking Mrs Evans if they might be able to spare a couple of places for you. She thought so, as long as we keep quiet about it. They do think well of you, you know. You could bring that Annie of yours.'

I was amazed and embarrassed at the same time, and stuttered out my thanks. Underneath, an anxiety was opening up for me: I wasn't comfy with the thought of bringing Annie. It was difficult to put into words because she was a lovely girl in so many ways. It wasn't her fault that she'd never had the chance to learn how to behave around people who'd had a proper schooling. I thought that she wouldn't know what to do, and that she might show me up somehow. I told Ernest that perhaps it wouldn't be her cup of tea. He gave me a piercing look.

'It'll be nice to see Alice with you then.'

I'd another idea, but I kept it to myself.

'It was the Style Forty-One. That's what brought you to notice, and brought us down here.'

'What's that, Mr Reynolds? Oh yes, 44906. I'll never forget that number.'

'I was proud of you, trusting your ears, and doing something about it.'

'I was only doing what you'd taught me. I thought if you'd

not been off sick that day it's what you'd have done.'

It had been in 1900, in the 'Chamber of Horrors'. It was as always: old man Brinsmead greeted the good pianos with a simple grunt, and there was a storm about each defect he found with the others. He'd got to that Style Forty-One Grand, inspected and played it, and moved on to the next. My heart had been in my mouth: I'd heard a defect in the treble. I'd breathed a sigh of relief then, but the thing worried at me all day long. I'd got up at five o'clock the next day and was working on the Grand before any of the men were in. It had only just gone seven a.m. when I heard my employer's commanding voice right up close.

'I passed that one yesterday. Why are you mucking around with it?'

I'd stood up. 'Yes, Mr Brinsmead, and I thought I could hear something not right in the treble. I couldn't rest easy thinking it might pass out from here less than perfect, so …'

I could see a moment's indecision on his face, as if he was torn between a feeling that he should scold me for my insubordination and a worry that he might have missed a fault. After a second he spoke. 'Play it now then, Scrivener.' The two of us had never exchanged a word before, yet he'd known who I was, just as he probably could put a name to the face of every one of his workers.

I'd played, staying right up at the top octave. 'Hear that sir, that there: it's not as it should be.' He'd been listening intently, but he didn't say anything about the defect, and I wondered if he'd actually heard it.

'You'd better sort it out then,' he'd said, before resuming his factory round.

'Mr Reynolds, you know when Mrs Evans came in carrying that note, did you realise we were wanted in the showrooms?'

'I wondered,' said Ernest. I thought it could only be that. If I remember right, the note didn't say much, something like: John Brinsmead Esq. would be obliged if Messrs. Reynolds and Scrivener would meet him in the office tomorrow, eight a.m. sharp. Suits are to be worn.'

'Ah, gentlemen.' That was all he'd said the next morning, reaching for his hat. 'We're going for a walk.' As the three of us set off down the Prince of Wales Road, Mr Brinsmead held forth on other British piano manufacturers. There were more than one hundred makes in London alone, a number he'd dismissed as ridiculous. He had an encyclopaedic knowledge of the larger firms, most of whom he thought produced inferior instruments. Stopping for a moment to let a smokey Great North Western train pass under the bridge letting into

49

Regent's Park Road, he'd told us that Broadwoods were the only other British company that had 'class'.

We'd walked briskly down Primrose Hill towards Regent's Park. Perhaps we looked like a family group: the old man was the wiry grandfather, his grandson a youth of twenty years, his son in middle age. Mr Brinsmead had continued to expound on piano manufacture, and then he'd told us what our walk was all about.

'In the Empire of the Piano, gentlemen, the ear is master of us all. Yet in its eighty-sixth year, perhaps my hearing can be forgiven for not being what it was when I was your age. I've decided that we should have a second check on all pianos in the showrooms. We shall walk on to Wigmore Street. Each of our instruments must be one hundred per cent, gentlemen, one hundred per cent. We cannot afford the smallest slip in view of what is going on down the street.'

So that's how we came to be at the showrooms every now and then. Mr Horace had continued the practice, and Ernest and I checked the showrooms' pianos a few times a year, depending on the work we had on at the factory. Sometimes we went over to Bechsteins and tried out their instruments. It always gave me food for thought.

'Some of those pianos are nearly as good as ours, don't you think, Mr Reynolds?'

'You're right, they're pretty good.'

But I'd be thinking, 'the Grands are better; the Grands are better than ours.'

The thing I wouldn't do is to give them money for a concert ticket, even if I'd had it to spare. So I was missing them all, from Busoni to Godowsky whose forthcoming concert they were even now promoting.

The Brinsmead showrooms closed at six and I headed home. Whilst I was working I'd been able to shut things out. Now, as I hurried towards the Euston Road, I was worried about Mother and about how Alice was coping with her. As I stepped by Fitzroy Square, I heard my name called.

'Hello, Jack. Stayed at work till they locked the doors?'

'Oh, Mireli, isn't it?' The twins were a few yards behind, their shawls over their baskets.

'I was waiting for you to come from Wigmore Street. And you have.'

'How did you know I'd come this way?'

'Because. Because the Walking People know a t'ing or two, Piano Jack. Buy a lucky heather from me, even though you can see that I'm the one who ain't had much luck today.' Her basket was still quite full of sprigs.

'Hmm, perhaps you need the ha'penny more than I do,' I

said, holding out the coin.

Mireli shook her head. 'It's tuppence. Tuppence for you, Jack, and a bargain too.'

'Tuppence! You must think I'm an idiot! That's no bargain.'

'Because I'm throwing somet'ing in wit' it. Somet'ing that usually costs t'ree pennies.'

I was immediately intrigued and suspicious too.

'He t'inks it's a kiss,' giggled one of the twins. 'He'd pay it too. He likes you, Mireli, he wants you to go wit' him!'

'Oh, if only I could!' I heard both the mock and the wistfulness in her voice. 'It's not a kiss. You must let me read your palm.'

'An' she never reads for gadje; she's taken a shine to you, Mister,' said the twin.

'Why me, why my palm?'

'Because. Because the Walking People know a t'ing or two, Piano Jack.'

I put my bag on the pavement, found a couple more coins in my pocket and handed them over to her. The twins huddled close, dropping their baskets to the ground. Both of them were empty. I snorted in annoyance as I realised that they'd given their unsold heathers to Mireli. The three of them had had pretty good luck that day.

It was intimate, Mireli taking my hand, as if, without meaning to, I'd allowed her to step close to my heart. I thought of Annie, and then of Priscilla. Yet I was uneasy because part of me wondered if it was all a routine designed to make me give myself away, just as I'd done when we'd met in the park.

'Do you want me to tell you them all, Piano Jack? Or just the happy ones?'

'Tell me what you see. Happy or not.' I told myself it was all nonsense.

'You're a practical man. Your life is concerned wit' wood and wire and such.'

'Of course,' I said, 'I work with pianos; anyone who knew it could say so without reading my palm!'

'Shhh! You see your path set out: learn and ply your trade, build and prosper. You have set your feet firm on the ground, Piano Jack. And yet … you don't admit it, even to yourself, but you're aware of another worl'.' Her slender forefinger traced a line on my left palm. And then she moved back to my right hand. 'Ha! Or maybe trut' is, it's aware of you.'

'What other world? What do you mean?'

'I mean the worl' of the noabyri. It's still here, underneath.'

'The noa … what?'

'There's a spirit in the swamplands, Piano Jack. We know it. When we wander in our country, some people see him walking, like a will-o-the-wisp. And there's a few that have the ear to hear his call.'

The twins said something to each other in their tongue. There was excitement, or maybe unease, in their faces.

Mireli put her finger to her lips.

'And what did he say? What are you telling me?'

'Your great London, rulin' half the worl', it isn't builded on rock, but on bog. You're the staunch man building up his life, t'inking he's on solid ground. All around you swirls, Piano Jack. What's underneath sees you. You'll hear him speak one day.'

What a nonsense! She must have seen disbelief on my face as I asked her to tell me about what the future held in store for me. 'And what else about my life? What about love?'

'The heart line is strong and steady.' Mireli moved her gaze between my palms. A woman will love you and give you child'en.'

Despite myself, I was pleased. 'How many children?'

'T'ree or four. And before you ask, I can't tell if they be boys or girls. Do you t'ink it good news, the child'en?'

'Of course! What else do you see?'

Mireli told me more of my character, but I can't remember

now what she said. She studied my palms one last time.

'T'ings from underneath can push into our worl', you know.'

'Can they?'

'Oh, the breat' of the marsh can raise a breeze that sets a man on a fair course, helps him build his life up high. And he wouldn't know it, see? Have you never t'ought what it is that lifts you up in your dreams? You fly then, don't you? Or have you t'ought where you got the music from? Not from your Ma or Pa, was it? Your Pa passed long time since, didn't he?' She went on before I could think of anything to say. 'Or happen, t'ings there whip up a quicksand and drag him down. His kin too. Men grow to love what they've builded, an' see it torn down back to eart'. Men lose what they treasure most. A short life can be a waste, a long one a burden, Piano Jack.'

'Why? Why should they drag him down?'

'Who can say where fortune comes from? Not poor Mireli. Some say it's to do wit' his deeds, good or bad, but it's not even a little bit of it.'

'What do you mean? It makes no sense!'

'There's deviltry in the swamp man's song. An' echoes follow.'

Mireli gently closed my palm. 'Oh now, you've had a good tuppence's worth from me.'

I looked into those beautiful eyes and was shocked to feel a tear start in my own. Without a word, she fixed a heather to my lapel. Reaching up, she gave my cheek a brief caress. Then she and the twins walked away, and were soon lost from my sight on the other side of the square.

Picking up my bag, I straightened my back and told myself it was all a trick. She wasn't even a proper Romany. Spirits ... swamps ... underneath! If she hadn't been so pretty I'd never have paid her to blather on. I'd been a fool to waste two pennies I could ill-afford on such twaddle. I put her from my mind and quickened my steps back to Barnsbury. To make the way home seem shorter I began to write a letter in my head. It was to a certain housemaid, asking her to take leave on a Saturday evening, and to come to a concert with me. Mr George Grossmith would be playing.

Riddlesdown
1934

The tram must have braked suddenly because I woke with a jolt. Norbury. I'd one arm around Kenneth's small frame and he was still nuzzled into me, fast asleep. I had his boater in my other hand, and an empty wicker picnic case on my lap. Somewhere in West Croydon I must have nodded off. In those few minutes of sleep I'd had something urgent I needed to talk over with Alice. She was on a tube train and I was in panic lest I miss her. I ran towards the tunnel, my boots deep in marsh, the mud clinging to them, slowing me down. I ran along the dark track, but Alice's train receded. The dread overwhelmed me.

Sometimes I still fly in dreams. Though, as I age, I spend more of the night under ground or deep under water. I don't know why that should be. Of course, Alice was the one person I couldn't speak to. It was Priscilla I needed to have a conversation with. There were a couple of things, both difficult, and I'd been putting off talking about them. I mean, I shouldn't have had to broach them with her, except she did go on so. I wondered if somewhere inside, she already knew the truth. That would make the conversations harder, rather than the other way around. Oh, and there was something I needed to do, that I'd put off. I looked up and four rows in front, saw Prilly and Harold chatting away, like once he did with me. I'd hoped that the two of us would sit together on the journey home, but he didn't want to. I sat back, and, as the tram retraced the way we'd come that morning, let the doings of the last few days pass by me.

'If the weather's fine this Whitsun we should go for a picnic,' Priscilla had said as I carried some boxes from Alfred's old room to our bedroom. Alf had moved to Notting Dale nearly a year ago, and Prilly had decided it was high time that we let his room to a lodger. After all, there was less money coming in. Nothing from Alf now, and I earned less than I once did.

'These'll never fit under the bed unless I move that old suitcase. I'll put it somewhere else.'

'Once we've had a bit of a sort-out, Alf's room would do nicely for someone,' Prilly had said. 'It'll be good to have a lodger again. A young gentleman, quiet, with an office job. Mrs Manzi has a nephew coming up to London to take up a post with the Sun Insurance people. I wonder if it would suit him? When you're back as a piano finisher, we can see if we want to continue with lodgers.'

I didn't want lodgers again, but our finances couldn't really be argued with. It would have to be a man. Prilly would never countenance another woman under our roof.

'Very nice, dear,' said I. 'Parliament Hill Fields and a view over London.'

'No, Jack! We always do that. We need a change. Let's have an outing. Let's go somewhere we've not been before. The question is: where to?'

I hadn't the slightest idea, but I knew that my wife wouldn't have put forward the suggestion unless she already had almost every detail of the plan settled in her head. It was a variation on a theme we'd often played before. I should suggest something, even if it was to be rejected or ended up as the smallest of flourishes in the finished score. Then I remembered a poster I'd seen. 'Kew Gardens? We've not been there for many a year.'

'Hmmm. I'd been thinking that we've never been out to the Purley Downs. If we get to the Embankment, the number sixteen or eighteen tram will take us right there, and we'll be in real countryside.'

The suitcase had moved with us from our old address, a few doors down Brecknock Road. This one was my house, saved for and bought on a mortgage so steep that it'd given me sleepless nights when I first took it on. It gave me some satisfaction when I reflected on my progress in life. In the drawing room downstairs was my own Brinsmead piano, a wonderful example of the Semi-Cottage Style Fourteen with a black finish so deep you could use it as a mirror. Yes, my own house with my piano in it and my family around me. Outside, men I hardly knew nodded to me in the street. As the years had passed, I'd become a fixture, established, respectable. And I knew what I should have done, that I should have unfastened the string around that piece of luggage, and flipped open the catches. Instead, I pulled up a chair, and hauled it to the top of the wardrobe. There are things nobody wants to revisit.

'You haven't forgotten, have you, that Alfred and a friend are coming over for tea today?' said Priscilla. I shook my head, though I hadn't remembered. 'Talking of Mrs Manzi, she told me a story against herself in the sweetest way.' Mrs Manzi was married to a well-to-do shopkeeper and Prilly had always wondered about it because Mr Manzi was so much older than his wife. But the lady seemed to be in her good books now. 'Her brother-in-law's family have moved up to Hampstead and she'd not been there before so they said to her, "get the number fifteen tram and we'll meet you at the terminus". Well, she says to me, "Dear Mrs Scrivener, I was too vain to put on my glasses that day and jumped on the number nineteen by mistake. I was so tired what with little Alexandra's nightmares having got me up twice in the night, that I fell asleep and ended up at the terminus in Barnet being woken by the conductor!" By the time she got to where she should have been, a policeman was there noting down her details! The in-laws had been to the shop, you see, and found that she'd left on time. They were convinced she'd been kidnapped! It's a funny story, isn't it, Jack?'

'I suppose the moral is: don't fall asleep on trams,' I'd said.

The car juddered as we neared the junction with the number ten line at Streatham. On our way up here this morning, Ken had asked me where the other line went. 'I'm not sure,' I'd said, 'Tooting perhaps.'

'When I'm grown up, Daddy, I'm going to be a tram driver and I'll explore all the lines.'

Setting out, the way is full of possibilities, this turning or that, decision points where, by choice or fate, you move onto a new track. Travelling back, the journey's very different. It all seems inevitable, going back to where you've come from. How could I be anything else than the piano man, married to Prilly, who's the father of three boys?

More than twenty years ago I'd had a premonition, not that I believe in such things, but I wouldn't know what other name it should go by. It had all come to pass, far worse than I could ever have imagined. After Robert Ernest, a wall had risen up between Prilly and me. Oh, we talked, but only about the business of running the house, or of Alf, or our money problems. Priscilla was down at St. Andrews every other day. Our rooms had filled up with prints of cherubs. She'd clasped her religion even closer, whilst I'd lost whatever belief I might once have held to. What sort of God would take an innocent? Why would he punish us? Whatever failings we'd had, we'd worked so hard to raise Alfred in the creed of the Church of England. We'd have done the same for Robert Ernest if we'd been given the chance.

Within months we were at war. Eventually, the Government dispossessed German companies, including Bechsteins, who lost their Wigmore Street showrooms, their stock and their fine hall, lost everything they had in Britain. Our piano orders fell off a cliff. Mr Billingshurst headed up the company then. He was married to one of old Mr Brinsmead's daughters. He got us work from the Army, making Uprights, and we made airframes for the Royal Flying Corps. My piano finisher's tools came out of their bag less often, and it was my carpenter's tool case that I took to work. There were compensations: the bright smell of wood as the crosscut saw sliced through it: having my hand drill comfy in my grip again. The younger men joined up, and Grafton Road became a ghost ship. The news trickled in: woodworkers, french polishers, labourers, the two idiots who thought they knew how to work the hoist. Young George. Our next generation of piano men: sons, brothers, fiancés, husbands. Not coming home. So the Great War doomed the Empire I cared most about. The Empire of the Piano drowned in wave upon wave of blood.

One dark January evening in 1917, I came home from the factory to find Alf playing alone by gaslight in the parlour. No supper was ready; my wife was weeping in our bedroom.

'What's the matter, Prilly? Come on, dear, stop crying for a minute and let me know.'

'It's Bessie Coombes, her cousin Larry.'

'Bessie from the church, from St. Andrews? I don't think I know her cousin.'

'Oh, we've not met him … He was killed on Thursday at Khadairi Bend.'

'Oh no, poor Bess. So many of them – gone.'

'It's … it's … all this death …'

I found that I was crying too, and we both sat on the bed holding hands. Prilly told me it was that night that she became pregnant with Harold.

The end of the Great War didn't end our troubles. That day

in 1919 during the Brinsmeads strike: it was a Sunday and I'd slept in, leaving Prilly to go to the service down at St. Andrews. I was in the kitchen shaving, when I heard her come in. I looked round to see her face.

'Good Lord, dear, what's wrong?'

Priscilla filled the kettle and put it on the gas. 'Alice. Alice is what's wrong. And not just her. On the way back, I dropped by to tell her about Mrs Smithson wanting new curtains made up – well, I thought she might be grateful for the work, Jack – and you know who was leaving as I got there?'

'Of course I don't blooming know.'

'Frank. She's carrying on with my own brother, and him a married man. It's ungodly, don't you think?'

A few days later, when I'd gone to Barnsbury to confront her, Alice had been combative.

'I can't see what it's got to do with you, or Priscilla for that matter. It's a new age now. I'll be voting come election time. Me and Frank is our business.' She'd taken up the scarf she was hemming and hadn't even put it down as she spoke.

'But he's married, Allie. And it's my brother-in-law we're talking about.'

She slammed her work down on the table. 'You don't care what life's like for me, do you? As far as you see it, I'm just here to look after Mother. And working all ruddy hours to keep a roof over both our heads. You'd be happy for me to be the drudge, the old maid!'

'No, Allie, I don't....'

'Hear me out, and like it or lump it. Frank and Lil don't get on any more. So why shouldn't I enjoy his company, why shouldn't I have a man around? There's plenty better than me who have different... well... arrangements, now. In case you haven't noticed it, there's whole armies of men that haven't made it back. So what if it's not got a blessing from Prilly's precious church? All those two-faced vicars and bishops... all that lot who were quick enough to cheer on those young fellers when they were being sent off to get killed! Frank and me will do what we do. Or don't, and it's not your business, Jack. Not Prilly's, neither.'

And that was it, more or less. Alice was never again invited to travel the long mile to our house. And I never visited her. Alf stopped asking about his Aunt. Priscilla stopped talking of Frank. After we'd held Mother's funeral at the church, Alice told me that she intended to move to 'Islington proper', as she put it. When she'd sent me her new address, I thought perhaps we could be repaired, but Frank had moved in with her. So she was sawn off, severed. I guessed that not even the strongest glue could mend us. At first it felt as though I'd lost a leg and would have to hobble through life like the men wounded in the War. Years had passed. I'd grown other limbs, suffered other amputations. And there was nobody I could confide in, the way I'd done with Alice.

Alfred was the only one of my boys who had his ears in music. He'd thrived on music lessons and had settled on the trumpet, and that's how he made his living now, as a jobbing musician. It seemed a precarious existence, but Alf said he was happy enough with it. When he'd rented a house with a couple of others, it'd been hard to see him go, but I knew he couldn't be tied to Prilly's apron strings forever. His friend turned out to be Eric, a fellow tenant in the house, a violinist with no permanent position.

'So how're things working out for you in west London? Isn't it terribly far away from … well, everything?'

'Not really, Dad. Latimer Road station is only a few minutes stroll away. Our digs are quite convenient for the main concert halls, you know. I so wanted us to rent that house round the corner in Treadgold Street, but the way it's worked out maybe it was all for the best. We thought we'd have lots of trouble with Parkin, he's the landlord, but he's not been too bad. He fixed the gutters, but wouldn't do anything inside. Though he's happy for us to spruce it up. Mum, I hope that you don't mind that I've not invited you both round yet, the fact is that it's all still a bit basic. And Eric, I hope you won't mind if I say that, of course, you're good at home decorating but you've not quite got a … a woman's touch.'

Eric looked flustered as Alf went on. 'So, Mum, I'd like to get it at least half as nice as you've made things here before you come over to tea …'

'Oh, don't worry about that, Alf, dear. Why don't you young men join us on Whitsun Monday for a picnic on the Downs? The two of you would be most welcome.'

'Oh that's very kind, Mrs Scrivener,' said Eric. 'I can't I'm afraid, because I'll be playing viola at the Wigmore Hall.'

'And I want to be there too,' said Alf. 'He's done well, hasn't he?'

'I'm impressed', I said. 'I didn't realise you played at such a high level. Alf, you once played at Queen's Hall under Sir Landon's baton.'

'That was just a thing for juniors, Dad. But yes, our Stoneleigh Street household is very … musical.' I caught an exchanged smile between the two men. 'And we're both playing on the bandstand in Holland Park on Empire Day this Thursday. If ever there was a day that should be a bank holiday, it's Empire Day, then you and Harold would have been able to come along.'

'Bank holidays good, Empire bad,' said Harold, 'only a fool would think the Indians and Africans want us to be in charge of them, any more than we'd want the Americans to govern us.'

'You'll learn, little brother, that it's our duty to lead the lesser races. And to keep them in line when it's called for. We have enough fine, fit, men in Britain to do the job. We need a strong man to lead them, that's all.'

Harold would happily spend the whole afternoon baiting Alf, and to change the subject, I asked if the money was alright for the sessions they played.

'So-so,' said Alf. 'Eric is aiming for a post with one of the orchestras. I'd like to get in with a band. Everyone wants a post, but you have to have experience and lots of contacts so that's unlikely for a while.'

'And when you've got a permanent position you'll be quite a catch, Alf,' said Prilly. 'There'll be lots of nice girls making eyes at you.'

'When I find one half as wonderful as you, Mum, then I'll let myself be caught!'

Priscilla flushed at the compliment, whilst I scowled at Harold because under his breath he'd said something that sounded like 'gut-spew'.

'Dad, you won't mind if I don't come to Purley, will you?'

'I would mind, Harold. Your mother wants to have both you and Kenneth there.'

'Well, I'll be doing something else.'

'What will you be doing?'

'Cycling out with Sammy, I expect.'

'You're not still spending time with that Jew-boy, are you?' said Alf.

'And why shouldn't I? I don't have to only mix with C of E just to suit you and your British Union friends! He's a Londoner and that's the best thing anyone could be.'

'I've explained it to you before, given you Sir Oswald's pamphlet to read …'

'Yes, and what a load of rubbish it was. A batty old toff who wants to march around with his arm out ordering everyone about! Cozying up to whatshisname in Italy and your hero, Adolf.'

'Herr Hitler is getting Germany sorted out. Clearing up the mess left by the Socialists, the Communists and the Jews.'

'You mean he's killing off democracy. You've been completely taken in. You've become a poodle in a black shirt! Woof-woof!'

Eric looked uncomfortable with the way the conversation had veered to politics again. 'What do you think about it, Mr Scrivener?'

The directness of the question took me by surprise. What did I think about it? I began slowly and then the pieces fell into place. 'I think ... that gentlemen do the best job of running a country. Men whose families have had generations of experience in doing it. They imbibe it with their mother's milk, as it were, looking after the nation. Men whose houses hold a grand piano or two, who grew up with fine paintings on their walls. We need gentlemen of refinement, who know the value of craft ... who support the craftsmen. We've no use for the blackshirts here. Hitler, Alf, he hasn't any class at all. Mr Churchill saw it at once. We've got a little martinet in charge of all the Germans. I hope he trips up before he gives us any trouble.'

'He has enough cultured people with him', said Alf, 'the Wagners, the Bechstein piano people ...'

'I don't know who supports him,' I said, 'but I'll pay attention from now on. If those Bechsteins are behind him, it doesn't exactly recommend him to me!' It still riled me that whilst Brinsmeads had gone to the wall, Bechsteins had survived the war, and were now flourishing again, even in London.

'And your father should have the last word on that topic,' Priscilla said. 'Alf, why don't you find a nice record or two to put on the gramophone? I've got a cake in the kitchen, I want to see you men finish it off for me.'

The tram halted for a while outside Streatham tram station whilst there was a change of crew. Ken stirred and looked up for a few seconds before settling down to sleep again. The baby of our family had come as a surprise to me. It seemed a long time ago already, in 1926, when we were alone one evening and Prilly sat me down because she had something she wanted to say.

'Jack, there's no easy way to break the news. I'm expecting again. It's a shock, dear, but I've had a couple of days to get used to it. Can you get used to it?'

I began speaking too soon. 'Good Lord, Prilly. I never even thought … we're not getting any younger, neither of us.' But I've never lived in a house that didn't have a woman in it. I've always known that you have to listen to them in a special way. Under the melody of their voices it's easy to miss a different song. Sometimes the motif beneath holds another message and sometimes it doesn't. So the descant in Prilly's voice told me that she was taken aback to find herself pregnant again, yet when I listened there was something else – a contralto longing perhaps – to hold a newborn of her own one last time. So I paused and said, 'How wonderful! That's a turn-up for the books.'

Kenneth was the most cosseted of our lads. Just three weeks ago I'd come home and Priscilla told me that she'd taken him to the doctor's surgery about his cough: 'Doctor took his stethoscope and listened to his chest and to his back. Our Ken wouldn't stay still, kept on saying that the metal felt cold, but Doctor listened carefully, and took his time. Told me not to worry because there isn't any fluid on the lungs. It was worth the money, just to stop worrying about him.'

'Isn't it amazing, he can tell what's going on just by listening?'

'Oh, I don't know, dear, isn't that what you finishers do with your pianos?' And it was true, though it hadn't struck me before. Often, just by listening to the instrument I used to know what investigations I should carry out, make a diagnosis, and even determine the treatments required by my patient, before opening up the piano case. This morning Prilly had referred, yet again, to my getting back to finishing pianos. But I won't be going back to it, ever, even though it's the best paid of the piano-making trades. I'm a general piano man now, and I can do most of the work that needs to be done around pianos. Once again, the hand drill is in my tool bag, and it feels almost part of me when it's in my hands. I suppose the drill is as emblematic of the piano man's craft as a stethoscope is of a doctor's.

After the War, my firm struggled on with a lack of orders, a shortage of skilled men to fulfil those we did have, and to cap it all, a union dispute. They were determined to have their strike, and I won't say that things weren't tough for us. 'Can't you lads see that the firm isn't strong enough to stand a strike?' I'd said. 'It'll fold and there'll be no work nor pay neither for any of us.' I'd taken no part in the action and had to put up with the bad blood that resulted. And so the Brinsmead dynasty limped to an end, with Cramers salvaging what parts they could, or what parts they thought would be of use to them. One of them was me. The Eastern end of the Grafton Road works was taken over by Dell's Confectionery, and it was good to see it have a second life. I continued with finishing and regulating until Cramers let me go, too. It was a relief, in a way.

As we clattered our way through Kennington Gate, Ken sat up and said he was famished. He smiled me that gentle smile of his, and I gasped as I always do since it so called back his long-lost brother. All I had was the remains of a bag of sweets, so I gave him a barley sugar.

'I'm going to take the bag to Mum and Harold in case they want one as well,' he said. Prilly refused, but his brother took one, nodding me his thanks, perhaps in a surly way.

Harold had turned out to be the boy who always had his head in a book. He loved adventure stories, and by the time he was ten or so he raced through them: Childers, Henty, Rider Haggard. Then, as he passed ten, it was science. Every sort, from astronomy to wireless. 'I'll be a scientist one day,' he'd said. I was proud of him, first or second in his class, in everything. All that book-learning was fine for a child, but not much use to a man. At least, not much use to a youngster growing up in our neck of the woods. When I collected my cards from Cramers, Harold was coming up for fourteen. I decided that he should leave school and learn carpentry. I'd got him in at Bovairds, cabinet makers. He didn't want to go. We got a visit from Mr Webster, his form teacher at Acland Boys School, pleading with me to let him stay on. Scholarship boy, higher exams, university, that sort of thing. I'd listened politely, though I wasn't to be swayed. How could I possibly support him when I hadn't got a job? Harold and I had quarrelled.

'I can't see what difference the few shillings that I can bring in will make.'

'It might be the difference between having a roof over our heads and a comfy home for Ken,' I'd said. 'It's time for you to be a man now, Harold, not a schoolboy. I had to when I was even younger than you.'

'You say you believe in progress. But not for me!' Harold had been hard to argue with. But I'd dug in.

It had been good as we'd travelled out in the morning, watching the strong, ancient core of London giving way to suburbs. Our city seemed sturdy and vigorous, even in the relative quiet of a bank holiday. Some force as mysterious as the electricity powering our tram was pushing it, pushing it out along the roads and railway lines, forming new houses and shops. I'd been glad when we'd got in sight of open country and when the conductor had called out, 'Purley. All change, all change.' We'd made good time and he'd have a few minutes for a mug of tea from the tram workers kiosk before he had to set off back to Streatham.

We followed the other excursionists up the trail to Riddlesdown; like them, Harold and I were weighed down: the picnic hamper, sandwiches, cake, Thermos flasks, bottles of dandelion and burdock, groundsheet, blanket, sunshades, Ken's cricket bat, Harold's books and the ex-army field glasses I'd got for him to take on his cycling trips. It was further up than I'd realised, and I began to puff.

'It feels as if London doesn't want to let us go,' I said to my middle son. 'It's making us sweat for the view of it.'

'Let's have an early lunch,' he said, 'at least then we won't have to carry the food around.' He found a spot with a view of the Downs, seeming like billows rolling into the Surrey countryside. We could see buildings in some of the hollows: London was pushing its way out even to here. When the time neared mid-afternoon, we left our picnic place and followed the circuit to Riddlesdown's other side. You get views of London from there, more distant than it is from Parliament Hill Fields. After he'd used the binoculars, Harold let me have them. I could see the wavering dome of St. Paul's and the East End chimneys, mostly smokeless today. It was clear enough to make out the tops of the dockside cranes. It puzzled me: the town no longer seemed so robust, fixed and solid. From here, London was fragile and temporary. It was an impossibility in the landscape, this mirage that I felt could melt away before I'd finished my scrutiny of it.

'It looks as if a puff of dragon's breath would blow it away,' I'd said to Harold as I gave him back the glasses, thinking that he might make fun of me for such a piece of whimsy. But he just chuckled.

'Then let's hope no dragons fly over to find us, Dad.'

'Careful here!' I called out, as the path became slippery. It was strange: we were near the foot of those dry downs and we had to avoid a section of deep mud. It was as if, even out here, those chalk hills had been dropped on top of a basin full of

Thames swamp.

The tram returned us to the Embankment and at last we scuttled underground to let the Electric Railway take us back to Kentish Town. After supper, as Prilly filled the sink with water, Harold carried the plates back to the kitchen and picked up a tea towel. Drying up was his task, but tonight he was pleased that I asked him to read to Kenneth instead.

'I'll do the drying up with your mother this evening, Harold.' When we were alone, I took the towel, and a breath.

'Priscilla, I want to mention a couple of things.'

'Well, mention them then.'

'Right. Yes, I … I've never told you the full story about stopping piano finishing, and I wondered if you'd guessed it.'

'What are you talking about, dear?'

'Oh, when did it start? A year or so before I got my cards at Cramers, I could see that a piano's Whippen flange was out of adjustment, but I couldn't hear it. I always could before. So I'd checked myself, and checked again. I'm losing my hearing, Prilly.'

She put the dish back in the sink, astonishment on her face.

'Why ever didn't you say? I mean, how could I guess it? You don't need to hear so fine when you're at home …'

'I was too proud, I suppose. I've lived by my ears for so

long, taken them for granted, never thought my hearing might leave me. Then I got the job at Challen's after what, only a month or two, and I thought I wouldn't need to spell it out.'

'My goodness and all this time I've been on at you to put in for a finisher's job!' There were tears in her eyes, so I hugged her. We stood together like that for a minute, she in her apron, and me in my shirtsleeves, looking at the lines in each other's faces.

'What's the other thing you want to tell me? You've got a fancy woman?'

'No! Of course nothing like that! It's about Alf. It's best not to bring up the subject of courting. He's best left alone to do things in his own way, with no family pressure. If he needs anything from us in that regard, I'm sure he'll ask. Not every young man wants to get married, you know.'

'I so want to have a wedding in the family. It would do us all so much good. I know you'll say he's got plenty of time, but one day he needs to find a lady and look to settling down. I suppose you're right though.'

So I left it like that. Not quite said.

Once the dishes were put away, I went upstairs to our bedroom, and pulled the suitcase from the top of the wardrobe, placing it on the bed. After fumbling with the knotted string, I slipped the catches and opened the lid. An instant later I was slumped on the floor, as if I'd been punched in the stomach. My eyes had taken in the contents: the exercise books I'd used when I wrote my journal twenty years ago; Robert Ernest's baby socks; the photograph, still in its frame, that, for a few brief weeks, had stood on the mantelpiece. But what took all the air out my body was what my ears had given me. It leapt out as if a roar of thunder had been held within that old leather. Though it wasn't thunder, it was that other crash I recognised at once, just as I knew the hanging chord in E flat minor that followed it.

I clambered to my feet and slammed the suitcase shut again. My ears were still ringing as I sat back down on the bed. Was it real or all in my head? It made no difference. I'd thought it'd gone away, that it'd sent enough misery towards me. It couldn't come back for more, could it? Even as I asked myself the question, I knew that it could. And it would.

John

Brecknock Road
2014

Young John held a hearing aid in his hand. In all his seven years, he'd never had charge of such an intriguing device. He walked with it on the path around the new house, precise and solid in red brick. He paused for a moment at the place where an old outhouse almost touched the side of the new house. He focused briefly on the point where the two structures nearly met. The outhouse was a dilapidated shed roughly built in brick with uneven tiles for a roof. It must have once been larger, or connected to another building that was there before the new house replaced it. The outhouse had no end wall, the roof ridge being held up by a stout timber upright. That yard of overhanging roof provided cover for a few garden tools his father kept there.

So I come to report my own history of that day in 1960. All these years after, it's not the easiest thing to do, because nobody made a record of it at the time. There was no fresh exercise book in Jack's careful handwriting, none of the Pitman shorthand Ulla could do as her pencil danced over her typist's notebook. Harold wasn't there, so he wrote nothing in his angular script. Later on, he used a dictaphone at work, but those devices hadn't even been invented then. Jane and Young John were children and never kept diaries. Yes, it's difficult. Everyone is dead and buried now.

Reviewing the previous sentence, I find it offends a certain punctiliousness that I've retained from my many years in the civil service. It's not quite right to say that they're all dead and buried because Young John was buried without being dead first. I've been told more than once that the treatment of him was somewhat uncivilised, but, I would contend, understandable in the times, in the circumstances. Anyway, I'm not sure if that makes him less, or more dead than the others. It's his memories I'm digging up, and the process isn't so much a remembering as an exhumation. Judging from what comes up, clinging to my spade, as Young John's personality leached away during his time underground, thoughts from the others mouldering there seeped into his bones.

The outhouse had two doors. At the far end there was an old privy which John had a dim memory of using before his father built a septic tank for the WC waiting in the new house. The near door was painted black a long time ago but had received no care since then, and the hinges creaked. The latch worked easily though, and led into a handyman's room.

John lifted the latch and stepped inside. There was a

workbench, complete with vice, and that day the only object on it was a black wooden toolbox. Along the bare brick walls were rickety shelves and nails serving as hooks to hold a variety of implements. There were two seats, a stool and an ancient captain's chair. Jack was sitting there, staring out of a window rich in cobwebs. He wore a waistcoat over a shirt with no collar; the brass stud showing at the top back of his shirt was a clue that he'd intended to attach the collar that morning.

'Hello, Granddad. Mummy says you left this in the kitchen and she really wants you to wear it.'

John waited a second or two for Jack to respond. He was used to that. The old man sometimes seemed to have travelled far away in his head, before his grandson's voice called him back.

'Ah, Young John, I was miles away, back in London, in our old house on Brecknock Road. The hearing aid, yes. Put it on the workbench please.'

Young John did as he'd been asked, feeling that it was a shame to part with the hearing aid. It was about the size of a packet of twenty cigarettes, and wired to an earpiece made of clear plastic, shaped to take sound deep into the deaf person's ear. The aid had a black wheel that clicked on and then controlled the volume. He'd already found that he could create squalls and whines by moving the wheel and bringing the earpiece close to the microphone in the box. He imagined the lucky wearer tuning out the world and stepping into parallel empires of whistle or hum.

'Why don't you wear it, Granddad?'

'I can hear well enough without it. It screeches in my ear. And sometimes there's a deep hum, in a minor key. I … I don't like it.'

The boy nodded. He'd heard those sounds too. That minor chord in E flat wouldn't have stopped him using the aid. And John knew the old man was quite deaf. He'd been speaking as loud as he comfortably could without shouting.

'What's in that tin?'

Jack looked down, his face showing puzzlement in finding he was holding a small can of glue.

'Oh this. I'd meant to put it in the toolbox. It's Cascamite wood glue, it makes strong bonds, young man. Do you know how long I was married to your Granny?'

'No,' said Young John. Priscilla had died before he was born, and was of no interest to him. He hoped that Jack wouldn't mention her again.

'Forty-two years. Strong bonds,' said Jack.

'What are you doing?' asked the boy.

'What am I doing, yes, glad you reminded me of that, I'm

going to pack away my tools. I don't suppose I'll be needing them now. I could use a hand from a nimble feller like you. Will you help?'

John thought about it. Somewhere inside him there was a sensitive barometer of the family weather. It told him that there would be no consequences if he refused. He felt no obligation to help, in the way he would have if either of his parents had told him, or even as he would have done if one of his sisters had asked him to fetch and carry. Without it ever entering his brain, he was completely aware that this eldest member of the household had less status than he himself did, as the youngest. He was interested in the woodworking tools but thought the job might become dull after a while. He didn't want to totally commit to it.

'Alright for now, I suppose,' he said.

John knelt on top of the stool so that he could better see the toolbox. It was made of wood with metal hinges and clasps for the lid. He read out the faded letters painted in a neat hand on the top.

'H-E-S. Why's it got Dad's initials on it?'

'Harold made it, all the young carpenters did something like that in those days. Harold stopped school and took up work when I lost my job at Cramers. Good firm they were too; we made good pianos, they were still Brinsmead ones really, but people didn't want them anymore. Bechsteined I was, Young John, Bechsteined.'

Much of what his grandfather said seemed to have washed over John, but there was nothing the old man said that he didn't quietly absorb. He was used to the silences, mis-hearings and strange expressions, but he reacted to the mention of pianos.

'Did you make pianos then, Granddad?'

The old man nodded back at him.

'Could you make us one?'

Jack's face lightened, and he almost chuckled.

'I'm afraid not, Young John, you need quite a few tradesmen to make just one piano, and you need a good workshop space too …' His voice trailed off.

'What about a guitar? Could you make one of those?'

The boy thought how exciting it would be to have a guitar – surely it would be much simpler to build one than a piano? Jack looked puzzled.

'The youngsters want guitars nowadays, though when I was a lad you never heard of them. Pianos were the thing; all respectable folk wanted one. Not just in London, but all through the country, it was the thing to have. And of course, we sent them all over the Empire.' Half a minute passed before he spoke again. 'Guitars, Lord love a duck no, I wouldn't know where to start.'

'What are these for?'

John was pointing to the toolbox lid. Attached to the inside of it were two small wooden blocks each topped by a thin piece of plywood that could be twisted round on a screw.

'They hold the saws that go in there. Let's do them first.'

He nodded in the direction of a shelf, and he asked the boy to bring them to him.

'Mind the teeth!'

'Why do you need three saws?'

Jack picked up the tenon saw.

'Look at this one, short and with the hard spine. See how small the teeth are? You can do fine cuts with them, so you can make dovetail joints, for instance. But it would be hard work to cut a thick piece of wood with it.'

He took one of the long saws and held it so that John could see the teeth. The boy thought that those old trembling hands looked as if they too had been fashioned from wood.

'This is a panel saw. The teeth are bigger than on the tenon, but they're not nearly as large as these.'

He laid the saw aside and picked up the third one.

'And this is the crosscut saw – this is the one to use for cutting through a thick piece, see those big teeth. Tell you what, I'll show you. Can you bring me that piece of two-by-two standing in the corner?'

Jack drew out two sawing trestles from under the workbench and placed the timber between them.

'Now can you hold onto that end?'

In a few moments he'd sawn the wood in half.

'Wow,' John said, impressed with the speed and neatness of the cut.

'Lots of practice,' responded his grandfather. His attention wandered and he looked out of the window. 'They've been cut away from me now. Priscilla, Alf, Alice and Robert Ernest. Life's a crosscut saw, young man; it saws off your limbs.'

John didn't know what his grandfather was talking about. He felt no curiosity to find out and put the first saw into the case.

'Though I tell you what, Alf did for your Granny, she never was the same after. Her poor heart had never recovered from the injury he'd given it months before she went.'

'Who was Alf?'

'Never mind.'

So here are Jack's memories, coming to me now, coming up as if I was lifting his body's compost from its place in the graveyard of All Saints church. It's not a place of rest for him because it was Priscilla's spot, not his. He'd never wanted to be there: if things had been different, he'd have chosen Thornhill Square.

On that day, his thoughts of Alfred brought with them the familiar bitterness, anger and despair. Jack supposed that he should have talked it all through with Prilly after he realised how things were, the day Alfred came round with Eric. That point was the notch, like the ones he made sawing wood. He'd take the HB pencil from behind his ear and draw the line. It had taken fifteen years or so, maturing as if it were timber in the Brinsmead warehouse, before the crosscut saw's sharp teeth had found the mark. And then those hard months in 1950. He couldn't but blame himself, feel that somehow he'd got it all wrong.

He could tell that John had asked him another question.

'What, Young John? Don't whisper, spit it out!'

'I said, what next?'

'See those two over there, they're planes and they could go in this bottom part of the case. Now, hang on, let me tell you how to hold them. They're on their sides, that's so the blades don't get blunted. You never hold them by the underside, because the blades stick through and they're sharp. You hold them by the handle and the knob on the front end. No, leave the jointer. Go on then, bring the jack plane, that's the smaller one; take care though, it's heavy.'

Once the plane was on the workbench, they both looked at it with respect. The underside had a hue of burnished silver, and the metal top bore the name 'Stanley' cast into the metal top. The wooden handle and knob were a deeply lacquered brown.

'That's beech wood,' the old man said to nobody in particular. 'I always liked the way it goes with a bit of varnish.'

'How does it work?'

Jack picked up a piece of the sawn two by two and placed it in the vice, and, taking up the plane, squinted along the underside to make an adjustment to the turning knob that controlled the length of the blade. He made a couple of quick passes over the stick and produced thick shavings. He made another adjustment, so that the shaving would be thinner and the plane easier for the boy to push along.

'Go on then.'

John managed to produce a satisfying curl of a wood shaving with a little practice. Jack rolled it up and gave it to him. 'If you smell it you should get a nice scent of pine.'

The boy liked the resinous aroma. He put the shaving into his pocket.

'Why did you call it Jack, when it says Stanley?' John asked.

'Golly, I don't know why the smaller ones are called jack planes. This one was made by a firm called Stanley. And that's a surname, I believe, not a Christian name. Your dad got these after the last war. Said mine had had their day. Maybe he was right, and these are a really nice set. American company, you didn't hear of them much before the war, but they bought into a Sheffield firm, what was their name ...'

Jack was absent for a while, staring out of the window. I have to admit that the fossil record is indistinct at this point, but let's say that this was what was going on for him ... It was something from a lifetime ago, when he was an apprentice in the soundboard workshop. Not having bothered to check the measurements, he'd cut a piece of best mahogany rather too thick. He hadn't wanted to admit to his carelessness, so planed it down to the right size. It took him all lunch break, but eventually he reduced it to the right dimensions. When old George came back he must have known what had happened but just told him to sweep up the shavings.

'What's Bechsteined?'

And here's a clear find. The boy's question had startled Jack. He was disconcerted by Young John's habit of picking up the pieces of conversations that had gone by. The boy listened closely, but chewed things over before he spoke. Harold had been like that too.

'What's that?'

'You said you were Bechsteined.'

'Did I? One of the lads started it. Way back before the First War. Tom his name was, nice lad and quite a good worker, never came in with a hangover or the like. But he had a sort of cocky manner about him, which maybe rubbed the Guvnor up the wrong way. I met him in the street once and he told me, 'I've been let go. The order book don't look too good – there's some others that'll be fetching their cards.' That means he was out of a job. And he said: 'We're being Bechsteined, I reckon.' So it stuck: whenever a man lost his job that's what we'd say.'

The boy nodded in that serious way he must have picked up from his father. 'Why did he say it though?'

'Ah, Bechsteins were another piano company, you see, German owned, and we thought it was unfair competition. We thought they were getting work that should have gone to us. They lost everything in the First War, of course. Beautiful pianos, but well, the owners were tricky people, bad people some of them, so it turned out.'

'Was that the end of them then?'

'No. They got back, Young John.'

'What goes in there?'

'What did you say?' asked Jack.

'What goes in there?' said John, louder, having forgotten to raise his voice the first time. He was pointing to three small drawers in the top of the case.

'Yes, well, see this drawer, that's for holding all those small boxes of screws. Let's get them out on the workbench, take the lids off. Now we'll look for any screws out on the shelves and we'll put them in the right box.'

'Granddad?' The boy was looking at the hearing aid on the workbench.

'Yes, John.'

'Did you go deaf overnight?'

'Deaf? I'm not deaf! I'm hard of hearing, that's quite different. And no, it wasn't all in one go. Each passing year pared it away, bit by bit. It's how life reduces a man, Young John. Not only with the saw, but with the plane too.' He turned away again, seemingly lost in his memories. 'A green-eyed girl told me how it would be, but I put her out of my head. Haven't thought of her for, must be … not far off fifty years.'

To John that was another unintelligible statement, so typical of what his grandfather sometimes came out with, bordering on the absurd, that did not deserve a reaction from him. 'What goes in the big drawer?' he asked.

John had done much of the work of filling up the small screw boxes, and though the task hadn't actually been finished, his grandfather seemed content to move on. He picked up a brace and released the long spiral bit from the grip of its teeth. 'This is what goes in there. Can you look to see if others like this are around, look there's a couple on that shelf.'

The boy scurried around picking up suitable bits and placing them in the drawer. Jack had fallen silent again. Then he was speaking, as much to the window as to the child. 'I'm not sure if it was nine or ten years ago. When I was sat here, in this captain's chair. Mrs Bridge was over from the vicarage calling my name. She'd rushed round to tell me about Prilly. Your grandma had popped over to the church to arrange flowers. There was no warning, nothing. She just collapsed. It was her heart … They'd called an ambulance but it was the doctor who arrived first. They'd rung him as well, Young John. He came right over in his car, but it was no good.'

Looking towards Young John, he spoke out louder, almost as if it was a rebuke.

'When I think of her now it's like somebody is using that one on me, using it here.' He pointed to the sharp end of the brace bit in the boy's hand, and tapped his own chest.

Young John couldn't see Ulla, not in those moments. She wasn't with him in the outhouse. And then, even when they were together in the same room, he would be only aware of her as mum, or mummy. All these years on, when her ashes have melded into the loam of the plot next to Jack's, I see her once more. I feel the light weight of his child's skull in my holding hands, and she comes alive again. This time around, I can look into her head and into her heart.

In the kitchen of the new house, Ulla put two spoons of sugar into a mug of tea for Jack. She placed it on a round metal tray next to a glass of milk and a saucer with four Rich Tea biscuits. At that moment she liked the kitchen, liked the cool of the quarry tiles on the floor and the capaciousness of the larder store. She was pleased by the care that Harold had put into the design, and his expertise in getting every last detail carried through by the builder. She was proud of the house because she was proud of him. She told herself that was a very different thing from being house-proud – something she wouldn't have aspired to. She smiled at the thought that she'd just avoided one of the many pitfalls of thinking in English.

Picking up the tray she walked across the glossy oak floor of the living room towards a side door. The house was too small with six of them living there. She needed to talk with Harold again about adding a couple of bedrooms. She put down the tray on top of a bookcase whilst she opened the door. It faced towards the outhouse. She disapproved of that ramshackle shed. It was a reminder of Harold's unfinished reworking of the land. And she frowned at the outhouse's proximity, at the way it seemed to claim a relationship with her home of comfort, progress and science. She wanted the outhouse removed, and the space paved over so that people would never know it'd been there.

Two paces through the side door took Ulla to the outhouse wall. Between the two buildings was a chasm of a hundred years. She felt a shiver travel down her spine. The past was sinister to her. She swung open the workshop door and set the tray down on the bench.

'I thought you men might like these.' Now Ulla was speaking loudly, the boy heard the accent in her perfectly precise English. He felt how she wanted him to, pleased because she was implying that he was already a man.

'I'm helping Granddad put away his tools, and look Mummy –' he produced the shaving from his pocket '– I can work the plane now.'

'He's lovely company for me, Ulla dear. Thank you for the

tea, it's most welcome.'

'Well done, both of you. John, in a few minutes I'll need to take you for your haircut.'

Suddenly the work in the outhouse appeared much more attractive. The boy had always hated having his hair cut. 'Do I have to? Granddad needs me here.'

'Yes, you do, you're beginning to look like a hairy dog.'

John was about to say that he liked to look like a hairy dog, but there was something in his mother's tone that told him it wouldn't be worthwhile.

After his daughter-in-law had left, the old man watched his grandson as he sipped his milk. Jack had heard the left hand of Ulla's voice, kind and caring of him. But he also heard the right hand playing something just as familiar: irritation, resentment, maybe. A sudden wave of anger swept over him at the thought that he was there on sufferance. Yet he knew that it wasn't part of Ulla's marriage agreement that he be in the household. He felt defeated and sighed. God knew that things hadn't gone to Jack's plan either. Alf!

Young John was soon back from collecting the spiral brace bits. 'Now look, Granddad, I've found these really small ones, bits I mean, for the brace.'

'Well yes, they're bits all right, but they're for the hand drill. Let's keep 'em separate. Can you see the hand drill?'

'I saw something high up behind those paint tins, is that it? It looks like Mum's whisk.'

Jack retrieved the drill. It was covered with cobwebs and dust; he wiped it down with a rag. Young John was speaking again.

'What's this funny one for? You couldn't make a hole with this, could you?' The boy was holding a drill bit with a conical end.

'That's a countersink. You use it to take the screw head under the surface of the wood. It hides it from sight, so nobody else knows it's there. Let's have a go.' The old man took the planed piece of two by two and returned it to the vice. Putting in a normal drill bit he drilled through it. Substituting the countersink bit, he gave the hand drill to the boy.

'You'll need to come up on the stool, just to get a little weight over it. That's it, now turn the handle.'

After the boy had made a reasonable indent in the wood, Jack took a small screw and showed how the head fitted snugly under the surface.

'But you can still see it, Granddad, and feel it there with your fingers.'

'Ah, well, you can hide it, with a bit of beeswax or filler. We could make it invisible with a wood stain, or french polish.'

'Isn't that a lot of work?'

'I suppose it is but it's worth it to hide the ugliness of the fix.'

'What happened when they got back?' Seeing that his grandfather hadn't responded he asked again. 'The Bechsteins, what happened when they got back?'

'They built up their business again, pretty quickly, pretty quickly. Including in London. Mind you, it was harder for all of us. There wasn't so much money around, and people had other needs that came first. And then there were gramophones and the wireless, so they thought they didn't need pianos as before.'

'What bad things did they do?'

'They helped Hitler, and I suppose he helped them.'

'How did they help him?'

Jack sighed. 'Well, I've not thought about it for many years. In fact I'm not sure I even want to think on it again. There was a time when nobody had heard of him. They picked him up, gave him gold, I don't know how much, but lots. They knew high society people, the rich, powerful ones. They introduced him to their circle. They raised him up.'

The boy knew that Jack had now told him of wicked things done by the Bechsteins. He thought on it for a moment. 'Were the Nazis their fault, did they cause the War?'

'Now, that's a question I used to ask myself. What would have happened if my employers had won out over Bechsteins rather than the other way around? What if the German firm had been the one to go broke after the First War? Is that what you mean, young man?'

Jack's question was much more exact than anything John had had in mind, but the boy nodded anyway.

'He'd have had less money in those early days, that's for sure. But I don't know the answer, Young John. I hope they didn't make a vital difference. I don't like to think of pianos hurting anyone.'

John removed a carpenter's set square from its place on the wall, and a made a gun from it. He was a soldier in the war now, fighting the Germans. He stopped his fantasy game and fired off another question. 'You know when the war started, what did you do, Grandad? Did you join the Army?' For John the war was part of things that 'happened before I was born', along with mammoths, building the pyramids, and the Battle of Hastings.

'I was too long in the tooth to do that. Sixty years old. I came up here from London with your Granny. Did some carpentry up at the airfield though.'

Jack's voice was silent, and Young John had no idea of where his mind had travelled to. Yet I find that it has left its traces in me as clear as grooves on the shellac they used for early gramophone records. I can hear his thoughts.

At that point. Jack had wanted to shout at his grandson, to say something like: 'You stupid child! You've no idea!'

Priscilla had been on at him for months. She'd thought that they should move from Brecknock Road to the safety of the cottage in which she'd been raised, up in rural Huntingdonshire. 'I've had enough of the blackout and everything ...'

'You're right,' Jack had said. 'No need to worry about that up there. There's hardly anything to black out! That cottage has three light bulbs and one electric point! No gas neither. I'm a Londoner, Prilly. It's all too backward in the village.'

'Yes, but what about rationing? We can get round it if we move. I'll turn the garden over to vegetables. We won't go short. Come on, Jack, we'll make the old place cosy, you'll see.'

In peacetime he'd been proud to have three sons, getting ready to make and remake the world. In wartime it was a gruelling agony. He went back to when Harold was first in uniform.

'*We're going to win it, Dad, we've got to. It'll be a while though. I just hope we finish off the Nazis before ... too long.*'

Jack had understood the pause. Private Scrivener had been going to say, 'before Ken is old enough to be called up', but held his tongue in the nick of time. Alf served as a bandsman and never left British shores. Prilly prayed every night for Harold, who was raised to Warrant Officer in the Italian campaign. Ken was called up in 1944. In June that year, news came in of the D-Day landings. He heard her prayer at the bedside. 'Sweet Jesus, please God, don't let 'em send my baby there.'

But Ken had already been spewed up on Sword Beach, barely eighteen years old and fighting his way up the Normandy coast. There was a particular sound Jack used to hear in the cottage. It was the tap-tap of his own footfall as he paced with a belly full of dread listening to the BBC news of the Italian campaign, and then of Normandy. He worried that he might hear the dark notes from the London marshes again, but he never did. Perhaps his move from the city had broken their grip on him.

'My Dad was in the Army,' John said, breaking the silence. 'He was. All my three ... your Uncle Ken was too.'

'You know when we won the War? What happened to them then? Were they put in prison?'

'What?'

'I mean the Bechsteins.'

'I'm not sure. I know the Yanks stopped them making pianos. They had to make coffins instead. The Americans took charge of it ...'

The door opened and a girl walked in. She was eleven years old. Her dark eyes had gravity and laughter in them. She had a copy of a children's encyclopaedia in a bag. 'Hello, Granddad. It's nearly time for Young John to go for his haircut.'

'I don't want to!'

'I'll come too, if you like,' said his sister. 'To keep you company. I'll keep an eye on Mr Richards to see he does it right. How does that sound?'

It didn't occur to Young John that this was a kind offer; that his eldest sister might have other things she'd prefer to do. It was part of his world that she looked out for him. He nodded.

'What have you been reading about today?' Jack said to Jane. There was so little for his three grandchildren to do in the village that they were always reading something. John's reading had raced ahead of his age. He'd leafed through his sisters' *Famous Five* titles without much enthusiasm. He liked the pictorial encyclopaedias best, but they also belonged to his sisters, and he needed their permission before he could look at them.

'The Great Fire of London happened in 1666,' said Jane. 'It wasn't all bad because it burnt the plague germs. Lots of people had died from it the year before.'

'I knew that!' said John.

'You're such a fibber! Mummy is always telling you.'

Jack fetched an old tobacco tin from his pocket and opened it. 'Have a barley sugar, Jane.' She took one and Jack passed the tin to the boy. Orange barley sugars were far from being John's favourite, but he'd noticed they were the only sweets his grandfather ever had, and he took one. A sweet was a sweet after all. Jack unwrapped one for himself and spoke whilst it was in his mouth. 'It's all wrong, what you've read, Jane. I can tell you what happened, I saw it with my own eyes, smelt it too.'

'Granddad! Now who's telling fibs? Not even you are that old!'

Young John used the next two or three minutes to bombard Jane with questions about the Great Fire. Then, turning to Jack, he asked: 'Your old house in London, did the bombs blow it down?'

'You're a dogged fellow, aren't you, young man? No, we were lucky. It was still there at the end of the war.'

Another fossil for the archeologist's brush: Jack was thinking how irritating the boy was. Why couldn't he be more like his two sisters, Jane and Hannah? Jack felt tired now, tired of struggling with his memories, fatigued by his grandson's questions. He yawned. He heard again the first bomb as it struck south of Camden Road. There'd been something in the noise that he'd recognised, but he'd not been able to place it, cramped down there in the Anderson Shelter. Although the Blitz tore at the bonds that held him to London, even those two nights right at the end of 1940 didn't make him agree to leave. Those nights when the Luftwaffe set the sky alight, when they filled his nostrils with burning. Those nights when half of the square mile of the City of London fell to the incendiary bombs. When Cripplegate was wiped off the London map, never to return. Leaving that unique smell of burnt building hanging in the air – that unnatural tarry smell, that made him feel sick. That was the real Great Fire. It was another time after an All Clear had sounded and he and Prilly were back in their kitchen, Mrs Smithson knocked and came in.

'Have you heard? Dell's been hit. It's just about all gone.'

He'd made himself go down in the afternoon to view the rubble, still smoking amid pools of water from the fire hoses. It was another amputation, this loss of his old workspaces. He'd felt the way he'd done when Robert Ernest died. Outwardly he remained impassive, whilst inside he was awash with tears. The next day he caved in. They'd leave London. 'I know we can't take much of the furniture,' Prilly had said, 'but let's have your piano taken up there.' The piano never finished the trip. It was stolen. Just an object after all, but it felt like part of him had fallen away. He missed it still.

Jack shut his eyes and let the memories take him back. He'd travelled up to London to see the house after the War. His street looked dilapidated, but then so did everywhere. The rampant fireweed on the bomb sites reminded him of the flames that had made him leave. The city of his birth, of his life, was wounded, grimy, all but ruined with rubble and dust.

He was back in the years when he and Prilly were in the cottage.

'Oh, I don't know, I suppose I'd hoped that he'd find a nice English girl, C of E perhaps, who could bring him back to the Church.' Priscilla had just read Harold's letter from London.

'Most of them have gone as GI brides, I expect, dear. Let's count our blessings. We have three sons strong and healthy

and there's many a couple who'd give up everything to be able to say the same.' Later in the year when the front door had closed after Harold and his fiancée's visit, he'd turned round to his wife again.

'What do you think, Priscilla? Does she love him?'

'No, I wouldn't say so.' He was shocked and it showed. Priscilla giggled.

'She adores him. Can't you see that yourself? Adores him. She'll do.'

Without meaning to, he spoke his next words out loud.

'That's where it went wrong again. When I got switched onto the wrong rails. We should've gone back, not sold up. From then on one bad set of points and then another … it's how I lost my … power.'

Jack's mind rolled forward. It was a Sunday and Harold had come down specially. They were inspecting the new house rising up on the plot right next to the old cottage. The footings were in, and fresh brick walls were clambering up around the robust wooden window frames. He'd sold the Brecknock Road house to pay for it. Harold and his architect friend had worked out that there would be just enough cash for building the new home. Yet the money had run out, though it wasn't that those two serious young men had made wrong calculations. Jack had given most of it to Alf.

The fellow had been on the edges of Alfred's group of musical men. He must have gained Alf's trust before betraying it. A nasty bit of work, maybe, but he had the evidence. Either he got the money he wanted or Alfred went to trial. Alf didn't have that sort of money. But they couldn't let him go to prison, could they? Jack wasn't sure why he'd paid up. Was it for love of his eldest son, or for fear of the shame that would descend on them all should it ever come out? Yet he'd known there would be consequences. The tension in his stomach had told him that the mark had been uncovered. He'd again feel the saw's sharp teeth.

'Why haven't you paid Bradley's next instalment, Dad? Stuart says he signed it off three weeks ago.'

He'd seen the colour draining from Harold's face when he'd told him. Not long after there was a family conference, without Alf. The only way out was that Harold and Ulla raise a mortgage to finish the build. They'd been saving for their own place, but now there was another plan. They would eventually live in the new house. Priscilla had wanted this to be her own home back in her old village. Ulla had wanted to live in London. Harold was submerged in fury with his older brother. Jack could hear the disgust in his voice.

'He must just go and never come back!'

That was it. The ugliness of the fix. What else could be

done?

Jack hadn't heard anything from Alf for nearly ten years. He'd no idea of where he was or what he was doing. It was the filler and varnish. His first-born child had been erased from the family logbook. He'd lost another son, and nobody now mentioned the fact.

'But not from my head, not from my heart,' Jack said, his eyes still closed. Jane was tapping his hand. The children had been speaking to him for a minute, trying to get him to respond. 'Granddad, are you alright? Were you dreaming?'

The old man opened his eyes. 'I'm Mrs Manzi. Fell asleep on the tram. I've ended up in the wrong place.'

Jane's eyes widened in alarm. 'Should I get Mummy?'

'Not a bit of it. Stop fussing, Jane. I'm alright.'

'Well, if you're sure … Mum will be ready to leave now. We shouldn't keep her waiting.'

'Of course, dear.' He picked up the hearing aid, switched it on and placed it in his ear.

Jane kissed her grandfather's forehead, flung the door aside and, taking her brother's hand, hurried with him to the new house.

So Young John left the outhouse, to go in the car with his mother and elder sister to have his haircut. Yet believe me, I know. It's cemented into my bones. I know what happened next.

It wasn't a windy day, but a malevolent sprite of breeze caught the open door and slammed it against the jamb. It didn't latch and creaked open again. Jack's hearing aid screamed out a chord in E flat. Something horrible was gathering. 'Leave me alone! Leave us all alone!' He whispered the words without the smallest hope that it would make any difference.

He rested his chin in his hands. There was nothing to be said, and nobody he could say it to. Priscilla had gone in 1951; neither Alfred nor Frank were at the funeral. The following year Frank and a few friends said goodbye to Alice at the Islington crematorium. He hadn't been there himself.

It was as if a conductor had entered that small workspace. The cacophony of his thoughts coalesced and he heard music play. As it grew, he heard his own struggle from the poverty of those Barnsbury rooms, the discovery of his aptitude for the piano, of Brinsmeads and Ernest. He heard Priscilla in his own house, his boys. He heard the pain of loss of the baby, the severance from Alice. The bell curve tilted down with the forlorn contest with Bechstein, the decline and fall of the Empire of the Piano, gradual deafness, the second War, leaving London. He heard his own piano disappear, the cutting off from Alfred, the loss of his own roof, of Prilly. And then there was something else, the termite onset of overpowering daydreams, of forgetfulness, of a pervasive vagueness.

Jack knew that he was lost in time; that somehow his era slept deep in the abyss between the outhouse and the new house. And he felt that he'd lost his place, which never had been in the village anyway but was back in London, back in Brecknock Road. Then the minute passed. He put aside the arc of his life. Turning round, he saw his hand drill on the workbench next to the toolbox. Picking up the rag, he gave it one last wipe down, placed it in the case and closed the lid.

Harold

In the Village
1970

'He came round last week and said I should give up living at my place.'

'Who did, Bill?'

'You know, Mr St. Lucia.'

By this he meant our neighbour, who had recently given out that he had purchased a property on that island on account of the British climate being 'too chilly'. We shared a quiet antipathy to the man. I knew him to be an avaricious and relentless capitalist, and had no doubt that in his dealings with the older residents he would be blunderingly unaware of where lie the sensitive tripwires of condescension. And if he caused offence, he wouldn't care. He'd be amazed that a man like Bill, who must have finished school at nine or ten years old, could see right through him and not let on. Bill had once remarked that the villagers were no longer invited to events at The Grange and I said to myself that a man with new money had acquired a manor house that was associated with a squire's privileges. Yet he had no respect for the responsibilities that traditionally went with them. The twists of the class system! It was the stuff of literature: a classic case of a parvenu lacking the attributes of a gentleman.

'Wanted us to move over the road into one of the places he's doing up. Said there would be all mod cons and it would be a lot easier for Mrs Mew.'

I fumbled in my pocket for a tin of Gold Block. 'Well, of course he was only thinking of benefitting you and Muriel.' It was understood without my adding ironic accents that the meaning of the statement was the inverse of what was said. I opened the tin and offered it to him first. There was a pause whilst we both went through the ritual of filling and lighting our pipes.

'What did you tell him?'

'Oh, tell him, well, I didn't tell him anything, asked him would he like a cup of tea.'

He looked suddenly intense and said, 'The thing is Harold, there are people who move, move on, and people who don't.'

There was a sound the car crash made. In the dark, through the fog, I heard it blast out over the countryside. At first, the squealing smash of metal on metal, and then, rolling on in a slow diminishment, a chord in a minor key. At the time, I thought those unsettling notes were caused by my bones breaking and blood welling out. The next day, when they told me, I thought it was what people heard when their child's life was stubbed out, as Jane's had been that night.

The stranger thing is that it's not the only time I've heard those sounds, since they've come back to me on occasions over the years. Though it was only after the third time that I realised that I hear it a few hours before she returns.

When it happened first, it was in the morning as I was getting up to make us both a cup of tea. I covered my ears and collapsed back onto the bed.

Ulla looked up. 'Harold, are you alright? You've gone white. What happened?'

'I think I stood up too quickly.' I didn't want to unpack it all for her. I don't suppose I ever shall.

It's the angle of the chin. That's how you know how old a child is, really from quite a distance. Their way of gazing out on the world. What I mean is that a younger child must look up slightly more to see into the faces of the grown-ups. And I realise I miss that, though it seems I hardly noticed it at the time when the kids were younger, that lovely trusting tilt back of their heads as they looked and chattered. Then before you can catch up, it's gone and when adolescence sets in, they suddenly grow and the girls move for a year or so as if their ankles were made of rubber, well, that's what I saw with Hannah. Their bodies changing shape.

So although she was right at the other end of the garden when I saw her again, I knew at once who it was, losing that angle of her chin, but not yet with the flexible ankles. As I strode over to her I saw she was in her green school uniform, and still wearing the school beret at an angle a little too jaunty to be conventional. She looked a trifle sadly at me but said nothing, and even in later times she never gave voice. Well, except the last time maybe she spoke, or I thought she did. As I approached, heart pounding, I could see her, perfect in every detail, far more than unaided memory could recall, down to each particular strand within the twist of her plaits. She had been dead for three years.

I'm a materialist, in the Marxist, philosophical sense of that word, not in the sense that I follow mammon. You have to keep a grip of reason. Ghosts don't exist, and there's no afterlife for them to be sent to. Yet what is the human mind to do with visions of the impossible? Had my nightmares faded only to be superseded by a new, daylight terror?

What we have here, I thought, even as my heart ached to bursting point, is an hallucination. That was it: a persistent hallucination and one that seemed more real to me than the people of mere flesh and blood of my every day. Perhaps I was in a waking dream, or perhaps I was the pilot played by Ulla's favourite, David Niven, in the film, *A Matter of Life and Death*. The accident had left me walking wounded, with an undiagnosed head injury, or maybe psychological trauma had altered the chemistry of my nervous system. Whatever the cause, the explanation must have been that some physical change had taken place and I was seeing what my reason knew couldn't be there. Jane stayed about five minutes, I think, although it felt like eternity, and then, perhaps feeling the futility of it all, she wandered off straight through the boundary fence and across the neighbouring field so quickly that I couldn't follow.

After that she visited me several times, but I could never find any pattern to it. The second time was a few months later, as I was driving home from work. She was there on the side of the road, a little down from where the small road crossed the A1, where the accident happened, of course. It was her, standing by the road in her school uniform. I was so shocked I had to pull over and stop. In the mirror I could see her walking towards the car and she got into the passenger seat, where she travelled the evening of the accident because usually I made her sit in the back. But she'd asked to talk with me and I caved in and let her sit with me in the front.

If I hadn't done that she'd have been all right.

So all that time later, I understood that once again she wanted to be with me in the front of the car. After a few miles of travelling with me, I looked over at her and she nodded, and I pulled over once more. She tried to say something but no sound came and again she left. The metal of the car couldn't contain her, nor could gravity hold her. She went through the car door and walked over the hedgerow.

After that I changed my route home. I would run further down south along the A1 to pick up another way home, simply to avoid the minor road. Then, probably eighteen months later, on my detour, I saw her on the verge side, and stopped in the lay-by there for her and once again she was travelling with me in the car. A few miles on I stopped and she left, like she did before. After that I realised that my roundabout routes were pointless so I went back to the B road again.

I told no one of these visitations. I knew they were my punishment, my private anguish. And yet at first somehow I found being back with my first-born child also a private joy. Later, that elation left me too, so I felt agony and terror unleavened. I had always thought that people who had visions saw them through a haziness, like a person glimpsed through a smoky room; or maybe they would be diaphanous, like a will-o-the-wisp. It wasn't like that for me. I saw Jane with such clarity: she seemed as real, more real even, than my everyday life. Yet she was invisible to all others, and I realised that I must accept my madness. It was my diminishment. I knew it.

My work life's been spent around builders, surveyors, architects. There's a sense in which building is also digging, and the deeper you dig, then the sounder you will build. Sometimes the contractor doesn't reach far enough down, since digging is hard and can be dangerous work. I've known excavations to collapse and strong men to be snuffed out in a trice. After the pandemonium, an unnatural hush descends on the site, like when the guns fell silent at Cassino and we knew it was only to pause for breath whilst something worse was prepared. But before long the vacant positions are filled, men are shouting, arguing and playing their practical jokes again. Grieving is left to the silence of the breast.

Experience taught me to keep impassive passing on the orders, it's better that way. There was one order I loathed getting, it sometimes led to … consequences, but in Italy it came time after time. The men would banter about it: 'Don't General Alex know how to write anything else: push on regardless! Must have learnt it on the pot at mummy's knee.' Someone else would chip in: 'Nanny's knee!' And it would be the start of a joke. Later on I suppose I made light of it myself and it was an expression I often used. A while ago I was working in the garden with John, when the weather took a turn for the worse. I said something like: 'Let's push on regardless.' His next question surprised me.

'What exactly did the Army want you to be regardless of, Dad?'

'Of loss, John; push on regardless of loss.'

'Oh.'

And he went silent and I didn't know what he was thinking.

After we were all demobbed I had to work out how I was going to make a living. I'd had to leave school at fourteen, but first the Labour League of Youth and then the Army had kept me reading. I knew that I could hold my own in conversation and performance with the university men, but was realistic enough to know that they would always trump me into the best jobs. The construction industry seemed to be a good bet. After the destruction of the war there was a great need for rebuilding, giving people the houses, the schools and hospitals that they deserved. And I knew I had a technical bent of mind; the maths that so many found hard was no problem for me. So I enrolled at Brixton College of Building and got qualified, and became a Clerk of Works. When you dig down in history you unearth important names associated with my profession; think of Chaucer or of Hawksmoor watching the delving into the soft London clays. They struggled to gain a solid footing amidst the Thames gravels and the tricky swamplands. Not much has changed for their successors.

When the pain of loss was sharp, Ulla and I circled round each other.

'Can't you see, Harold, there are too many memories for me in this house. Even the happy ones have shadows in them now. It's your fault! It's all your fault! Listen to me! I want to live somewhere else, to start again. Let's make new memories somewhere else. Or maybe I should just take Hannah and John and go.'

When the pain was just the old, constant, familiar pain, we still circled around each other.

'Let's move to London,' she'd say. 'There's much more to do there, for both us. Theatre, galleries. And it would be good for your work, you could land the best jobs.'

I knew she was right. It was all my fault. I was in charge, and she died. I would do anything for Ulla, to make it better, to lessen her torment. But I couldn't do what she wanted most. Neither could I find a way to tell her why.

'Doesn't it mean anything to you, that this plot of land was my grandfather's? That my parents lived here? Isn't it something that we're raising the next generation here too?' All the time I'd be fighting off a kind of dread. Dread of going back, returning to the people all pressed together in the damp air. More than that. I couldn't leave, I just couldn't leave. In my mind I saw my daughter wandering in our garden alone, desperate to find the father whose mistake had so surely crushed her out of the world and who would now have surely abandoned her.

'I'm not going to be pulled back down to London,' was all I said.

I swept away the old outhouse in the garden and began work on a house extension. It would be perfect in every way and meet the solid and detailed specification I'd developed. Hannah and John would each have their own new bedroom, the car would have a garage for the first time and a new garden room would connect with the existing house. The only way to do it properly was to do most of the work myself, getting help from John of course. And with the slowness of a growing tree, the construction moved from my mind into bricks, mortar, windows and doors. Ulla and I argued about it.

'What's the use? The children will have left home before it's finished.'

She wanted to take out another mortgage and get a builder in to take charge. But slow was the way I needed it to be.

I've been functioning pretty well really, for a haunted man. I've provided for my family, involved myself in the local

122

Labour Party, helped Ulla manage Hannah as best as could be done, and have been as jolly as could be on family occasions. But I suppose I can say that if some builder, or some archaeologist perhaps, was to dig down inside me, they'd find there a cavern the shape of … Jane.

I finished building last year. The day after I'd completed the last act of construction – creating a path to the door of the garden room – I walked into our neighbour's field to check that elevation. I was alone: Hannah was travelling before going up to university, John was away with friends and Ulla had gone in the car to get some groceries.

Coming back into the garden I saw Jane sitting on the low wall by the drive. As I moved over to her I felt that old familiar panic coming close to a paralysis. Struggling to breathe, I gazed at her, once again wondering at the clearness in which she appeared to me. She'd draped her school cardigan over her arm, and I could see the name label Ulla had sewn into the collar all those years before. A crease hid the last two letters, but 'Jane Scriven', red thread on white, was fully visible.

She smiled at me, maybe a little wistfully, and said something, well, I could see her mouth forming a few syllables, and then again, and again. At last she pointed behind me and I turned round to look at the completed

123

extension; when I turned back she was gone. At first I thought she'd dropped down behind the wall but there was no trace of her there. There was something about this visit that felt different from the other times. I'd had no warning from the dark music that she might come back that day. I wondered if she was saying a final goodbye. In my head I heard an echo of words.

'Let me go, Daddy, let me go.'

I collapsed down onto the low wall and wept.

We spoke only infrequently, Mr Mew and I, perhaps when I had some heavy digging for him to do, or was in the garden when he walked past, and there was a certain formality, a certain procedure, in talking with him. We would acknowledge each other:

'Good morning, Mr Mew,' I would say, and he might respond:

'I think it's good afternoon already, Mr Scrivener,' and then we could get on to using our first names.

'You know, Harold, it looks to me as if your apple trees could use a tar wash this winter.'

Or I might say: 'Bill, I've been wondering about turning this corner over to asparagus – what do you think?'

It was only this once that he departed from our way.

Sitting on the low, hard wall, racked by my tears, twisted by a cry that would not take voice, I felt a hand on my shoulder and turned round to see Bill Mew. I suppose he must have been on his way to the local for his Saturday lunchtime pint, though I'd no idea of how long he'd been standing there. And he said:

'Alright, Harold, alright.'

As he looked at me I knew that he knew, and later I remembered what he'd told me before.

'There are people who move, move on, and people who don't.'

Temple Fortune
1975

'Whom shall I say is calling?'

'My name's Scrivener. Harold Scrivener.'

I heard clicking on the line, as the woman threw a switch. Then his voice, instantly recognisable, as if we'd spoken only a couple of weeks ago.

'Ah, hello, Harold. I was wondering where you'd got to.'

And that was it. Picking up again after thirty-five years.

The weather had been fine that late September morning as I motored through Hatfield. On the lower reaches of the Great North Road the haze started to thicken, so that by the time I was down in Hendon I was sliding under the cover of London cloud. I knew that sky. For half my boyhood it'd been above me. It seemed metallic, impermeable, nearly as dark as pewter. The lid that fitted over the bowl of London, trapping us inside.

I never knew how many trains moved each day through our part of town, bound for Kings Cross, Euston or wherever. But it seemed that each one vomited up an ounce of smoke for every yard of rail it travelled. Then there was the industry nearby: Careeras cigarettes and the boilers stoked by every piano manufactory. One breeze brought the stench of East

End factories; another gave us the grit from Bankside Power Station. A particular southerly wind produced a gentle rain of soot, which people said was the gift of the Lots Road plant that made electricity for the Underground. London was a beast ravenous for coal, mountains of it, mashed into fumes in the blink of an eye. On some winter days we breathed in the tarry astringency of coal fires, millions of them. That's what warmed every hearth. Well, every hearth where they could afford the coal man's prices. Odd that I only ever get that coaly smell nowadays in the village, in the evenings of still autumn days like this one. Today in London I smelt only the vehicle fumes sucked in by the car heater.

So there in the driver's seat I was already going back, thinking of those times. Thinking of when a north wind would clear the air, only to produce draughts that whistled into our house through those ill-fitting windows and doors. It was the same for everyone we knew; it's only now that people are putting things right, installing properly made ones that fit. About this time of year Mum would be searching for the door blankets and window bangs.

'I put them away somewhere, Harold, still in the brown paper from the laundry. Have you seen 'em?'

'Yes but I can't think where. Under the stairs?' Door blankets! Window bangs! I bet Hannah and John don't even know what they are.

The traffic had gradually thickened up. I decided to keep to the A1. But on the Falloden Way I got stuck fast in a jam. On the spur of the moment I squeezed a right turn into the Hampstead Garden Suburb and began to navigate through the complex streets. I'd never driven it before and yet I knew my way through without missing a turn. I racked my brain as to how that could be. Instead of remembering, my head was filled with last week when I'd walked in St. James Park. The lake there was a leftover from the time when the Serpentine River was subjected to human will. Although the ground felt solid enough, the waterway was still there, somewhere under my feet. There's a similar set-up nearby in Hyde Park. For the most part, people have forgotten about the little rivers that feed the Thames, but builders should remember them. Much of London sits on marsh, clay and gravel. The boggy water shifts and slides in unexpected ways. The whole system is in motion, a slow-breathing thing, as the Thames tides drag and press through the gravels. My work was near the Park – a high-specification office block to be occupied by a government department. Ground conditions weren't easy. In the early days of the contract, a pit flooded without warning. The digger operator said that it was as if he'd removed a plug; in a minute he was in four feet of water. He'd hit an uncharted little brook that flowed like a capillary towards the Serpentine. It had forced itself up into our awareness.

I turned onto the Finchley Road, the stretch of it called Temple Fortune. It's an in-between place, little more than a parade of shops on a through road. You can drive right through it and not know you've been there. You might say that it doesn't exist at all, that it's just an estate agent's or map-maker's conceit. It doesn't seem to have a locus, a heartland. I stopped at a Belisha Beacon to let some school kids cross and glanced to the side. The office premises there had a sign that read: Lemann and Weinberg: Chartered Accountants.

Lemann. Sammy Lemann. I'd not thought of him for years. We were on bikes, he with the new one his uncle had bought for him and me on Alf's. Even with the saddle right down I could only touch the ground with the end of my toe. We'd cycled up from Kentish Town and then round the suburb, picking out the houses that we'd live in one day when we'd made our fortunes. Clean air, proper gardens, all mod cons, we'd have cars outside our gates. Clever boys' dreams we had then.

'When you're Professor of Maths at London University, Sammy!'

'And what will you be?'

'I'll be a scientist. Chemistry. I'll make new materials, things that don't exist in nature ...'

Of course we didn't know then that we were nearing the end of our schooling. Mine was only a few months away when my father lost his job at the piano factory. He told me I had to get earning, to leave school and get work. I was fourteen. Sammy hung on for another year or so. And we didn't know we'd have to fight, to spend our youth at war and not in college.

As the car dropped down towards Golders Green I got to wondering if it could be the same Lemann. Not a common name. At our school there was only one boy better at figures than me and that was Sammy Lemann. Had he become an accountant along the way?

We were winding up at Queen Anne's Gate. After my delayed journey I'd hardly a minute to spare before the Monday morning walk-out. The usual sort of issues: most of the boxes ticked, but there was some shoddy finishing needing to be redone, a subcontractor waiting on drawings that hadn't appeared, that sort of thing. Then we were in the staff restaurant, which was a favourite place of mine. The civil service had been used to having separate eating rooms for juniors and seniors, but the egalitarian idea here was that everyone, from porter to permanent under secretary, would dine together in this spacious room. As we arrived, the electricians were completing the installation of scores of red glass lampshades over the ceiling lights.

The architects' man was the first to speak. 'This isn't what's intended. Each shade is a completely different red. That one's orange, for pity's sake! They should be uniform. See how the jangle draws the eye. It's supposed to be restful. Mr Fitzroy will have kittens. And I don't want to be the one accompanying Sir Basil at the official opening.'

I spoke for the client. 'I agree. Unacceptable.'

Young Hodgkins from the contractor's side looked sheepish.

'The supplier is saying ten weeks to replace, which probably means twice that.'

We'd got only six weeks before the handover.

'So if the client won't accept as is, we'll have to deal with it under snagging.'

The architects' man shook his head in disbelief.

'Andy, let the two of us sort it out over a mug of tea,' I said.

Later, I suggested that he get the 'sparks' to take all the lampshades down and put them on the floor.

'Make them grade those shades. Palest reds towards the

windows, darkest ones in the centre. Make sure they do it well and put them up in the same order. The colour difference between adjacent lights will be tiny. My bet is that the eye will never pick it up.'

Hodgkins was looking at me with – dare I say – respect.

Then I had space in the day to get out the London telephone directories.

'I'd like to speak to Mr Lemann. Mr Samuel Lemann.'

On Friday morning I inspected the canteen again. I knew those different hues of red were there, was looking for them, but now that the lampshades had been rearranged, I couldn't see them anymore. I left work early for lunch with Sammy near the Lemann and Weinberg offices.

'He's talking with Mr Weinberg.' I recognised her voice from the phone. 'He's expecting you, of course, and asked if you would mind waiting in his office. May I bring you a tea or coffee?'

'That's kind, but no thank you.'

She looked at me with interest, as if I were a VIP guest that she was showing in. Sammy's office wasn't large, but it was neat: a desk by the window, in the corner two armchairs and a coffee table with some magazines on it, filing cabinets and shelves with box files, and books. Some old accounting textbooks, next to which rested a much-used volume: *An Introduction to the Theory of Numbers*. Another shelf held two heavily bound Hebrew titles, and one entitled *Myths of the MesoAmerican Peoples*. I was surprised to see a couple of books by Carlos Casteneda – I knew the name because John had had one when he was a student – and a Huxley. Not Thomas but Aldous.

There were some children's games too: a small wooden case of dominoes, a battered cardboard box that declared itself as Snakes and Ladders. I took that one and set it out on the coffee table. We'd had a similar set when the kids were small, and we'd play together, the five of us. The kids would be over the moon if they won, and down in the dumps if they lost. When Young John was tiny, he'd be tearful at losing. As they got older they worked out that it's all down to chance, and stopped caring so much. Later on, after … after it happened, Ulla put the game away somewhere, as we didn't do things like that anymore. I'd not seen it since.

Sammy came in. I'd have passed him in the street, but there was no mistaking him now. Taller than me, his grey hair somewhat thinned and rather long. He'd swept it back behind his ears and fastened it with a clip at the back. He was in shirtsleeves and a bright floral waistcoat. Not at all what I expected from a man of my own age, and – how can I put it?

– an accountant.

'Harold – it's grand. Grand to see you.'

We shook hands. It felt a bit awkward.

'Hope you don't mind, but I was just looking at the board game. It brings back memories. We used to have one just like it.'

'Be my guest. When my kids were small they'd sometimes come to the office after school. This was to keep them busy until I'd finished work.'

I pointed to an issue of the *London Philatelist* magazine on his coffee table. 'And do you still collect stamps Sammy?' He'd had the best albums of any of my friends.

'No – had to sell my collection twenty years ago. Needed the money. It did quite well though. I still take an interest – out of habit.'

Then we got to talking about our families. I told him about Ulla and my two kids. Hannah embarked on an academic career, John starting in the civil service.

'Do you see much of them?'

'Not as much as I'd like. John's in London now and I see him from time-to-time. Last week I showed him round Queen Anne's Gate. We had a sandwich lunch in the room I'm using as my office. I think he was interested, but he's quite reserved with me, so I always find it hard to be sure.'

Sammy had married in '52. Two girls and a boy. Girls doing well. The lad was giving him some worry. 'He's got in with the wrong crowd at school. You know, not doing his homework; even playing truant when he can. We're thinking of moving him.'

He'd said it in a matter of fact way, and I suppose that's why I was less guarded than I thought I'd be:

'I did have three kids actually, but Jane died when she was twelve.'

In the silence that followed I saw him studying my face.

'What happened?'

'An accident. I was driving.' There was another pause, and he took my hand and squeezed it.

Seeking to change the subject, I asked him about his war.

'Because the last time I saw you, if I've got this right, was for a pint near Camden tube station, in the Mother Red Cap, before we joined up.'

'Got posted up to Scotland to guard the bases. I've never been so bored or so cold! Mind you, I got to doing some of the back room jobs and that gave me the idea of taking up accountancy. When we were demobbed my uncle put in a good word for me and I got taken on as clerk by a practice in Golders Green. Did my exams the hard way, you know, evening classes, correspondence courses. Got my letters in fifty-one.'

'But you left and set up your own partnership?'

'Too many family members for me to go up. I'd never have made partner. Not good for a man seeking to start a family of his own! So yes, I left and came here, so as not to fish in exactly the same pond.'

I told him about Italy, as far as I could. And more about getting into the building industry, about landing a job in Ghana, and our wonderful years there.

'What are you doing in London, Harold? You always said you'd live in the countryside, somewhere with fresh air and a garden. It appealed to me too – I suppose I've made it as far as Barnet!'

'Oh, I did it. I built a house in the village my mother came from. We still live there. But it's the work, Sammy. The best jobs, most of them are still down in The Smoke. I wanted the chance to work with a top architectural practice. London's winched me back in, so to speak. I stay up here Monday to Thursday nights and drive back on Fridays. That's what I'll do after lunch. It's not ideal for Ulla and me, but it's for a limited time. The thing about the building industry is that nothing lasts because you work yourself out of a job!'

I'd called London by its old name, The Smoke. But it's not a good one anymore. 'Mind you,' I said, 'the air's much fresher in town than in our day. And you know what, all over Westminster they're washing buildings, getting the soot off with pressure hoses. Soon we'll just have Big Ben and the Houses of Parliament to remind us of how it was.'

'Not just in Westminster, in our old stamping grounds too, some things are getting spruced up. The bomb sites have just about been inter-filled. It's really getting quite nice, even at the Tufnell Park end of your road. My God, a lot of bombs fell there.'

'It used to be depressing coming home, didn't it? I know I never thought it would take twenty-five, thirty years to rebuild. Perhaps I should have stayed around in Camden or Islington. But no, I'm glad the kids had breathing spaces, a big garden to play in, fresh air.'

And we moved on to talking about our health. Sam looked fit and energetic: I told him I could see him carrying on for another thirty years.

'What about you, Harold?'

I said I'd been fine till the last few years when a heart issue, diabetes and one or two things like that had thumped me.

'All manageable though,' I said. I think I succeeded in sounding upbeat. The reality is that I'm gradually being worn down. Anyway, he didn't seem to notice that my guard was up.

'Harold, was there any particular thing that made you look me up? One of my old Golders Green mates got in touch a few months ago. He needed someone he could trust to give him advice about money. Is there anything like that? It's good to see you and it wouldn't bother me at all.'

'On no, nothing like that. All I wanted to do was to see how things had turned out for you. And I suppose I feel a need to look back, to see how I got to where I am now … but the road from the past seems to have faded. Things happen and you block the past off, don't you? You don't look back; a man's got to live in the present and plan for the future …'

'Except that now you want to remember it?'

'Well, I suppose so. I suppose I've been stirred up a little by being in London again, and the prospect of leaving soon when the job's over. It's made me feel the passing of time: familiar places looking strange, young people in them doing what they've always done, what we did …'

'Go on.'

'I'm happy for the youngsters and sad for myself, perhaps … Sammy, you know what's just come to me? The finish of my last job. I was used to walking on site to a cheery greeting from the security man, not even needing to show my pass. A couple of weeks after it ended I went back there to retrieve a favourite slide-rule that I'd left in my desk drawer. The client had moved in and there'd been a changing of the guard. There was nobody who knew me, or who even recognised an old staff card. The world had turned; that slice of earth had new occupants.'

'Harold, I'm not sure what to say. Except that the world turns as it should. And the past must be remembered to be honoured. The human mind forgets nothing, you know. Most people don't realise what a glorious thing the mind is, that it doesn't need to be stuck inside the body. In our culture, most people keep it trapped, stopped up. Sometimes it needs help, that's all, help to loosen off its moorings …'

I wasn't sure what he meant but before I had the chance to ask, he squared his shoulders and said, 'I'm famished. Fancy going for lunch right away?'

We ignored the nearby Jewish eatery and went to a café. Sammy put on a pair of half-moon glasses to read the menu, even though it was just a card.

'The gammon, egg and chips is good here. That's what I'm having.'

'I'll have the same,' I said. 'You're still not keeping kosher then, Sam? A week or two after your bar-mitzvah I remember you telling me that your father had taken you to the Lyons Corner House where you each had a gorgeous sandwich. And you said: what meat is this in here, Dad?'

'That's right! And Dad said: it's bacon son. And whatever you do, don't tell your mother!'

We were both chuckling.

'Some days I go kosher but it's just because I fancy latkes or salt beef with pickle! I'm a member of the reform shul – it's a community thing. Good for business too. Maybe I put on my yarmulke and roll up a couple of times a year. But no, I don't believe in any of it. I'm involved in … other things. What about you? Did you go back to the C of E like Mrs Scrivener wanted you to?'

'No. I've not changed. Philosophically, I'm still a materialist. Although I try to keep an open mind. You know: there are more things in heaven and earth, Horatio.'

He peered at me over those half moon spectacles, his eyes as intelligent as ever.

'Hmm. Hamlet. He saw his father's ghost, didn't he?'

Was there another question in the air? Had I lowered my guard again? I changed tack and said: 'I suppose we've both ended up working in the definite, physical world. Me in bricks, mortar and reinforced concrete, you with figures. The thing with a number is that it's what it is and can't be anything else. No room for whimsy. Oh, don't you agree with me Sammy?'

'It's just that I used to think that too. Then I came across imaginary numbers. Have you heard of them?'

I hadn't.

'Things like the square root of minus one. Logic tells us they can't actually exist, but we can pretend they do. And in maths they turn out to be incredibly useful. What blew my mind, as the kids say, was the realisation that the laws of physics rely on them too. The universe seems to run on imaginary numbers.'

I couldn't see how it could be. So Sammy talked on about the mathematician Euler, who I'd heard of, and then about a wave equation by Schrödinger, whose name was new to me. He declined the suggestion that we have a tea or coffee saying that he had better fare back in his office.

'I'm going to make us a special tea,' he said as I settled down into one of his armchairs. 'I got it in Mexico. It's tea but with herbs added. A bit of cactus flower, that sort of thing. I usually drink it without milk, but it's fine with. Stimulates the memory.'

I didn't say, but I've never been keen on mucked-about tea. Earl Grey with his bergamot and all that. Sam poured from a small teapot into cups without handles. It had a pungent taste.

'Now I've got some things here you might recall. Part of

my collection.'

He went behind his desk, picked up a fat briefcase like accountants carry, and pulled out a battered loose-leaf binder. Flicking through the pages he took out several polythene wallets. He snapped one down on the coffee table as if it were a tarot card.

It was a duplicated letter headed Acland School for Boys, Kentish Town, informing parents that an outing had been arranged to Staines Town Rowing Club, please would they sign the attached slip and provide a packed lunch, etcetera. It meant nothing to me. I'd no memory of it at all. Then it hit me. My body felt light, weightless. And I was suddenly back there, back then:

'Hey! Stop flicking water Sammy!'

'I'm not doing it on purpose. I've never rowed a boat before!'

'Neither have I! You're putting the oar in like this.' I flick some water over at him. A battle develops and we get quite wet. My legs are cold and then prickly as the moisture soaks into the cloth of my shorts. A voice shouts.

'Oi you two, pack it in!'

We settle in to row upstream, as we'd been told. Once we get the hang of it we move quickly forward. Too quickly, as we're soon tired.

'Let's just rest a minute.'

'What do you think it's like living in one of the river houses?'

'Wouldn't it be great? Look at the size of that lawn! I'd have a dog.'

'If you worked in London you'd keep a boat and sail down to town.'

'Or row upstream for river bank picnics.'

As we talk our hard rowing is being undone. At first only imperceptibly and then, with increasing speed, we're drifting, being pulled back down the way we'd come.

'Come on, we've got to keep rowing! We'll end up back in London!'

'Pull as hard as you can or we'll never get anywhere!'

My body was heavy again as if gravity had suddenly doubled; I was back in the armchair in Sammy's office. My mouth was dry. Sam was staring dreamily out of the window. Then he focussed on me. 'You alright, Harold? You've been … um …very quiet.'

Was that archness I'd heard in his voice?

He put another polythene wallet down and then another beside it. I knew they both had a connection with me. I rummaged through my brain to think how. A leaflet advertising the Clarion Cycling Club excursion to Box Hill and a printed letter from the Spanish Youth Foodship Committee. I took another gulp of tea. For a second gravity didn't exist anymore and when it came back I was cycling hard up the Dorking Road. On my own bike. In the summer of 1934. Sammy was shouting:

'I'm just a pool of sweat!'

'Me too! But let's try to get up the hill without walking the bikes up.'

And we do. I've a stitch as painful as if I'm being stabbed in the ribs. Panting, we throw the bikes down on the grass and open a Thermos of tea. Although we're hot, somehow the tea seems to cool us down. Sam opens a parcel of sandwiches. Bread from the Jewish bakery with some sort of seed in it. I don't like it much but I accept the offer for the cheese and pickle it contains.

We try to make conversation with a couple of girls who arrive walking their bicycles up to the top. They're friendly enough but there's no disguising that they have no interest in us. We're back on our bikes and freewheeling home, coasting along, surrendering as we fall. The breeze is a welcome wave of coolness that soon becomes chilly. And then it must have been another journey. There's four of us wheeling back down from the Clarion Hostel in Hoddeston. Me, Sammy, Connie and Emily. It's sunny and we stop off somewhere along the

River Lea. Sam and Connie have paired off. Emily and I are in the meadow grass.

'You're sweet, Em.'

'That's what you tell all the girls.'

'There's no other girls!'

'You can kiss me if you mind your hands.'

Then we're all back on our bikes and sliding down the lane. Falling back to the place where we started.

Yet not quite. For the next instant I'm fastening my cycle to railings at the bottom of Lloyd Baker Street, near Kings Cross station. It's opposite Rowton House Hotel or, as we call it, the Rundown House Hotel. A ramshackle building that's home to packing cases, cans, bags, boxes of every conceivable type of produce. At the back a grocer's van is being unloaded. It's full of cardboard boxes that could almost have come from a hundred harvest festival collections. There's a small office in the back. A couple of desks and typewriters that have seen better days. Teddy Willis comes out, walking up and down with a telephone on a long lead. He finishes his conversation and slams the receiver home.

'Ah, Comrade Scrivener! How are you, Harold? Have you brought Sam with you?'

'He's here already, I think.'

'Tell you what we've got to do, we've got to get this lot

sorted and stored so that Jones's man can drop off another load before the end of his shift.'

'How come Jones's are delivering here, Ted?'

'Don't ask! I didn't. Their driver's a comrade and they're contributing to Spain, and that's all I know!'

He opens the phone again.

Sam trots down the stairs with a notepad and pencil. He's muttering to himself.

'Six, no, say seven, tons … thirty-two on the second floor … Hello, Comrade! Maybe it's been a bit ambitious saying we'll fill a ship.'

I could feel a drag on my head pulling it down towards my knees. A jarring, jolting feeling and once more I was pushed down into the armchair in Sammy's office. Sam was staring out of the window again.

'It's strange. It felt as if I went back for a while to those days of the Foodship campaign. You know, if we'd actually sent it I'd have gone with it, or tried to, out to Spain. The load went overland in the end.'

There was a pause before he replied, as if from a long way away.

'So when was that – thirty-eight?'

'Must be. Remember in those days before the war, Sam, just about everyone we knew was a Popular Fronter. So many

147

of us, yet so many more with their heads in the sand. Then there were the outright fascist supporters, of course.'

'Remember when we two went down to volunteer for the International Brigade? You said that it was our chance to get out of London, and do our bit for the cause and to see La Pasionaria herself.'

'There was three of us who went down. Wasn't Dickie Smith with us?'

'God, yes. And we two filled in forms after which they told us that they'd closed ordinary recruitment to the British Battalion.'

'I suppose two scrawny working class lads weren't a very promising prospect. I mean compared with famous writers, intellectuals and so on.'

'Wasn't it Dickie's idea that we go down to the East End to block the Blackshirts that day?'

'Yes, only we didn't get to Cable Street, did we? Because there were thousands of people at Gardiner's Corner.'

'Refill?' he asked.

'No, thanks.'

He poured himself another cup.

Sammy placed another plastic wallet on the table. In it was a cutting from The Times. At the top he'd written 'Nearly copped it! 3rd October 1937'. Thirty-eight years ago to the day.

'Hooligans in Bermondsey

Communists and Mosleyites

Police kept busy'

I started to read the report of the Battle of Bermondsey, when the Blackshirts had tried to march again, down Long Lane. I knew it was biased. I'd been there that day, with Dickie and Sam. The office melted away, I was there again, in those narrow, dirty, dangerous streets. Shouting. Swearing. Someone letting off fireworks. A few ragged men bring out an old settee, which is the start of a barricade. Many hands bringing out poles, metal, masonry. A young lad, he can't be more than twelve, shows me a bag of marbles.

'They don't like these, Mister!'

'Who don't?'

'Fuckin' cop 'orses.'

And we're waiting, shouting and singing. It seems forever until the word goes round:

'They're in the Lane! They've reached the Lane!'

Only it's not the Blackshirts, it's the police. People surge back from a charge. Bloodied heads from batons. 'Stop 'em! Don't let the bastards through!'

Overhead bricks and stones fly towards the police. Cheers.

'They're scarpering! See 'em run!'

We don't see the fascists. They've gone down Tooley Street and we all run down Tower Bridge Road, but we've missed them. We end up going for a drink in the Royal Oak. We're fired up afterwards, and step out onto the dark street. The two of us start the walk to Waterloo Station, humming The Red Flag.

Sam's voice sounded far away: 'Remember when we met those fascists coming back from their rally at the Mill Pond?'

There's only one of them. In a pool of light from the lamp on the other side of the road.

'Fucking yid lovers!'

Sammy shouts back. 'I'm not a yid lover, I'm a yid! So put that in yer pipe and choke!'

I give the fascist the two fingers. Sammy likewise. A bit further on and he's back with three others. A couple of them are big fellers.

'There they are! Bastard yiddo reds come and get yer faces shoved in!'

We run. There's more of them ahead. We dart down a side street. Running through arches under the railway. One of them's gaining on us. It's very dark. Round a corner, my heart feels like it's going bust. There's a factory yard behind a brick wall.

'Over here!'

We both jump up. I get over. Sam's trouser snags on a projecting nail. He's stopped on top of the wall to free it. Only a second's pause but then he can't move his foot. The Blackshirt's got hold of it. I leap up to help free him. The top brick is loose and comes away in my hand. I jump up again, and smash the brick down into our pursuer's face. There's a crunch. He falls away. Sam's free. We run through the yard – there's a tall iron gate leading to a side lane.

'We've got to climb this!'

'Shit! It's taking too long.'

We fall as much as climb down the other side. We rush through the lane to Borough High Street.

'Hey! I think you broke his Nazi nose for him.'

We avoid the big stations and cross Waterloo Bridge to pick up a number three tram from Holborn. My clothes, skin and hair are begrimed with London black. Back home in Brecknock Road, shivering, scrubbing myself hard in a cold bath – no chance of hot water on a Sunday evening.

'In the morning my skin still seemed grey. You know, the London dirt had got into my pores. I wonder if I ever got it out, if it's still there, mixed up with the Cassino mud.'

Sammy somehow got the sense of what I was saying. 'It'll always be part of you, Harold, just as those days are part of me.'

'For all the camaraderie and laughs we had, wasn't London a witches' cauldron back then? And when I eventually got out it was from the frying pan into the fire.'

'What do you mean?'

'Nineteen forty-three. The ship that took us to North Africa. I reckoned I'd been so much part of London that it took all of the million horse power of the Eighth Army to get me out! That's what made me feel that I'm not just a Londoner any more, that I've seen a bit of the world.'

And Sam told me of his travels, all in the past few years, once he'd finally got himself established.

'You know what?' said Sammy. 'You always said you came from Kentish Town, though your side of the road's the wrong side of the borough boundary. You could have said you came from Islington; that would've have been a notch above hoi polloi like me who were Kentish Town born and bred.'

'Ah well, workers lived in Kentish Town, things were made there. It always seemed that was where things happened. Whereas Brecknock Road isn't quite Holloway, nor the Nag's Head, certainly not Tufnell Park. I couldn't identify with it.'

'I think it shows what sort of chap you are, Harold. Who you identify with.'

I glanced at the clock on the wall.

'I'd best be getting on the road.'

In the way of things we talked on for nearly an hour after I'd said that. About politics, on which we mostly agreed. Grudging respect for Wilson, frustration with his cautiousness; excitement at the final triumph of the Vietnamese. Franco was on his last legs – we worried that Spanish fascism might outlast him.

'It's fascinating to me, Sam, how things turn out. How lives take the paths they do.'

'I often think of it too. We're the product of the things we came from, the things we lived through, you know, the fight against the fascists, joining the army and so on ...'

'And of how we responded to all that. The things we made, we did, for ourselves. How does it all fit together? Perhaps someone could put together a maths for all that!'

'Perhaps one day a calculus will be developed for it, Harold! Though the equations would need their constants, and I'm not sure what they'd be. Our characters maybe? We remain ourselves amidst the hurly-burly of the world.'

'Yes ... but we do change too. Or at least I've changed. Things happened to me, or should I say I've made things happen to me, sometimes without meaning to,' I said. He looked at me over his spectacles. I felt exposed again. Sammy picked up the dice from the Snakes and Ladders game and dropped it into its plastic cup. 'You've got to allow for chance.' He took a deep breath before continuing. 'Sometimes when we do well we think it's all down to us, to our abilities and merit. Though some of it, all of it even, may be down to chance, our good luck. Or we blame ourselves, as you blame yourself, for a disaster, when it might simply be awful ill-chance.'

I could feel a tear starting in my eye.

'Sometimes I wonder,' I said, 'if there's such a thing as chance. If it's just a way of letting ourselves off the hook, the hook of responsibility. If you throw that dice we'd both say that there was a one in six chance of a particular side being on top. But isn't that just a cover for ignorance or laziness? If we knew everything about the dice itself, about how you threw it and the surface it bounced onto then surely we could work out which side must come up? We could alter the way we roll the dice so that our number would win.'

Sammy was studying my face. 'It might work better than blowing over the dice cup and saying the number you want, which is what my girls used to do … In principle, you've a point. Or would do were it not for natural laws that stop us either getting all the information we need to do the calculations, or having the consistent scheme of maths that

154

we'd need to do them.'

'Obviously we don't know everything, there's a lot to know. But why shouldn't we eventually be able to know it?'

'Oh, take it from me: we can't. There's Heisenberg in physics, Gödel in arithmetic. Not even you can do away with the messiness of luck, old comrade of mine.' We talked on about it.

I looked at the clock again. 'Chance or not, we haven't done too badly, have we, Sam? For two North London boys.'

'We've done OK, maybe better than was to be expected. Considering what we had, and the times we've lived through. Would you say that you've fulfilled your potential?'

'That's a hard question. But no, not really. I never ended up with the education I wanted. And war, well, it changes a man. So I've done what I did, did what I could. It's up to the kids now.'

Back in the car, I thought that I wouldn't be seeing very much of Sam. We'd travelled very different paths since that pint in the Mother Red Cap – the long years had stretched and strained the strong connection we once had. Yet I was glad I'd made the telephone call. Out of our meeting I'd got some things that I must have wanted without my even realising it. It came to me, the question that Sammy helped me with, and I hadn't even asked it out loud. What is the equation for a life?

I thought of all the things, nature and nurture, that had formed us, Sammy and me, with our similarities and differences. The left hand side of an equation with a hundred thousand terms all joined together by the long S of the integral calculus. And there, on the right hand side, after the equals sign, you'd have his life, or mine: Samuel Levy Lemann, Harold Edward Scrivener. But then, there's a storm of integers swirling between everything like a will-o-the-wisp. So the calculation is changed, and the result uncertain. I tried to grasp where my luck, both the good and the terrible, had come from. Probabilities? Imaginary numbers? Fortune: an iridescent flight of butterflies; or else a darkening swarm of locusts.

As the car nosed north I was thinking about the glass lampshades again. We'd hidden those different tints in broad daylight, in full view; was it the eye or the mind that we'd deceived? We could undo it, and the colours would clash out again. I was thinking of all the things that must be around us, but we're blind to; blind until there's another rearrangement, a reordering, so to speak, and then, only then, do they stand out to us.

I found myself listening to the car engine. It seemed to be softly complaining as it pulled me up the long, gradual slope that was the road out of London.

Ulla

The Royal Free
1983

I was dreaming in German. I'd not done that for years. A boat on a river, it might have been the Rhine once but now it's the Thames. I'm not on the straight, wide flow any more, but have gone up a meander, a stream. It's an oxbow, and we're cut off. Where I'd come from was far away. I'm carrying that old leather suitcase; it's heavy in my hand. Children are calling out the rhyme that Mainz kids knew in those days: *Willigis, Willigis, Denk'woher Du kommen bis*!

Someone gentle took hold of my hand. Before I was properly awake I said:

'I'm not going for any more tests. Leave me be.'

'Ulla, it's Lore.'

I opened my eyes and saw her there, sitting in the bedside chair.

'Lore, is it really you?'

'Of course it's me.'

'It's just that … oh, never mind.'

I took a gulp of water from the beaker on the bedside unit. 'I thought you were one of the porters. They've been taking me everywhere in their wheelchairs. It feels like I've been down miles of corridors; I must have been through every one

157

of those double fire-doors.' The porters don't push you through the doors front-ways. They do a sort of flip turn, pushing the doors open with their back so you actually move forwards in reverse, looking at the previous set of doors, and then you're spun around to face forward again. 'Sometimes the porters hurry; they send me giddy with the speed they turn the chair and back again, as if they were moving a sack of potatoes around, and not a patient, not a person. These Royal Free Hospital doctors, they do love you to have tests. But I don't see the point of them any more. Sorry, Lore, I'm rambling, something they've given me, I expect.'

'Last time we met up we were going to talk about your time in Africa, but we never got round to it. Should we do that now?'

'Not now, later maybe. Everything's a bit of an effort today.'

'I thought I might see John or Hannah here.'

'They were here earlier, said they'd return tomorrow … Detta's coming back soon.'

'Detta!'

After the astonishment, I saw concern on her face. 'Don't look so worried, Lore. I am dying, you know. I'm allowed my stupidities.'

She tried to move the conversation on. 'They've

transferred you since I last came. Good to have your own room.'

'It was yesterday, I think. The staff nurse said that I'd be more comfortable here, but we both know what she meant, that everyone else would be more comfortable eventually.'

'Oh, Ulla.'

'I do like that I can see the sky from my bed. A London sky, London air. Do you remember when we first saw it on the train; I mean it had that bleary quality as if there were milk droplets in it?'

'Your first words to me then were "so this is England with misty skies", or something like it.'

'I suppose it's all that moisture around. Being an island. Anyway that's what struck me at first – all that milky damp sky wrapped into the smokiness of London. Look at those clouds now – they're moving over Hampstead Heath. They remind me of Turner. He painted the air, didn't he? Though you'd need to come to England to really understand him.'

We started talking of when I first came to the village. The old tumble-down thatched-roof cottage, with no running water, just an open fire for heating and no oven; a central bulb in three rooms was all the electric there was – and just one power point. There was no ring main. God, I didn't know such primitive houses even existed in England of all places.

The new house was being finished on the next-door plot. Somehow we managed to live in the cottage for a while before we went to Ghana. It was still called the Gold Coast in those days.

'When we lived in the cottage, Miss Saunders would come up from Chapel House to sit with me so that I wouldn't be all alone, and then – perhaps I mentioned it to you – after the accident, in the new house she was sitting with me again. She had a kindly heart; one day when it was bad for me, I mean I couldn't cook or anything, and she took hold of both my hands and looked right into my teary eyes and said, "Ulla, you have two lovely living children, you must carry on for them". I knew she was right. I put my tears away.'

I moved further up the bed, catching at the dream she'd broken in on. 'Lore, do you remember that rhyme about Willigis we all learned back in Mainz? I was dreaming about it.'

She thought for a moment. 'Willigis, Willigis, remember where your beginning is.'

I liked her translation. I told her so. 'Is he still celebrated in Mainz?'

'Not so much. The town still uses his coat-of-arms.'

I was thinking of him then, the wise bishop of a thousand years ago. His father had been a working man, a wheelwright, and he was taunted by opponents who brought two cartwheels to his mansion. He refused to be ashamed and displayed the wheels outside the palace. And he put them into his emblem. Perhaps he was a lucky man, the local Catholics still think him a saint, and even after all the cruel twists of history, he's still remembered.

'I always asked myself why they made such a big deal of it,' I said. 'It isn't a shameful thing that he was announcing in his coat-of-arms. I wonder if there were things in his past that he did feel guilty about, and would have kept quiet, if he could.'

'I expect so. Isn't that true of most people?'

'It's true about most Germans; shameful, wicked things they still keep under wraps. I don't know how you can bear to go back there without having to. I only went twice. There was the time three years after the War when I went because Papa asked me to, and in 1964 I went to see Detta one last time. I never liked going back. All those Germans with their dead stranger's eyes, I didn't know what was going on behind those eyes, behind the "Ja Frau Scrivener, Nein Frau Scrivener". I mean Lore, what did they say, what did they do in those years? Everyone there has amnesia about that time, nobody saw anything, nobody heard anything, and of course nobody actually was a Nazi.'

'You're certainly right. But there's another generation now, they've been brought up differently. They believe in rights, in democracy and not what happened under the Nazis. They're like young people here, or anywhere probably. And they don't want it all swept under the carpet. So unless you believe that children carry the sins of their fathers …'

'It's just how I feel about going back. And no, I don't think they carry their fathers' sins.' My thoughts had moved on. 'I don't know what it is they get from us, Lore. Kids, I mean. There's the things we know we're giving them. We worried about their schooling, got them the right books, kept pets for them, took them to their after-school activities, had the children's parties. The whirl of all those things. But the kids get other stuff from you, that you never thought about, or intended.'

'Such as?' she said.

'You know what comes to mind? In Ghana, Harold had this way of turning his shoes upside down before he put them on in the morning. He'd bang the heels sharply together. It was something he'd learned in the war, when he was in North Africa. It was to dislodge any scorpions that might have crawled into them in the night. He wasn't scared of much, Harold, but he hated scorpions. I mean, the point I'm getting at is that a couple of years later when we were back in

England, I saw Young John do exactly the same with his little wellington boots. He was only six or seven. And muttering something like, "Go away, horrid scorpions!"'

Lore was smiling.

'Yes,' I said. 'It's a charming picture at first. But when you think about it, it's not quite like that. I suppose what I'm saying is that children also get ... the fears, the absences, the shadows ...'

I always forget how quick she is. With hardly a pause she said, 'You and Harold suffered a terrible hurt. You coped, you managed. Your loss. You kept going, kept your marriage going. Raised Hannah and John. Ulla, believe it, you did really well. I remember you telling me that though Hannah went off the rails for a while, John just sailed on. That he was too young to be much affected. Look at them now: both stars, both doing well, aren't they?'

In my head I saw an image of Young John sitting in his uncle Ken's car. Small on the back seat, a suitcase next to him. The day after the accident. Wide eyes. Silent. Seeming not to realise that I thought he'd be in the way. Not complaining that he was being sent off to boarding school for a while. For the first time a knife twisted in me: the memory of the look, frightened, yet halfway to a glare, that he gave me then. It'd taken twenty-two years to strike home. I took a deep breath and pushed the memory away. Lore was waiting for me to say something.

'Yes. And sometimes I wonder. As he got older, it was as if John gradually cut himself away from us. He became rather – I'm not sure how to put it – inscrutable is maybe the word. You know how he was as a kid: question after question and then silence, working it out, I suppose, trying to make sense of whatever it was. Eventually he'd speak about it. Then he stopped asking and stopped sharing what he thought.'

'But don't boys do that anyway? And he always seemed to me to be very caring of you and Harold.'

'Yes, he was, and I was glad at the time; looking back I wish he'd rebelled a little. I remember something. About a year after the accident I was calling him – no response – and I found he'd taken the stool from the outhouse and was sitting on it in the garden, back against the outhouse door and just staring into the distance. So I asked him why he hadn't answered me.

"I was listening with the hearing aid."

"What? I mean whose hearing aid?"

"Granddad's."

'So I said the obvious. "But John, Granddad's one is with him at your Uncle Ken's."

And he looked at me as if I'd said something incredibly

stupid. "I don't need the hearing aid actually with me to listen with it, Mum." Then he clammed up and that's the most I ever got out of him.'

Lore told me to stop worrying. But I couldn't.

I must have fallen asleep again. Dreaming about 'Kristallnacht' and it was 1938 again; well, sometimes it does come back to me when dreams go bad. Another time, and I'm a girl again, struggling with my suitcase. It feels heavy. I need something it contains, though what I can't recall. There's a fearful thing inside: I'm too frightened to open it.

I awoke with a start. Lore wasn't in the bedside chair any more. Detta was. I hadn't been thinking when it had slipped out about her. I thought: oh dear! Lore will have left agitated. She'll suppose I'm losing my mind.

'Hello, my little Ulla.'

'Guten Tag, Detta. Thanks for coming. Good to hear you speak English again.' If there was a hint of sarcasm in my voice it was because she never could speak it when she was alive. It was a nuisance: people visiting who weren't real, but I couldn't think of anything to do except playing along as I'd done earlier.

'It's the least I can do. You did come all the way to Frankfurt for me when I was at the same point as you are now. Anyway, I made a promise.'

'A promise? To whom?'

'Your Mama. Her road on Earth was so short. When I took up being your nanny, I said I would still look after you when she was no longer there to do it.'

My memories of my own mother were hazy, and I didn't feel like making them any sharper by talking with Detta. In fact, I was irritated with her. This time was my time, or should be, shouldn't it? I mean, my last days in the world. I tried to think of something else to talk about.

'Do you ever go to galleries?' I asked.

'*Kunstgalerien*? Not really, angel, why do you ask?'

'Sometimes a gallery exhibits the life story of a painter. You can see how the artist started with small canvases and then progressed to larger ones. In those days when the Nazis were in power, each year we painted on a smaller canvas. People left if their families had got permission to move abroad: France, Palestine, the USA. It was a horrible feeling, the community evaporating like that. I didn't always realise it when I was a kid, but our world was in reverse. It was shrinking; we were getting hemmed in.'

She nodded. I wondered for the first time if even she'd felt threatened working for our family: a woman without a Jewish heritage, who on Sundays went to the Lutheran service at St. John's church, the Johanniskirche. If she'd been a year or two younger it would have been illegal for her to have stayed on as our nanny.

'At first I used to walk with Papa from our house to the shop.'

'Of course. Kahn and Metzger, he was proud of it, though he said it tied him down.'

'And he would do some work, and then we two would go round the corner into the square and there was a small café where he'd have coffee and they would make their special sweet home-made lemonade for me. Then we all had to leave our house and live in the flat above the shop.'

'I remember! It was cramped, wasn't it?'

'Yes, it was! I'm not sure how we managed it.'

'It felt exciting living in the centre of town but after, after that November, it felt unsafe. I mean we didn't sit anymore in the cathedral square cafés … Of course that was some time after we hadn't been allowed in the state schools anymore and …'

She butted in, 'Terrible…'

'But I liked the Birzeitschule. Though the synagogue wasn't the best place for a school of any kind. Looking back at the teaching though, it was good, Detta, I mean really good.'

'They fired all of those clever people from university jobs, and they came to you. Your small school probably had the best-qualified teachers in all of Mainz. Herr Robert always used to say that Dr. Mannheimer had a brilliant brain. And then it all ended. I still shudder at what could have happened to you that day. I should've been listening to the wireless.'

'Detta, don't blame yourself – you couldn't do everything. It would've been different if Papa had been there in Mainz, he always listened to the news. And then I wouldn't have walked to school in the morning.' As I talked to her the years fell away. I was back in my nightmare; in Newtown, where the synagogue was. Where are all the other girls? What's that in my nostrils? The acrid smell of burning, maybe something from the river port is being burnt. I come round the corner: it's the schul and a group of Hitler Youth cheering, jeering, shouting: '*Saujuden, wir werden euch alle töten!*'

Turn back, get back to our place. Another group of them are in the way, moving over in the direction of the town centre and blocking my route. They're quiet, menacing. No way through! What'll I do if one of them grabs me? Where can I go? Lore! She lives nearby; run down her street and bang on her door. Nothing happens – have they gone away? What can I do? Keep on banging so hard my fist hurts. At last Lore's mum's head appears out of the top floor window.

'My God, Ulla, is it you? Is this the day to go for a stroll?'

She rushes down to get me. Run panting up the stairs and up steep steps. There's furniture in their attic. We three hide behind it. My face up against the harsh fabric of an old armchair with horsehair showing through it. It's horrible, waiting, waiting with dread. Shouting, banging and crashing next door where Frau what's-her-name lived, a harmless old widow but everything she owns is being smashed or looted. Only a few more minutes there and they'll come to Lore's house. Might they set a fire like they did to the synagogue? Then another voice, very loud, very authoritative, shouting in anger. *'Halt Stop! Der Führer würde dieses Treiben nicht woollen.'* Everything went quiet. We could hardly bear to hope they'd gone away.

'It was the headmaster of the High School, Detta. Thank goodness he lived nearby. He must have taught some of those young thugs, and Lore's mum told us they came over all hang-dog and embarrassed and melted away.'

'I remember the next day walking across Hindenburgstrasse, where the big houses were, and they'd thrown people's things onto the street. Did I tell you that there were two pianos from houses side by side?'

'I'm not sure. I suppose you must have.'

'There was a beautiful Bechstein Grand, and next to it an English one, a smaller piano with lovely inlays. All destroyed.

And then I knew, really knew, not in my head, in my bones. That our time together was coming to an end. That what Herr Robert believed was true. He simply had to get the family out. It was the madness of it all. Such hard work to lift up those pianos and throw them through the windows. They could have taken them and sold them for as much effort, but no, they wanted everything to be wasted, and all to no purpose except to feed the Devil.'

'You know what the worst part was for me, because it wasn't then? It was when Papa rang from Zurich to say he was going to stay there. There was fear, fear in my stomach like I've only felt one other time. And you held me, told me it was going to work out, that Papa would keep us safe, arrange for us all to go to Australia, or to join him in Switzerland, or maybe we'd all go to England.'

'His heart wanted to return but his head told him "no". It was right. They were going to take his passport.'

She paused and her eyes had a far-away look.

'What was the other time?'

Her question had surprised me. 'The night when the hospital sister called, they had Harold in the ward and he was in pain but was out of danger. "What about my daughter, my daughter, what about Jane?" My voice had become shrill. She said she didn't know about Jane but I felt she did but she

170

wasn't allowed to tell. I missed you then.'

What could she have said? So we talked instead of the long months before she was getting me ready for the train. We were allowed a crate, what everyone called a 'lift'. Everything that could fit from our crowded rooms was marked to go in there. But there wasn't any guarantee that it would arrive. We got to take a suitcase each. Only one. So that's where there's a certain benefit to being a refugee, choosing what goes into it. I mean one has to look back on one's life and decide what's important, what will be of help in the next stage.

'Do you remember talking about what you should take with you?'

'I packed clothes – as many as I could, since England was a land of fog, of rain, of cold; I'd read Conan Doyle and Dickens and I thought I knew about it – a spare pair of sensible shoes from the Mainz Schuh-Haus, spare underwear, though as I was still growing I wondered how long it would do. You gave me sanitary pads telling me that such things may not be so easy to get in England.'

'We were both so practical, no room for sentiment. Only useful things in the suitcase.'

'Well yes, except that I did bring my photograph albums.'

'I remember it wouldn't all fit and you had to sit on the lid to get it closed.'

171

It came to me in that moment, part of me had always been stuck there, then. Fifteen years old, forcing shut the suitcase lid.

So that's how we were scattered, all but one. Papa in Zurich; me, Rolf, Lore and our three friends on the London-bound train. Our Nadetta, she went to Frankfurt. We were the lucky ones. Lore's mum and dad were deported – and murdered. And then, the Lancasters came by night, the Liberators by day, and they burned it. They burned Mainz down: the old town, the Johanniskirche, the Cathedral square, the little café with its home-made lemonade, Kahn and Metzger, Newtown, the river port, our old house on Tannausstrasse with its windows looking out to the Rhine; they sent it all to flames and rubble. Nazis, the many who followed them because they thought they could make a few marks out of it, those who kept quiet, those who silently hated them, those who opposed them when they could, they were blasted, burnt, asphyxiated with no distinction made, they died side-by-side as they cowered in their shelters and cellars.

'I read in the newspaper that Mainz had been bombed. Perhaps I should be a little ashamed now when I think of my reaction: I was glad.'

She nodded.

'But I did remember and prayed, because there was

nothing else I could do. I'd lost any belief I had, but I prayed to the God I didn't think existed: please God look after her.'

'You never did tell him, did you?'

'Harold? No, nor the kids. To spare them from such things. Or because I felt guilty that it wasn't me. Or because it became a habit, shutting things away. You know, Detta, when I came to England I thought of paintings again but in another way. My life was the canvas. Yes, I started it in Mainz. And now I was going to overpaint it. Did you know they examine Old Masters with X-Rays?'

'Yes, *liebchen*, they used do that in Frankfurt. It was in the papers.'

'And sometimes there's an altogether different painting underneath. The artist felt that the original didn't work well enough, there was no future in it, so he started over again. That's me too. I took control. I repainted myself as a modern British woman.' I sat up in bed, feeling energy flowing again as I remembered the many things I'd done. 'I wanted to stand on my own two feet, not to have to depend on a man for money. Learning to type, the shorthand, learning all the secretarial tasks, they were my ideas for myself. The strange thing is that it worked doing it all in my second language, exactly because I'd learned it from books. So after a while I'd be asked to set down what the manager said, but in 'proper'

English …'

Detta was looking quizzical. 'As long as you don't forget that first painting, the Mainz one.'

'I've tried so hard to forget it. But I never could find a thick enough paint to cover it.'

I'm sweating in tropical heat. My small boat slips down an African river. It must be the Volta, as the Adomi Bridge is in front of me. There are many eyes amongst the reeds near the shoreline. The unrelenting stare of crocodiles; their malevolent greed, their long-suppressed rage, lying just beneath the dark waters.

The door opened; Lore came in and sat back down in the chair.

'You'd dozed off, so I went down to the café. I hope I'm not tiring you.'

'Not in the least. I like having you here. I wanted to say that you were right. I couldn't do a Willigis and celebrate the past. Yes, I did slam shut the doors of my life in Germany. I wanted it all to be …'

'… behind you?'

'Well, yes, but more than that. Erased. Part of me wanted it never to have been. I wanted my life to be as though I'd always lived here, here in England, to always have been British. I suppose that in my mind's eye I tried to see myself as a woman from misty, rainy, Turner's island. So I faced forward to it, happy to be a subject of King George, with a passport in my handbag to prove it. I read and re-read those words written in it. I knew they were pompous but I loved them anyway. "His Britannic Majesty… requests and requires all whom it may concern to allow the bearer to pass freely without let or hindrance and to afford such assistance and protection as may be necessary."

'I never wanted a German passport either. I felt such a sense of relief when I got my British one; so much was riding on that small, dark-blue booklet.'

'It was too. The British were quite kind, I mean I found friendliness in them even in the War when I had a stronger German accent than I do now.'

'Hmmm … I was never happy at being called a Friendly Enemy Alien.'

'An oxymoron,' I said. 'No doubt a civil servant thought it up, someone senior who felt that the rules of English, as far as they have them, could be dispensed with. And the rest, well, the way some of them speak you would think they hadn't even heard of Sir Ernest Gower or opened a copy of Fowlers. Of course they haven't. When I first lived in London I had so much trouble understanding what they were saying. I mean it wasn't only the accent, it was the slang …'

'We were totally unprepared for it. And the humour, at times when one should be serious!'

'I grew to like it actually,' I said. I don't think Lore ever did. 'But it was disorientating. Do you remember how the BBC man always said "This is London" and he sounded so solid and secure?'

'Yes, confidence, even in dark days,' Lore said.

'I mean I was lucky in a way, because when it was time to move from Hertfordshire the first Blitz was over. London was so exciting, so free. Somehow even the dirty city air was lighter than the air in Mainz had been since the Nazis took over. Then came the return of fear and I think I've never quite outrun it. Not even in the bright African sunlight. When we took the car to the Cape Coast we saw the traces of things done in the slavery days. People take wickedness with them wherever they go … London became home but it was often a strange place as well. When I lived in Pimlico and Battersea in those early years, the Thames always seemed in the wrong position. I wanted red name signs for the streets that went towards the river …'

'And blue ones for those that ran parallel to it? You were still a Mainzer girl!'

'Yes. Though it would never work because the Rhine at Mainz is straight whilst the Thames makes London bend, fold in on itself ... Oh yes, I was going to tell you about Ghana. Those years were an adventure. At the time, you think you'll remember it all, but much of it fades away. I mean I know I've done it, was out there, but the order of events gets lost. Much is gone forever, I suppose, yet some things I can recall in fine detail. The light is different there: the colours are so vivid. People sometimes say they're brighter, but in fact they're drawn from an entirely different palette to what we have here. I wish Turner had gone there, Lore, to see what he would've made of it. The Africans have a totally different sense of colour – did you see those kente cloths we took back home? I mean nobody in Britain would ever have made something like it; everything here turns out dark or dun-coloured even if there are vibrancies within it like Harris tweed.'

'I remember you showing them to us when you'd settled back in the village. Have you still got them?'

'Put away, behind the studding,' I said.

We used that phrase, got from Harold, I suppose, when we spoke of the eaves cupboards in the new house. We had an old chest stored there. The kente cloths are still in it, along with all the things I thought I could never see again but didn't want to throw away. After Harold died, I felt London pulling me in, and moved from the village to a flat not far from here. The

177

removals men put the trunk straight into the back of the largest cupboard. It's been more than twenty years since it was last opened. The kids may unravel it, John might, that's how he is, there's that sneaky, ferreting, sleuthing way of his. I'm not sure if I want him to rummage through all that past; I mean sometimes I do and sometimes I don't. Wouldn't he be better off getting on with his life? Oh, I suppose that if I had really wanted them not to know, to remain an enigma, then I would have thrown it all away, or made a bonfire of it.

'Yes, Lore, they were a high point, those African days, if only we'd known it. And yet, and yet ... Once I was driving our live-in help, and the three kids in the Morris Minor. On the track we saw a puff adder with its sinister brown bands of scales. Vile, lethal.

"Drive over him or he'll bite someone for sure, Mrs Scrivener." She never would call me Ulla. Anyway, so I did run over it; but in the mirror I could see it still worming its way across the road. I reversed over it again, and once more forward. Then we couldn't see the snake anymore. Where had it gone? Was it lurking in the wheel arch? Perhaps it could slither inside and sink its fangs into the precious cargo on the back seat. I reversed again, and drove slowly forward, both of us looking out: we still couldn't find the adder's corpse.

That sense of looking out for something malevolent I'd

thought dead, killed, I get it sometimes even here in London. Maybe it's the way they keep things hid here. Those fortunes of gold coins and ingots locked in city vaults, Harold used to say they were first built up from the likes of the Cape Coast fort ...' I could tell that Lore wasn't following what I was saying, but I persisted.

'London has such a long history, Lore, and it's not been like the postcards the tourists buy: all jolly red buses, telephone boxes or guardsmen in tall busbies. Not all heroism like in the Blitz. The wicked things have been hidden, they're not talked of, but they're still there, beneath the paving stones. I mean, the things we thought had been banished by our generation's sweat and blood. Look under the facades, Lore! Rip up the tarmac, and you'll find them there.'

We were quiet for a minute or two before she said, 'I think I've tired you out, Ulla.'

'Sorry. Have I been quiet? Here's another memory. When it was time for us to leave Africa I had to clear out the cupboards. Some of the stuff had been there since we'd moved in. There was a built-in cupboard, full of spiders' webs, that went far back and you had to go into it on your hands and knees. I'd taken out everything from the front, when I thought of how scorpions hide in dark corners, how they'd love to nest in the back of a cupboard like this one. In

179

the end I left the last box where it was. For years afterwards when I couldn't find something I wondered if it was there, in that box, amongst scorpions.' How curious they are, these cobweb memories! Insubstantial; blown away on the wind; incredibly strong.

It's grown heavier, but I'm still carrying my suitcase. I battle on with it banging against my right leg. Moving it over to my left side, it slips to the ground and the catches spring open. I stare at it, realising that I must now face what's inside. Ashes. The suitcase is full of ashes. I hear myself say that I've been carrying the cinders of Mainz all my life. And then I know they aren't just those ashes. I feel overwhelmed by horror: some of them are from the Auschwitz ovens. All mixed up with another casket-full: Jane's.

When I next awoke there was nobody in the bedside chair. Just me and my cobwebs.

One Saturday morning, a couple of months after Harold got out of hospital, we were all sat down for breakfast. There was me, Harold, Hannah, Young John and Jack. It hadn't been mentioned, and it never would be spoken of, that there was a spare chair now.

The post arrived with a stiff-backed envelope for me and I opened it. I screamed. Because it was Jane's school portrait photo and I was weeping and shouting at Jack, that stupid old man who'd sent away for it. I meant to throw it away, then found I couldn't bear to. I opened the cupboard door and crawled behind the studding. Lifting the lid of the storage chest, I reached in to get our first photo album for her, full of baby pictures, and hid the school photo in the back. It was too painful, I could never see her again. So she was locked up in the trunk with the other things of long ago. I told myself that I'd taken my one look back at her; let someone else find that picture.

I spun around to face the day, and I needed to take Hannah to the shops for new shoes.

John

Maggie Blake's Cause[1]
2013

It was one of those songs that you know right from the opening bars, at least if you're my generation you do. So there, walking out of Charing Cross tube station, rushing to get to the bank before it closed, the busker took me back fifty years or so. *Concrete and Clay*: the speeded-up cover version, so that it comes out in D flat; I knew it before he got to the words. The busker was a few years older than I am, and greyed like me. Life had dealt him the tougher hand though, by the look of his grizzled face and grubby jeans. I hurried past in my suit, avoiding eye contact, coins staying in my pocket. This was where the years had taken him, to the ugliness of that underground concourse, strumming out hits from the sixties, his guitar as loud as his battered amp and speaker box would go. 'Unit 4 + 2, I remember them,' I muttered. He called out the song and got his revenge.

The concrete and the clay beneath my feet ...

Days afterwards I was still hearing the parasite he'd inserted, writhing, in my head. Sidewalks crumbled, mountains tumbled, yet the lovers were in love for ever. And isn't that the way it's meant to be?

1 A version of this chapter appeared in *21 Stories of Love and Loss,* ed. Donna Hillyer (2017). Hunstanton: Witley Press.

My bank is on the Strand. I'm in there quite often, keeping tabs on everything, making sure it's all in the black. It took only a couple of minutes to make the transfers even though I wasn't concentrating on what I was doing. I had to find a way of telling Becky that something had come up at work and tomorrow we'd have less time together than we'd planned. Duty. Responsibility. McGhee knew how to make me run. And now, the earworm wriggling on my brain.

Back on the Strand I bought a *Big Issue*. I don't usually buy the magazine as there's little in it of my world, but I think that day I felt guilty about my earlier rush past the busker.

'There's another issue out next week, come here then and get it from me,' the seller said.

'Ah, this is your spot, is it?'

'Yep, I'm here, till I win the lottery or somethin'. In the morning I always say: "I'm off to the beach." My little joke, isn't it? It used to be near the shore once, beside the Thames it was, right here.'

'Oh, I suppose so,' I said.

'And it's still warm, this pavement, warm from when the sun shone on the beach. That's why it's the best place, see?'

'I'm not sure I follow …' I was saying but he'd already lost interest in me. He was trying to catch another passer-by.

'*Big Issue*, luv?'

The visit to the bank had meant I'd left work earlier than usual. I came up from the station at Kennington and walked towards our house. Ten minutes later I opened the front door in happy expectation, as if my return in good time justified congratulations. I was hanging on to a refrain, to that dream of domestic warmth. Music coming from upstairs meant that our son was in. And Becky was already home.

'John. How lovely. You're back and I've got you to myself until Monday. Let's go to the café for breakfast tomorrow so it'll feel like a holiday right from the start. Oh, you bought a *Big Issue*, I'll have a look at it later on.'

It was like it once had been, and I could tell that she was full of hope about our next days together, longing to believe that we had at last found a path through the landslip that had strewn boulders in the way of our marriage. And I'd been holding the knowledge that my day off had been shortened.

'Well ...'

I saw a shadow in her eyes.

'What is it that you're not telling me?'

'It's just that I've got to attend one of McGhee's ruddy meetings at the Department.'

'Got to? What do you mean, got to? You booked it as leave, didn't you? It's a day of your holiday entitlement. You won't use it all this year, just like you didn't last.'

'Yes, but the thing is, this is important stuff.' I could hear McGhee's words in my head: 'It's important stuff, old chap'. Now I was parroting them, even though, deep down, I felt that nothing would come of his working group. 'Look, I'm really sorry that McGhee's eaten away a little of our time together …'

'Is it him who's done it, or you?'

'It's a nine o'clock start. We could meet up for a coffee at eleven and then get on with our day.'

'That's not the point. Why is everything else more important than our time together? You could have sent someone else.'

'McGhee wanted me.'

'So what? He's not your boss. What do you want, John? That's what I always ask myself. You never bloody say. I'm worn out guessing … and all day you'll be in your fucking … exoskeleton!'

'And what's that supposed to mean?'

'You'll be in your suit. You won't be you. You'll be the version of you that fits into the Department.'

'Rubbish! I'm me whatever I'm wearing.'

'I'm telling you what I feel.'

And it went on like that, voices raised. I was fighting my corner. Well, perhaps it was my corner, perhaps not.

Underneath I felt bad. I'd tried pleasing everyone and had ended up disappointing her.

In a sullen mood I went upstairs. Jake's door was open and the music quietened.

'Hi Jake, I'm home!'

'I heard.'

I came into his room. Our son was surrounded by cables and boxes of electronics, which was how he made music. Against the walls were special storage containers that held vinyl records. There was little enough room left for his bed.

'I thought you'd still be at work,' I said.

'I did too, that's what they'd told me, so I turned up. But in fact they hadn't anything for me to do. I'm pissed at them – I could use the money, Dad. That's zero hours for you!'

I nodded, thinking of the various paths I'd offered up to him in the past that would have led to professional employment. He'd dismissed them out of hand. I couldn't resist saying, 'Do you ever wish you'd taken up one of the those internships we'd sorted out?'

Jake looked amazed. Then angry. 'Not for a minute. I work to live, not the other way around. Music is what I want to do. Internship! Internment, being interred. No, thanks!'

'Yes, that's all very well when you've got parents to house and feed you through your twenties! I was twenty-one when I

came to London and I pretty soon knuckled down to a career.'
I'm not sure why I was being like that. Was I trying to make
him feel guilty or unwelcome? I turned to go to the main
bedroom.

'Yeah. Well, I guess I'm not like you,' he said. I might
have imagined it but I thought I heard him say sotto voce,
'thank God'.

In our bedroom I changed from my suit. Sloughing off my
carapace, if Becky was right. I supposed that I could still
slough it off? Over the years it hadn't fused into my skin, had
it? I sat on the bed and wrenched off my tie. As I lurched into
each row with Becky, it felt like I'd crashed into it. The
arguments caught me unawares, as though I'd tripped into an
uncovered manhole. But then, turning around and reviewing
the sequence in my mind's eye, the conflicts seemed horribly
familiar, as if I was doomed to blunder into the same obstacle
again and again. The worm under my skull twitched out the
busker's words.

I wondered what it was about *Concrete and Clay* that had
got to me. I'd been a child when I'd first heard it, and even
now I was still unsettled by the notion that solid worlds might
crumble and tumble. It came to me that the song released a
colder music, the icy fugue that had taken grip of my boyhood
years. I thought I'd silenced it, yet there it was again,

demanding to be heard. I didn't sleep well that night, woke early and pulled on my running kit. There was already a grey light at five as I headed for the South Bank. Running along the river towards London Bridge, I found the words of that damn song supplying the beat to my breathing.

The concrete and the clay beneath my feet ...

I know the way along the south side of the Thames. Running through the arch under Tower Bridge I came into a narrow street paved with stones. The nineteenth-century commercial buildings on either side have been converted into cafés, offices and apartments. The road surface is no good to run on and I prefer the air by the river, so as usual I swerved into a narrow passage – Maggie Blake's Cause. It's an odd name. Out of curiosity, I once looked it up. It's named after the campaigner who secured the riverside public right of way from the developers who would have kept it all private. It was a London story: the famous landmark drew the attention, but real life was played out in its shadow. Maggie Blake's short pathway took me to the river embankment and the growing morning light.

Later, when I was showered, besuited and on the tube, Unit 4 + 2 played on. I'm used to the sort of absence of mind one gets on the Underground, when passengers are all packed in together, when you're standing and there's no room to read.

I loathe those rush hour times when it's hard not to breathe in someone's exhaled breath as if you weren't strangers, but lovers. When it's like that I turn an imaginary wheel and tune the world out; this time my head supplied the song I was already sick of. Again, the concrete and the clay cracked open, again true love triumphed.

It put me into a trance. That was my explanation of it, a bout of vacancy. At St. James's Park I stepped from the train and followed the herd to the exit. Above me the sky was uniform white and bright. In front there were two low-rise brick buildings. Sandwiched between them was a Starbucks café fronted with Graeco-Roman columns and pediment. It was bolted-on fakery – the outside pretending to be something the inside gave the lie to. Some buildings are like that. Some people too. I blinked and recognised nothing, feeling as if I'd stepped through a portal into another town, or into a parallel universe that contained a London, but not the one I lived in. Turning left and walking on confused, I found myself on Victoria Street. I realised what had happened: the station had two exits and I'd walked out the wrong one.

After my detour, I was the last one to arrive, walking into the meeting room with a smudge on my brain.

'Good to see you, John,' said McGhee, indicating a chair.

'I've got to be away for ten-fifteen.'

'We'll be done long before, old chap,' he said, and inside I groaned. He'd drone on until the morning was done. It was an act, this old chap business; he was a grammar school boy. He wore the affectations of the Inns of Court and Civil Service as if they were his own skin. In that moment I hated him. Yet maybe it wasn't *him* I hated. I sat with something creeping up on me. A growing unease, as if a hidden loudspeaker was sourcing a chord sequence in E flat. At first it clashed with a slow-motion version of *Concrete and Clay*, deep in the bass, yet then I heard the two merge. Where the ardent accents of young love should have been there was only sarcasm. I fought to quell a rising wave of panic. I was seized by a sense of menace. I wanted to rush from the building into Queen Anne's Gate and breathe free in the park. But I said what I needed to and remained silent as the others spoke. I knew, more or less, what they were going to say. I turned down their speech and concentrated on the texture of their voices. Each one was different: public school, state school, Yorkshire, Estuary. But they shared a family resemblance. I could hear the comfort of suburban houses with neatly cut lawns, the clink of end-of-day wine glasses in the pied-à-terre, the pleasant buzz of a restaurant working lunch. Throughout their careers they'd grown a cadence, month on month, something in the voice that comes from the security of a good salary easing its way into your account. I must sound like that too.

McGhee was saying something, whilst around me the dissonance was growing again. I shook my head to try to clear it from my ears. No one else seemed aware of it and I realised that it must come from inside me. There was something about the room that made me uneasy. I seldom visit the Ministry of Justice, and I'd no recollection of ever being in that room, yet I felt as if I'd been there before. Part of my brain started to peel away the carpet tiles, to remove the wood panels from the walls, to take away the false ceiling. I saw it stripped back to a box made from reinforced concrete and breeze blocks. The bass was jagged now, like a saw. The beeping of the alarm on my mobile phone killed it.

'Excuse me, colleagues, but I must leave in five minutes.'

So McGhee wound up and people left; he was still full of himself, and for form's sake I exchanged a pleasantry with him whilst nibbling one of the sweet biscuits.

'You were quiet,' he said.

'Oh, a touch of déjà vu, you know.'

'Ah, yes, old chap, we've all done it before, helping our politicians off the hook when they've over-promised.'

It wasn't at all what I meant, but I smiled and took my leave.

Becky and I had agreed to meet at a café on the South

Bank that we go to sometimes. Before she saw me, I caught a glimpse of her, nursing her cup of tea. Despondency was on her face. She tried hard to be jolly when I arrived. I got an Americano.

'How was it?' she said, her voice a little bit too bright.

'As expected, I mean OK. I had this tune going round in my head.'

'Go on ...'

For some reason I couldn't. 'That's about it. You were right. I didn't really need to be there.'

'You must prefer being there rather than spending time with me.'

'No! It's not like that ...'

'Oh, for God's sake, get a life! How many times do I have to say it?' She got up abruptly and strode along by the river towards Bankside. I set off after her, leaving my coffee unfinished.

We walked in silence towards the Design Museum[2]. The sun was out now and in front of City Hall tourists were photographing Tower Bridge. Becky approached a couple who were taking it in turns to pose with the Bridge as a backdrop, and asked if they would like her to take a

2. Author's note: When John and Becky visited it, the Design Museum was on the riverside. It has since moved to the Holland Park area of London.

photograph of them both. They beamed at her and accepted. I felt annoyance rise within me.

'We're supposed to be doing something together for once. You're the one who just can't concentrate on it!'

'I was being nice, that's all. They're young and in love, probably on their honeymoon.'

'You think you're being nice, but it's not about nice. It's about boosting their narcissism! They're not really interested in the view, in remembering it. They're not interested in London. Not interested in Tower fucking Bridge! They're going to take that photo and post it on Facebook! It's just self-aggrandisement. Look where we've been!'

When we were first married, and when Jake was small, we'd both take photos and eagerly wait to retrieve the film from the chemist's shop. The best ones were placed in a growing collection of albums. At Christmas we'd bring them out and laugh over them. Then Becky got the idea of making photo collages and putting them in large picture frames. They're still on the walls of our house. Sometimes I stop and remember the holidays when they were taken. With digital cameras and smartphones we take many more shots. And once Jake was grown we hardly ever celebrated the pictures. I thought of all the photos in our phones and computers that have never been printed out; images captured, then locked up behind our passwords and seldom seen again. Becky was looking at me, narrowing her eyes.

'You know what? You've become a grumpy old man, a misanthrope. God, I don't even want to talk with you – you're so stuck in a rut!' She strode off once more, soon swallowed by the summer's dense crowds of tourists.

The museum was right on the riverside, not far downstream of Tower Bridge. I continued on the road I'd avoided on my morning run, because Maggie Blake's Cause is easy to miss, and I thought Becky wouldn't know about it. But I couldn't see her as the crowds thinned. So she must have taken the cut-through to the riverside. In my head Unit 4 + 2 thrashed away at *Concrete and Clay*.

The two of us were walking separate, parallel paths. I envied her those few lost yards of mine, those spectacular river vistas. At least we were heading for the same place. And then, quickening my step, I wondered if we still were.

The proprietor of the small restaurant took my coat.

'Good evening, sir. It's been a while, hasn't it? Good to see you again. Your lady's not arrived yet.'

I discovered this place years ago and I've been there many times with Becky. It's an uncommon thing in London, an eatery that's changed little over the years. It was reassuring, the owner and I going through the familiar ritual, older versions of our former selves. The kitchen never failed to come up with tasty dishes but it was with unusual anxiety that I walked up the stairs to the table. I heard the band in my head strike up again:

The concrete and the clay beneath my feet ...

I ordered a glass of merlot whilst I waited for Becky. It crossed my mind that she might not come. My wine arrived and I sipped at it. I'd just glanced at my watch when she was there, only a few minutes late. I stood to greet her; she looked down so that I was forced to kiss her forehead rather than her lips.

We were both trying but our conversation was mechanical: 'I'll have a starter and main, the fish looks nice.' That evening it seemed as if we'd become one of those couples we swore we never would be, partners who ate together in silence, making only occasional comments about the menu or the weather. People will tell you that such couples have nothing left to talk about. It's not true, though – the reality is that they can't talk about what's going on underneath. At least neither of us got out our mobile phones.

'So,' I said, trying to be cheerful, 'Gauguin tomorrow. Where is it again?'

Becky looked exasperated.

'I thought you weren't listening when I told you. That's what you do, go away in your head like... like you're trying to catch a tune no-one else can hear. It's at the Courtauld. Don't you remember my saying that I wanted to go there again?'

'Ah yes.'

'There's a small gallery of Gauguin's work. After we could walk on the Heath if we want.'

'Why are we doing another exhibition? We did one today.'

'Because it's what I want to do, OK? I arranged it, like always. If you'd suggested something we'd have done that instead. You've not contributed any ideas about what to do on our weekend.'

I felt the attack, and became defensive. 'I booked the restaurant, didn't I?' I realised that somehow it had turned out to be my sole contribution to the weekend itinerary.

'Yes,' she said. 'You made a phone call. And I did the rest. John, I'm fed up with being your social secretary.'

The Courtauld Gallery is on the Strand, so that's how I came to be walking out of Charing Cross tube again on Saturday morning, this time with Becky. We looked like a couple, I suppose. We were about the same age, had a certain similarity of style and, in London's cacophony, we still must have sounded out our shared notes. Over intertwining seasons, without our meaning to or even being aware of it, we'd grown to mirror one another's posture and expression. Yet that day it felt as if we'd lost the curving together that we once had. Neither of us spoke. Perhaps she was determined to be active, to fight off despair. I was quiet for another reason – the song was still echoing around the inside of my head.

At first we took no notice of the gridlocked traffic in the street. It's common enough. As we walked along in the direction of the gallery, we saw flashing blue lights. Smoke was sidling upwards. I pushed forward in the gathering band of onlookers. The smoke came from an open pavement; paving stones and earth had been flung aside as if by an explosive charge. Copies of a magazine were scattered on the ground. A paramedic was treating a bloodied man lying in the road.

'What's happened, what on earth's happened?' Becky said.

'It's the chap who sold me the *Big Issue*.'

'Pavement explosion,' said a man. I wasn't sure if he was a know-all or if he actually knew. 'Faulty old power lines under the ground. They smoulder for ages, gases build up, boom – they explode and then a fire starts. There's been quite a few of them.'

A woman turned to a small group of tourists. 'It's neglect,

neglect! They haven't invested; they've taken it all for granted, they've not made the effort to maintain it.' There was anger in her voice. I wasn't sure the tourists understood: they looked on with uncomprehending expressions. I turned to Becky; her face was white.

'I can't do this anymore, John. I just can't'

I hoped that she was talking of the exhibition, hoped that another time we could journey to the warm sensuality of the painter's Tahiti.

'Yes, of course. We can turn back.'

'We can't turn back, John. I wish we could, but no …'

There were tears in her eyes. I couldn't think of anything to say so I just held her. She was weeping in my arms.

In that sunny morning, I felt cold seeping into my limbs. I should have said that she was the rock of my life, that she was my life. Should have said that I was scared. But I didn't. My voice was frozen. In my head I was running by the Thames, longing for the lonely riverscapes you get downriver of Tower Bridge. I was sliding away from the jostling crush of London, with all its contrary demands, as I slipped along the thin aisle of Maggie Blake's Cause.

Exhibition Road
2013

I was walking up Kennington Road when I first saw him, pootling out of the park that holds the Imperial War Museum. Several steps away I realised he was going to talk to me. He was elderly, well into his eighties, I guessed, and there was something odd about his gaze, about his rheumy eyes. I knew, without knowing how I knew, that the trace of uncertainty in his gait showed that he was not quite living in the moment, as if his legs were preoccupied with a walk from long ago.

'Excuse me, can one get a bus to ah, Streatham, from here?'

He had a high and slightly tremulous voice. I paused a second for my glance to take him in before responding. The stranger was dressed in red pressed corduroy trousers, a light zipped jacket under which he wore a freshly ironed blue shirt and pullover. He was neatly shaved without the telltale of razor cuts or missed tufts that marked many men succumbing to the curses of dementia. I'd stayed in enough hotels to have noticed the commissionaires' technique for distinguishing the dressed-down from the pounds-down, so I looked at his feet. And the footwear failed my test. The white socks over which sat open-toed sandals were not right for his age and for the time of year. It was early autumn and, although it was bright, there was a chill in the air. An early gale a couple of days before had plucked leaves and small branches from the roadside trees.

I was no expert on the routes of London buses; in fact, it must have been years since I'd even been on one, preferring tubes or trains to the frustrations of the undetermined wait for a bus. I never thought of getting about by means of one. London's geography had atrophied in my head to that of Harry Beck's London Underground map, and I no longer reflected on the real distances and relationships between places, as they appear to the surface traveller. But I'd walked this street many times and thought I remembered the head codes of the buses.

'Yes, they go from that stop there,' and I pointed to the shelter just beyond the pedestrian crossing. 'The fifty-nine and the one-five-nine, I believe they both go to Streatham.'

'Thank you, that's good.'

Since the man did not make any attempt to move out of the way, to progress with his own journey, I found myself saying: 'Are you, I mean will you be, alright?'

'Yes, indeed, *I'm* alright.'

He gave out a penetrating stare that led me to feel that there was something evidently wrong with me.

From that feeling there welled a miserable certainty that I was definitely not alright. I'd only been back home to pick up a couple of letters as I wasn't living there anymore. Becky had asked me to move out. She said she found me impossible, vague about what I wanted for myself. Often silent. She used to say that I mostly lived inside my own head. Jake was furious with me, alternately sullen and accusatory. The bonds that had held me were breaking, dissolving away.

In my head I was telling the stranger about myself. 'I rush around looking after everyone else. That's what I do. It's not that I chase other women, I'm not a drunkard. I try to do the right thing. But maybe Becky's right, I don't talk about what really matters.' I was like a dog chasing its own tail. Always busy, not stopping, not easy in my own skin. Didn't travelling shows once have motorcyclists who roared round the inside of a cylinder high off the ground, just kept attached to the wall of death by centrifugal forces? That was what life was like for me – I had to keep motoring round on the road to nowhere lest I fall, lest others should fall. In silence on that pavement I wondered how things could be like this. I was a failure at what counted for most. At that moment I felt that I could collapse into nothingness, let air out of the balloon that was my body, forget about posture, about the form expected of a professional man. Why should I not admit that I was overcome, hopelessly out of my depth?

Then I heard it: a low chord, dissonant in E flat and quite loud, but declining in force over a few seconds or so. I looked around me, but no-one else seemed to have remarked it. I couldn't work out what it could be, and yet there was something within the sound that led me to think I'd heard it before.

The man was looking at me. I wondered how long the two of us had been standing there, he in a perhaps quizzical silence, and me with a head full, a body full, of melancholy. With surprising nimbleness he stooped and from the pavement picked up a large Y-shaped twig that must have come from a roadside tree. He gave it to me.

'Put that in your briefcase. It'll be handy for finding water.'

I must have shown my astonishment.

'You should try it, maybe you'll find your river.' The stranger pointed to the plane trees lining the other side of the road. 'They're astronauts, those trees, but you have to look to see,' and he ambled forward towards the bus stop. I flung the twig aside as I took a few brisk steps in the opposite direction. They always pick on me, the helpless, the nutters.

I was late setting out for a work meeting that I didn't want to attend anyway. I'd always been keen, interested to get to work, to be the regular, dependable guy who cared that the job was well done. Commitment had drained from me that day. A vision of my work life came to me that tainted all my motivation. What was it but endless rounds of meetings, reports on things that didn't need to be reported upon, reorganisations that put things back the way they had been five, ten years ago before the last three reorganisations? It depressed me to think that all the restless managerial activity of my career concealed the state's grand decline, a long retreat from the high standards of care and professionalism established by my father's generation.

I was undecided. It was hard to walk on with Jake's angry words still shouting in my head. Perhaps I should go back and try to leave things with him on a rather happier note. I turned round wondering if a retry would backfire, and leave Jake angrier than before. A single-decker number three-sixty bus came by and pulled in at the stop. The old man got on it.

"Oh, jeez! He's got on the wrong bloody bus." There was no reason for it, but I felt responsible for the man's mistake. I had no idea where that bus went, and imagined him ending up at the terminus wondering why he wasn't back at Streatham, in his wardened accommodation or whatever. Turning back again to my own journey I saw another three-sixty coming along the road. In sudden impulse I jogged back to the bus stop. If I took it, the second bus might catch up and overtake the one ahead. I mean, I'd seen buses leapfrogging each other like that. I'd dismount and board the earlier one to speak with the old chap. I'd be even later in at the office than I'd said, but I told myself that work had already had its pound of flesh from Mr J Scrivener. And now? Now I feel the need to bring to mind, to record, how I started my voyage that day. It's one that I'm still on. Not the bus journey through London, I mean that was just a short trip, but a voyage through my heart's inside.

Single deckers always seemed like short change to me. They're half a bus, a sort of bungalow on wheels. I like stairs, the separation of floors that provide the different modes of being you can experience in a house. I was someone that until then had always chosen to live in a house with a staircase, like the one I grew up in, and I felt diminished in my small one-bed flat, as if I'd lost a crucial aspect of my personal space. I'd moved down from three dimensions to two.

The previous three-sixty had picked up the others who wanted this route; I was the only person to board at the Imperial War Museum stop. Nevertheless it was pretty full. The experience of boarding was very different from the every day of getting on a tube train. All those pairs of eyes facing forward and, without exactly focussing on me, seemingly regarding me with a mixture of curiosity and suspicion. I felt like a museum specimen in a glass case.

That step up to embark gave out a cadence from my childhood days, climbing onto the school bus in the morning; mine had been one of the last stops before school and as a small kid I'd always got on with a kind of apprehension. I suppose it was an inward tension between my wearing of the school uniform and how I felt about it. I never really felt I belonged in it. Something I couldn't pin down, but part of me always sensed that I was an outsider, so I wore the uniform with the anxiety of a pretender. Would I be scrutinised, found out and picked on by the older, tougher boys? Looking around, I saw that the bus had embraced a different city from the one I circulated in; my companions were mainly female, and were more representative of the diverse ethnicities that comprise today's London. I took the strain in some of their faces as an indication that money was tight. There was only one other man in a suit, right at the back. My dark-grey pinstripe declared me as a member of a different tribe from most of the other passengers on the three-sixty. Once again I felt uncomfortable in it, as if it was a restricting suit of armour as Becky had said.

All the seats had someone sitting on them. Lone travellers

tried to avoid sitting together with another stranger – it's difficult when seats are set out all in pairs like that. It's a sort of enforced coupledom. I cast a quick speed-dating glance at each occupant. It felt awkward because it meant that I had to look without catching an eye, without breaking the cardinal rule of civic inattention, that rule that minimises interaction between the city's strangers, the rule that allows each rivulet, each human stream, to flow free of whirlpools, a rule that allows it to be a quiet tributary to the ebb and flow of the tides of London. A young couple resumed their conversation in French. I needed to sit on the left side so that I could see through the front windscreen. Ignoring one large woman who had left little space next to her, I chose a younger, slimmer black woman who stared out of the window.

The autumn sunlight streamed in and my mood lightened. I fancied I was within a dome of metal and glass. I could watch out for the bus in front and still enjoy the view. As we turned right into Black Prince Road I thought of the Prince, that victor of Poitiers, whose homely court, well, a portion of it, was now occupied by an office block of profound banality. Coleridge's words were running in my brain:

Where Alph, the sacred river, ran
Through caverns measureless to man
Down to a sunless sea.

Up here on the surface I was in my version of the pleasure dome the poet had dreamt of, not shuttling underground as I usually did. How many months, years of my life had I spent in those long, dark caverns with my face harsh in the fluorescent light? Sometimes the underground railway shared the same space as the old London rivers; I'd once seen a photograph of workers on the then-new Metropolitan Line shoring up the breach made by the River Fleet. It had wanted to break free from its confines and return to its old haunts beside the Farringdon Road. I was far from the Fleet here, but not from the Effra, which was likewise deep within its brick tube, the tube Bazalgette had built for it. As the bus reached the Albert Embankment, I thought of the massive subterranean red brick sepulchre that was the great man's homage to the spirit of the troublesome river he'd finally buried. It was somewhere near, under the slipway next to the MI6 building, I supposed, where the tamed Effra met the Thames.

There's a story – just an urban myth perhaps – that in the nineteenth century a coffin was found floating on the Thames. It had proved to come from the cemetery miles south at Norwood, but on the surface the grave had not been disturbed. It was supposed that the interment had been made too close to the Effra's course, and the coffin had been borne upon it through sunless galleries to its confluence with the Thames at Vauxhall. In a stab of recognition, I thought that in my commuting journeys I too was a corpse, carried far below the earth in my metal coffin, swept along on the quicksilver races of the London Underground.

Looking ahead I could see no sign of the preceding bus. It had slipped around one of those peculiarly unlovely London islands, the Vauxhall gyratory system. As we came into the aluminium and glass of the bus station, I saw the earlier bus pull out. I couldn't see any trace of my quarry at the station and told myself that he must still be on board.

My seat mate had made some small alteration of body posture, a slight turn forward and a hand placed on the bar of the seat in front, that, without actually involving her trying to stand and without communicating directly with me, let me know that she wished to leave at the stop. I angled right to let her out and tried to empty my mind of the clatter of thoughts whilst I shuffled over to the window seat. After a long pause at traffic lights the bus set out over Vauxhall Bridge, a glance right showed me the sealed pile of the secret service building, and further along the improbable curve of the London Eye. There was a delight in not knowing the bus route, in having no power to direct its course or destination.

'I'm carried along by this little stream, I can simply enjoy the ride.' My barque pulled me past Pimlico station. I concentrated on the bus in front, and searched the pavements near each stop; it seemed to me that it would be easy to miss the old man if he alighted there. I turned to look round at the other passengers. There'd been a changeover of passengers, and I wondered if I was the only person still remaining from when I'd boarded. It was disconcerting, as if I'd awoken from a Rip Van Winkle sleep to find my familiar domain occupied by strangers. My companions were all white, and I fancied were rather more smartly dressed.

Once I saw researchers taking water samples from the Thames. From their boat they lowered a plastic container and then hauled it up full of water, before moving downstream to the next sampling point. This bus was a sort of scoop, each stage of the journey bringing in a cross section, one that could be subject to scientific demographic, sociological analysis if one had the mind to do so. With each stop of the bus a fresh sample of the human pool was taken up and the previous ones gently decanted. I supposed that most of my fellow passengers did not need to travel far. Nobody travelled from terminus to terminus.

The Thames was in front once more. I'd thought that it was far behind over my left shoulder. We were moving along the end of Grosvenor Road under the railway and I felt disorientated again, as if old man Thames had taken up his bed and walked out of position. As we returned to full sunlight on the other side of the bridge, a single decker passed in the other direction and I turned my head to look at it. I gasped in annoyance; the old man was sitting in a seat by the window. He turned his head towards me and then faced the front again.

I'm an idiot on a wild goose chase, I thought. He's realised his mistake and has taken a bus back to Kennington.

I wondered what to do. I didn't want to alight, didn't wish to return to the work world of demands and decisions. The damn phone was vibrating in my jacket pocket. Removing it, I could see messages from the office, you know the sort of thing – will you sign off on the project I sent you, have you got an ETA? I put it beside me for a moment on the seat.

The three-sixty stopped and turned sharply right in front of the Royal Hospital Gardens. There was a bus stop in the oxbow on this northern side of the road. The driver paused only for an instant and moved back onto the Embankment, now heading back into town, his manoeuvre having turned the vehicle completely around.

'What's going on? Why are we going back?' I knew an instant before the driver swerved left into Chelsea Bridge Road, that the purpose of the strange course, this horseshoe bend, had been to avoid making an awkward right turn from the riverside. I told myself it should be called the one-eighty, it makes a half circle turn.

The pursuit was still on, because the man had not changed buses after all. As we moved up to South Kensington, I kept a sharp look out on the streets, but I didn't spot him, not even as we threaded our way up Exhibition Road. At the Royal Albert Hall there was another three-sixty bus standing at the stop. It must have been finishing there, as it was completely empty of passengers. I thought for a moment and rushed from my bus. I was on the north side of the Hall, and, seeing nothing of the man I'd followed, walked around it.

He stood at the entrance door to one of the nearby red brick blocks of mansion flats. I walked towards him, thinking that the chap might have lived there once and in his confusion had returned. That sort of thing happened when people had Alzheimer's disease or the like. He pulled a bunch of keys from his pocket and opened the door. As he disappeared into the flats, he gave an almost sly glance over his shoulder straight at me.

I stood on the road, dumbfounded. There had been a flicker of recognition in that backward look. It's as if he was pleased that I had wasted my time in following him there. He never was going to Streatham. I felt foolish, and was undecided what to do with the day. My energy had deserted me; my body felt heavy. I walked back to the bus stop, crossed Kensington Gore into Hyde Park. I pondered walking along the Serpentine: a few minutes walk away was the place where the dark waters are released from their underground straight-jacket to pool in the park. In the end I decided against it. Instead, I climbed the few steps to take in the Albert Memorial. Conservators had spent many years restoring it. It had looked grim before but the end result was a disappointment – a gilded gothic kitsch.

'Victorian rococo. I wonder if that's what Albert would have wanted; wasn't he the man who endorsed the simple elegance of Paxton's designs for the Crystal Palace?' Maybe the whole district was the true memorial to the German prince. This bit of London was far from being a favourite of mine, so I'd never before focussed upon it, never marshalled up what I knew of it. It had been bought from the proceeds of the 1851 Great Exhibition. Albertopolis, they once called it, with a note of disparagement perhaps, and the name fell out of favour after the untimely death of the Prince Consort. The neighbourhood kept its peculiar mixture of Empire puff and educational or cultural institutions of extraordinary reach and influence. He was worth remembering, that man so interested in promoting learning, art and science that some cited it as evidence that he must have really been the son of the Jewish chamberlain to the Saxe-Gotha court. I chuckled at the thought that the compliment to Jewishness was a backhanded one. There's a strand in British society that finds enlightenment so uncomfortable that it must tag it as doubly alien, not just German, but German-Jewish.

So I was mulling over Albert, and that he has a whole district through which he is remembered. And that he's remembered again in the unfashionable Kennington Park through the Prince Consort Lodge – his sturdy exemplar dwellings for artisans with their simple, clean lines. Why should some be remembered and others more or less obliterated, all but forgotten? Chance? The unthinking tunnel-vision of those who remain post-mortem? I'd just missed the green man on the pedestrian crossing. The driver of a small car stalled his vehicle, and the lorry behind him blared its horn. The chord was ugly and long in E flat. And it sounded loud, ear-piercing and amplified as if by hearing aids. I covered my ears with my hands until it ceased. I was shaking when the green man illuminated and it was my turn to traverse the road. Without any plan at all in my head, I turned round again and walked down the steps towards the Royal College of Music. A group of half a dozen schoolgirls, perhaps eleven or twelve years old, were waiting at the entrance, neat in their claret blazers and grey skirts. I wondered what concert it could be that started so early in the day.

'No, not a concert, we've been waiting for the museum to open, we got here a few minutes early. It's just about eleven-thirty now, so we'll get on in very soon,' said their teacher in response to my question.

As the school group entered, I wondered what to do next. I told myself that the day was wasted. I hadn't known there was a museum here, and thought to take a look at it.

The museum hall was small, and since the group's project must have related to the historic stringed instruments on the balcony floor, I stayed downstairs and perused the old wind instruments with mild interest. Looking up I saw that another girl, who had her back towards me, had joined the group. She was the same height as the others but must have come from a different school with a green uniform. Over her plaits she wore her school beret.

'Maybe she's a new girl, she hasn't got her new school uniform yet. Damsels with dulcimers! It's Samuel Taylor C again!'

I never actually had to learn Kubla Khan at school, but certain lines seemed to have velcro-stuck to the inside of my skull.

216

A damsel with a dulcimer
In a vision once I saw
–something something, whatever–
Could I revive within me
Her symphony and song,
To such a deep delight 'twould win me
That with music loud and long...

I gave up trying to recall the rest of the lines and engrossed myself with the British pianos. A couple of Broadwoods, a Clementi, and an old Collard and Collard. I wanted to bring forth a note or two from these survivors of a bygone age, but notices on the keyboards told me that touch was forbidden. So I contented myself with reading about the piano craft tradition that went back to the end of the eighteenth century. It was now largely forgotten. My grandfather had made pianos, but it was odd how little I knew of it, even though music had always been an important part of my life, albeit listening rather than playing. I saw that the oldest firms had set up in the Soho area and had moved out to Camden and Kentish Town once they outgrew their premises. Of course! Granddad had lived in that part of North London and that's where he'd raised his family. The bumping noise as the hall doors closed interrupted my reverie. Looking up again, I realised that the school group had gone.

A few minutes later I decided that I'd had enough of the museum. I would walk to the tube and go back to the flat. On my way down Exhibition Road to the station at South Kensington, I passed the white steel pillars of the new Imperial College building. There, in the foyer, was an exhibition about the history of the college. I paused, idly looking in through the plate glass at those display stands, and people-watching those inside the building. When I refocussed my eyes I could see the reflections of passers-by in the street behind me and took a minute's enjoyment watching them as they flowed past. It was a mix of tourists and young people I took to be students. A couple paused to look at a map together. And next to them there was a schoolgirl, in green uniform, like me looking in at the window. There was something about her that I recognised, and after a bit I found the sense of déjà vu unsettling.

That's it! I realised. She's the one who was at the Music Museum, but she's on her own now.

I turned back to concentrate on the display, and then, wondering what the kid might be doing away from her group, turned around to look at her. I became more unsettled, because she'd completely disappeared. When I turned back to face the window I could see her reflection again, as if she was standing a bit further back from the pane than me. I walked along a few paces to change my position, yet still the girl was reflected in the glass. I could see her looking up and down the street. She turned and gave me, I thought, a slight smile. I told myself that modern plate glass was a complex, laminated product and it might be she was standing in a quite different location, and she could even be somewhere inside the foyer. Or perhaps we were separated in time rather than in space. Maybe the scientists at Imperial were showcasing their new invention: a glass that took in images and held them back for minutes or hours as the light travelled across the width of the pane. In which case the window was showing me the image of the schoolgirl as she made her way up to the Royal College of Music.

I smiled to myself – slow glass! Now that really would be a miracle of rare device. I knew a little thermodynamics; I didn't think the laws of physics would permit an object to store the energy from years, or even hours, of light-fall. Wouldn't it heat up, melt or even explode? Slow glass was fiction, and I half remembered that it came to me from a sad short story[3] I'd read way back when I was in my teens. It had made an impression on me at the time, yet I hadn't brought it to mind since then. The gist of the tale was that urban dwellers could purchase panes of slow glass for their

3. Author's note: *The Light of Other Days*, by Bob Shaw.

windows, matured in the countryside over decades. And the light so harvested would be given out to them over subsequent years as it traversed the width of the glass. Bright country vistas would replace their dark street views. There was something in that story that appealed to me again, now. Hadn't I been a subterranean traveller, who today had been journeying on the surface, in the daylight?

Looking in at the window I saw the schoolgirl move away, as if she was walking up Exhibition Road towards Kensington Gardens. So I thought to move too, to return home. I walked down the street and crossed Gloucester Road on my way to the Underground. I would phone into work to let them know I wouldn't be in that day. At the bottom end of Exhibition Road there were several cafés. Choosing one, I ordered my Americano. The Poppy Day collection box on the counter reminded me that it was getting to be the season of remembrance, and I dropped some change into it. Catching the barista's eye, I dropped another coin onto the tips saucer and she smiled her thanks. Sitting by the window, I let a wave of aimlessness wash over me. My life, to me then, was like my day had been, without achievement. I doubted that my parents had ever had a day like this. Granddad Jack neither. They always had purpose. I had become wealthier than they ever had been, but there was no point to me.

I tried to focus on work. There, at least, I had a certain status. Yet the work that used to be compelling, today seemed to have only a synthetic importance. The career that had consumed my energies for so much of my life seemed distant now, as if I was staring at it through the wrong end of a telescope.

'Oh, fuck it!' I was feeling in my pocket for my mobile phone. It wasn't there. I'd left it on the bus. I sat slowly sipping coffee whilst watching the people passing. Some were hurried, others, tourists perhaps, sauntered down Exhibition Road. A chattering school group walked on excited by the prospect of a museum visit. A family headed off in the direction of the Science Museum, two young women deep in conversation, crossed over the road. They were on their way to the V and A, or perhaps to the Knightsbridge shops. A man was wearing a poppy in his coat lapel. So that's what I was thinking about in the café. It felt as if there was something I'd forgotten, something I could nearly but not quite locate, like a word on the tip of my tongue. Didn't Coleridge say that the arrival of a visitor interrupted his dream memory and that's why he didn't finish the poem? Maybe I'm my own person from Porlock, maybe I spend my days distracting, blocking myself from remembering.

It was like the Thames at tide-turn, when the waters were

confused by two strong forces working in opposite directions. What was it that part of me wanted to suppress? And that another part was struggling to make me remember?

I took another sip of coffee. For some reason *The Light of Other Days* came back to me again. In the story, a couple go to a Highland farmer to buy their slow glass. Through the window they see the neat farmhouse interior with the farmer's happy wife and child. But when they open the door they find the inside of the house to be deserted and unkempt. The light-harvester's family had died many years before in a road accident. The bereft man had kept the windows that held their image.

Then I was gripping my coffee cup so hard that it's a wonder it didn't crack. I was cold in my coat and a knot of fear twisted my stomach. Muscles taut, I fought down the panic. In that moment I knew who the schoolgirl in green was … had been. She who had not been a schoolgirl for fifty years. Had not been anything. She who had hardly been spoken of for the last half-century, though her absence now seemed to loom large in my soul.

So there you are: slow glass did exist. I was it. It was me. Images, feelings I had taken in long time past, they were seeping, leaking, out of my brain. And I was seeing things, no, seeing *her*, as she once was. And I'd thought it was the old man who was losing his marbles, when all along it was me.

I finished my coffee. Was it the caffeine or something else that made me shake and sweat? I sat there struggling to control my panicked breathing over my empty cup. It seemed to me then that my professional life – no, my way of being in the world – had been a monstrous diversion; it was the overbearing levee that I'd built to dam the bubbling, disorderly stream of my life that would have, should have, flowed. Holding my body in my usual workaday posture seemed to require an all but superhuman effort. In that moment everything about me felt wrong.

The barista was circling around picking up the used cups. As she came to my table, I saw her give a start. I suppose I'd come in as a buttoned-up professional chap, and now looked as if I'd seen a ghost. In a way, I had. My memory trawled up an unwanted echo of Coleridge:

And all should cry, Beware! Beware!
His flashing eyes, his floating hair!

I set off to South Kensington Station with the feeling that I would drown in my old life, the routines of my way of being, that I must find a new watercourse or sink without trace. Something held me back from going through the gates into the Underground. I turned round, and walked to the nearby bus stop. The bus timetable said that a number fourteen would take me to Warren Street. I'd work out the rest of the journey when I got there.

Barbican
2014

The first foot in the water was the hardest. It was an overcast February morning and Hampstead Men's Pond was ice-cold. It hurt. I forced myself off the walkway into the pool.

'Bloody hell! Whose stupid idea was this?'

'Yours!' Tony called back.

He'd changed quickly and immersed himself before I was even in my swimming trunks.

The two of us went around in a circuit – breaststroke because neither of us wanted to put our heads under the water. It was muddy and you'd not want to get a mouthful. I pushed some floating feathers away from my face.

'Well, where else can you swim in real water in London?' I called over to him.

'Hyde Park: the Serpentine,' Tony said. 'People swim there'.

'I wouldn't; what about Weil's disease? It's just diluted rat pee, that place.'

'What, and they don't have rats here?'

'I suppose they do, but I've never heard of a problem.'

'Yep, better class of rat in Hampstead. That's why I live

up this way,' he said.

Our talking was often a form of good-natured jousting, and we went on like that, as best we could, between breaths. We'd known each other for many years, Tony and me. When we'd been junior at the Department we discovered we were both runners, and that had created a link. He pursued his running with a huge energy that I could never match, and with a competitive spirit that I'd never had. But I think we're quite alike, both of us introverts, and that was probably why we'd gotten into the habit of having something active to do when we met up. I wasn't surprised when he'd told me that he was retiring early. His mother had died after a long illness, and he'd said that he needed to rest and 'get his head in order'.

'John, are you getting any support?' I didn't know what he'd meant, so he'd explained and given me an introduction that led to Benjamin's consulting room.

'Did you know,' I said, giving up my attempt to match the speed of a nearby duck paddling through the water, 'that people used to bathe in spa water in London? In Bermondsey there was a spa, there were baths at Sadlers Wells for a while. You know those public baths near the roundabout at the end of City Road, at Ironmonger Row? When they were first built they used their own spring water.'

'Why did they stop?'

'I'm not sure,' I said, 'I'll have to read up about it.'

'Please do, John, then you'd be even more of a mine of information. Much of it useless, of course, but you bring up an occasional diamond.'

'In the context, I think you mean a fount,' I said. 'Of wisdom. And pearls!'

'Now you're just further muddying the water! If that's even possible,' he said. 'Hey, I'm getting cold; think I've had enough. See you dry side.'

I wanted to swim another circuit. Half way round I took air into my lungs, closed my eyes and plunged under, hoping to find the bottom. For a second or two I powered down, and then I broke through a thermocline. I'd moved from the fridge to the freezer and the deeper cold knotted my stomach in fear. I surfaced without having touched the mud below. After showering, shivering in the freezing tap water, I dressed hurriedly as the changing space was perishingly cold, being open to the elements.

'I'm pleased to have done that, even if it's the only time I ever do it,' Tony said. 'Let's get on with the plan!' The plan was to warm up by walking over the Heath and getting some breakfast in Hampstead. We chatted at first: about the Department, swimming, about the green parakeets we'd both seen on the Heath before. Then came an awkward pause and I knew he was building to a different sort of question.

'John, I was wondering how you were getting on with Benjamin?'

'Yes, OK, I guess …'

'I mean I don't want to pry; what's your stuff is your stuff.'

'That's OK. No, it's good. I'm seeing him every week and he's got me keeping a journal. I write down dreams and feelings and things like that. My blue book. Though it's got all mixed up now with my research notes.'

'Do you think you might get back together with Becky?'

'Sometimes I think so, sometimes not. I actually hope so, most days. It can feel fractured, fractious. I'm on a journey, Tony. I've got to go back, to go deep to find out who I am. I guess I'm impossible to live with right now. And will she be there for me later on? I mean she's got her own life to lead so who knows?' A silence fell between us and to fill it I found myself talking on. 'What's worse for me right now are the nights. They seem awfully long. I don't sleep well. That's when I hate it really. Being alone.'

'It sounds horribly tough. What's it like for you living in the Barbican?' he asked.

'Well, OK. At times I quite like it. I mean it's simpler. No, it's strange. I bought the flat ages ago to rent out. Never thought I'd live in it. I guess I feel there's something carefully planned and totally inauthentic about the place. It's a bit like I'm living in a film set.'

'Hmm,' he said, 'it's got that fifties look of what people thought the future would be like: all concrete, houses perched up a floor or two from the street, or way up in a tower block. High-up walkways without cars, roads without people.'

'Did you know it obliterated a whole district that was there before? It was burned down in the Blitz and the Barbican Estate was built instead.'

'What was there before then?'

'Warehouses, shops, streets, homes. It was known as Cripplegate for something like a thousand years. Then in a generation or two, well, it's been quite forgotten, hardly anyone's even heard of it now.'

'I've heard of the name because it's on the Barbican church – St. Giles Cripplegate – they have concerts there from time to time. I've never understood why they left that church there. It's incongruous, isn't it – like a sailing ship stranded on the red slabs of the pedestrian precinct. No, like a barnacled old whale beached on the shore of modern times. One of those things you get in London, I suppose; survivors from the past.'

'Ah, it wasn't so much left as reinstated. It was destroyed

in the Blitz, but the sixteenth-century plans were found at Lambeth Palace and it was rebuilt more or less as it was.'

'Ah, a resurrection!'

'I guess so … don't you think it's hard to really delete something? I mean the memory keeps on coming back, so you have to continue to work to keep it away.'

'Even if it's destroyed?'

'Even then. If there's a memory of it, it may try to come back in one form or another.'

'If that's so the Barbican Estate better watch out,' he said. 'Cripplegate might come back!'

A few months before I'd left my phone on a bus. It had all sorts of information on it that I wouldn't want a dishonest person to go through, so I sent out a remote wipe instruction. A week or so later I found that it had turned up at the Lost Property Office. I went down there to Baker Street and retrieved it. When I switched it on I watched it wind back to ground zero. I hadn't made a backup for a long time, so when I restored it, I got a truncated, stunted, version of what it had been.

'So is that what you're researching? You said you had research notes.'

'Sort of. My notes are histories. Things that came before,

before us. Like Hampstead Ponds: dug out as reservoirs in the seventeenth and eighteenth centuries. Fed by streams that flow into the River Fleet. Themselves part of a glacial system, you know.'

'Bloody right I do, after this morning!'

'No, I mean they're a hangover from the last ice age. The glaciers came as far south as the Heath, melted, and the waters washed away a layer or two of soil from London. Took it back to the clay.'

'Oh right.'

'In that period the Thames flowed into a freshwater sea, as did the Rhine, so they were joined.' By then I could see that he wasn't impressed. 'Sorry Tony, it's a compulsion I seem to have acquired. To peel away the surface, to look back at how things were. You know I'm half-Jewish? I'm wondering if it's a gene from that side of my family, people of the book, who look for the truth in old pages.'

'Hmm, Rabbi John, eh? I don't see it myself …'

'Yes, well, maybe I should talk to Benjamin about it.'

'So is that what you're currently diving into? Hampstead Ponds and the Fleet River?'

'No, and it's only a hobby of course, but I'm chasing a big fish. Shakespeare in London, to be exact. Not sure why, but maybe living where I do put him into my mind. I'm going to walk around some of the places he knew. Of course it's all changed since those days, but I don't know, maybe one could get an inkling of him.'

'That sounds more like it! A lot more interesting than rocks and soil!'

'Hey, why not come over some time this week and we'll walk it together?'

Over breakfast Tony and I got to chatting about running, about routes, and things that had happened to us on those early morning excursions. Our sort of running springs from a solitude, and flows back to it too; we do it away from roads in London's shut-away back tracks. And we run in shut-away time too, at the interstices of days. In winter we set out under the yellow glaze of the street lights and see daylight spread, pale and grey, as we toil around our circuits.

'So what's your route, now you're holed up in Mountjoy House?' he asked.

'Down to the Thames, over the footbridge to the South Bank, down river to the Greenwich Foot Tunnel and back on the north side. And I always do it that way round. If I start off on the north side, by the time I hit the South Bank crowds have built up – commuters, tourists gawping at the sights. You know how bloody irritating it is to have to slow down and weave through them.'

'Yep, there's some narrowish places there. You know that place a little upstream from the Globe Theatre? It's still called Gabriel's Wharf, though of course there's no dock there now. I remember running through there one time. There were busloads of tourists milling around, window shopping or gazing at the mural there.'

'Oh, that one, on the side of the TV studios; the one of Georgian houses.'

'Last time I was there I thought it was fading, the paint had flaked off the wall. It's a *trompe l'oeil*. How does that translate – a trick of the eye? Anyway, hopefully someone will maintain it: London doesn't have enough *trompes*.'

'Do you think so, Tony? They make me uneasy – at first I don't realise what I'm seeing. Then I do, with a frisson of excitement. Because it's ingenious or whatever. Then finally it's just plain spooky. It must have a reason, surely, for pretence, for not showing itself as it really is?' Then Tony told me about the time he'd been running, very early in the morning, along the New River Path. There was a woman's body floating face down in the water.

'I'd been making good time and for a second didn't want to stop. Then I thought, fuck it, she may still be capable of resus, though I didn't know what to do if she was; I was actually hoping she was stone cold dead. So I got in and sort of swam-waded over to her. Grabbed her frock, pulled her towards the bank and then it hit me – she was a ruddy mannequin!'

'What!'

'Yep. I said to myself that I'd ruined my run, was wet and covered with all sorts of goo from the River so I might as well make sure nobody else made the same mistake. Sort of manhandled the thing onto the side. And there I am panting on the path with this shop window dummy and a woman comes by with her dog. Looks at me as if I'm some sort of weirdo. I felt like a fucking idiot.'

My first response was to laugh, but I choked it down when I saw that beneath the bravado, the memory upset him. So I said, 'You're no idiot, Tony. The whole thing shows that you're a decent feller, that's all.'

Then, perhaps too soon, I moved to tell him of something that happened to me. 'You know when, years ago now, Becky, me and Jake lived out on London's southern boundary, near the Purley Downs.'

'Sure. Before you moved into London proper again.'

'It was brilliant running country, trails through woods like Foxley Wood and Dollypers Wood, and over the Downs. Anyway, one bright, frosty morning I went out running to

Farthing Down. Furthest away from home my circuit took me down into a valley, it's actually called Happy Valley, only that day it was anything but happy. It was in a shadow so deep that from above it still seemed to be in night. When I entered it, I felt an intense, unnatural cold. I could feel my body's core heat pumping from me. Something told me that if I stopped or slowed I'd go hypothermic in no time. I picked up my speed, and I swear I was running hard and yet shivering. I ran the mile out of the valley as I'd intended, but with an awful sense of dread.'

'God, you must have been pleased to get back into the sun. How did you feel about it?'

'You know I'm not in the least bit superstitious, but I tell you, it was like, like Death was there, waiting for me in Happy Valley. And I'd outrun him. That time, for now.'

I woke suddenly that night. Reaching for the blue book next to my bed I wrote:

I'm walking into a valley with mist clinging to the hilltops, so that as the eye moves upwards the thickly wooded hills disappear into cloud. Becky and Jake are there; he holds her hand and turns his head to catch his mother's words. He's eight years old.

That was as far as I wrote before I lost the rest. I knew the place where my dreaming had taken me. Dollyper's Wood, set in my once-familiar suburban hills, out on the map's edge where those northern outposts of the Surrey Downs reach up like fingers into the underside of the London boroughs. Then another part of the dream came back to me and I wrote it down.

I call out to my wife and son, but they're deep in conversation and walk on heedless into the wood.

The clock dial showed 4 a.m. I tried to sleep again but couldn't. My body was tired but my mind was running on.

And the following night I went back to Dollyper's Wood.

Running, running in panic searching for my wife and son. In a clearing there are steps leading up to a tree-top walkway.

I'd dreamt more, but it had drifted away like smoke. Eventually I gave up on sleep and changed into my running kit. I did some stretching exercises out on the elevated walkway. There's a network of them here that were intended to be the start of a city-wide pedway system, but these were the only ones ever built. As I looked down at the large rectangular pond in the Barbican courtyard I had a feeling as if an insect was crawling down my back. I tried to remember when I'd had that sensation before. It came to me, that's how I respond to a *trompe l'oeil*. There's a trickery about water that hasn't found its own level. I reckon the pond is on the first floor. Those ducks swimming in it must be completely unaware that it's all made by men and not nature. Why had I chosen to live in a place of blatant artifice, opted for a *trompe* instead of the real thing?

It was still dark as I ran past St. Paul's Cathedral and down the steps to the Millennium footbridge over the Thames. On the South Bank I faced the growing dawn and ran near the riverside, under the London and Tower bridges. I was following my usual route downriver, along the great curve it makes from Rotherhithe. Daylight saw me in the grounds of the hotel in the old Surrey Docks: they have ornamental pools there. One of them has a statue of a heron in it, and my habit was to give that metal bird a nod, a sort of marker that I was through a stage of my route. By some magic that morning there were two herons: a real one had joined the bronze *trompe*. The living bird hardly moved, only turning its head to stare at me as I passed by.

I ran past the Greenland Dock, huge and improbable; along the bridge that crosses muddy Deptford Creek to Greenwich. Taking a gulp of water from my bottle, I jogged down the steps into the Greenwich Foot Tunnel. That morning the thermocline kicked in half way down the spiral stairs. There was a sinister cold in the belly of the tunnel, and thoughts of death came to me. I was alone here. My heart might give out and it would likely be an hour before another person came this way. A thug with a knife could despatch me with impunity. What were these feelings of menace? All those tons of water above my head? I was wondering if this is what submariners felt in the War, far underneath the Ocean. I sensed the Thames seeking for the slightest weakness in the builder's work that would enable it to push down, to flood, to wash away this underground exemplar of human arrogance.

Back in the flat, my priorities were water, shower and food. Then I put out the maps and walking guides on the breakfast table. Boiling water had just gone into the cafétière when Tony rang the bell.

'Hey John, are you working again?' He'd glanced at a pile of papers I'd printed off and left on the kitchen table.

'No, not exactly. The Department asked if I'd be interested in doing a quick piece of consultancy. Might do it. I've not looked at the paperwork yet.'

We stood cupping our mugs of coffee in our hands as we stared out over concrete and brick.

'So what's the route?' he asked.

We turned to the guides and maps on the table and worked it through.

'What do you make of this map, Tony? I got it a few days ago.'

I opened up *Holborn and the City in 1914*. He poured over it for a couple of minutes.

'Strange! Some of it seems completely familiar, and then much of what's here now isn't shown. Not very good for us today ...'

'Yes, see how Cripplegate was still there then, and now it's gone. From where we are now, going south towards the Guildhall is shown as a maze of narrow streets and alleys.'

'I guess the Barbican Estate paves over most of the district in the north.'

'See on the modern map, at the Estate's south side, there's a short dual carriageway road, London Wall. See how it barges through the old street pattern just inside of the Roman wall.'

'It's a bit pointless, don't you think? That new road?'

'I bet you that in one plan there would have been other dual carriageway roads, linking up to this one. But they never got built. Hey Tony, take this and look here.'

I handed him a magnifying glass and pointed on the old map to a place just south of the wall.

'Can you see it?

'Yes,' he said. 'Actually not very far from here,. if we

239

could find our way when only a few of the old streets remain.'

'We can, Tony. We shall.'

We spent ninety minutes in the City, having decided not to go south of the river, and curled our way back towards the Barbican.

'It must be around here,' I said.

'How can you possibly know?'

'Ah – well, I can't really. I'm going from what's online. These people use software to knit together the past and present landscape. So the house in Silver Street should be down here.'

We started to step down into the Corporation's subterranean car park.

'Ruddy hell,' said Tony, 'I should have known. We'll be spending the rest of the day chasing his ghost underground. All because of some digital … geomancer.'

We stood in gloom watching bay fourteen. 'Here's where it was then Tony, Mr Mountjoy's home, thirty-six Silver Street, where his lodger, one Mr Will Shakespeare, wrote *King Lear*.'

There was silence between us for a minute, as if we were mourners.

'In one way what nonsense this is,' I said. 'Because Shakespeare isn't here. And yet I'm getting something from it. I'm moved.'

'I'm getting something from it too,' he said. 'Incipient carbon monoxide poisoning. Fumes hanging around in here, can't you smell 'em?'

'Oh, come on, Tony, where's your sense of mystery? Of time. Can't you feel him willing us to rediscover his house, at least to put up a blue plaque for him?'

'I suppose the house in Silver Street could be half here,' Tony said as we walked to the exit. 'Dead to me and just about everybody else to whom this is just a car park. Alive to you and to all your fellow obsessives. Thirty-six Silver Street lingering on in a state of half-existence, like Shrödinger's Cat!'

'Don't you feel like we're the ones who've discovered it, Tony, as if we're archeologists? Don't you get a buzz from that?'

'No. It's hardly Troy or Mycenae. Though somehow I'm not surprised you think that, John.'

Back in the daylight we chatted on, about London, about the destruction of the town the Tudors knew. Silver Street had been completely destroyed in the Fire of 1666. The judges of the Fire Court had rejected grandiose rebuilding plans, so the street came back, in brick and stone, not timber and wattle. And destruction came again in the much bigger arson of the twenty-ninth and thirtieth December 1940. A mile-long stretch of the City disappeared. Nearly every building in Cripplegate had gone: hardly anyone lived there after the War.

'Of course, no Fire Court after the War,' said Tony, 'and rubble and fireweed have no voice.'

'So most of the neighbourhood could be written off and written out. And who would want cramped alleyways again? Not big business; it needs big buildings, of course.'

'So Silver Street gets cut from the postwar maps.'

'Leaving number thirty-six to cling on best it could, leading its ghost life. Sort of erased and yet still there.'

'Poor old Shakey, over time gravity's dragged him underground like the rest of us. And you want to dig him up!'

'Oh, I don't want to dig *him* up,' I said.

'Who then?'

'Me, I guess.' I'd said it without thinking and then wondered if I'd said too much.

Tony paused looked at me as if something had just occurred to him. 'Maybe that's your journey then, John.'

We strolled on, walking up to the high walks, until a thought struck me. 'Hey, I understand now why there's a tower named after Shakespeare in the Barbican, why my block is called Mountjoy House. It's something akin to an apology, you know, like the way a pickpocket might tip his hat to the chap whose wallet he's just quietly nicked.'

'Ah, the cutpurses are purloining still,' said Tony. 'I think I hear the Bard chuckling!'

Back in the flat after we'd had our coffees and Tony had left, in my book I jotted down a quote to get it out my head. It was from Fitzgerald's Rubaiyat:

As, buried once, men want dug up again.

And then I wrote:

This man at least.

That night I set out from Dollyper's Wood on my elevated walkway.

Running: running hard on my elevated path. I'm high over Happy Valley. Now below me is the house we'd had when we lived in the suburbs. I'm yards above Riddlesdown. Then I'm running back over London, pausing over our first terraced house where Jake had been a baby. Then more of London, but it's not mine. It's a London of small shops within Georgian dwellings. Shoppers come and go. I recognise the street: it's the mural from Gabriel's Wharf. The bronze heron is in front of me. He turns head and speaks as I run past. 'You and me, we're both trompes l'oeils.'

My sheets were clammy. With a sweaty hand I wrote other

lines under that journal entry:

I'm reversing time, racing towards my past. I'm surveying my life's path. Benjamin told me that everything in my dreams are from me. So even the heron's voice is mine – and is that how it is? John Scrivener: a trick of the eye?

The rest of the dream had melted away. I retrieved the consultancy documents from the kitchen table and in the still-dark morning, started to read them through. After the first page I was forcing my way forward. It was the sort of cloth my whole work life had been cut from, yet I found it inexpressibly restrictive, impossibly dull. It felt as if it was work that once had interested another man, not me. It was only 7 a.m. when I threw all the paperwork away.

Another dark winter morning, and I was shivering as I read through my blue notebook. I came to the entry I'd just made:

I'm back in the village now above the new house, where for a while I'd been Young John. The outhouse has been replaced by the extension that I helped to build. I feel there's something I've forgotten or lost. That I've only a few moments to call it back. Water is encroaching on the neighbourhood, rising rapidly over the gardens, spilling over thresholds and up to the sills of the ground floor windows. It's clearer than the most pristine pool. Crouching down on the walkway I try to touch the roof, to reconnect with times past, but it's just beyond my fingers' reach. I lie face down on the now translucent walkway to make contact with the past but my hand touches only ice-cold water and in the eddies my submerged life dissolves away.

Beneath it my note read:

I want to revisit it as a time traveller. If only I could find the point where the track turned towards the wilderness. That's where I'd make some small change, some alteration. I'd correct the flow of events. I'd repair things broken in my life.

I paused, feeling dissatisfied with all I'd written in that succession of four o'clocks. Now that it was lines on a page, my sleep world seemed diminished. I felt as if I'd put a precious bejewelled possession under a road-roller: now I had to be content with the trail of ruined gold and crushed gems. Or I'd flattened the arc of the rainbow and mangled out most of its colour. I wrote in the book once more:

At least I may have avoided turning it all to battleship grey. Maybe I've preserved just enough of the dark turquoise of dreams.

Walking to the window, I opened it to let the night air clear my head. Inhaling, I listened for the city's night breath, that low hum I knew from other sleepless hours. This time I imagined that faint strands of music were reaching me. Or perhaps they really were there at the brink of my hearing. Somewhere, someone was playing a piano. Straining my ears for a minute, I believed I could just make out the ineffable beauty of the Chopin Nocturnes. I threw on some warm clothes and went out along the Barbican High Walks. I couldn't hear the piano, even near the Guildhall School of Music, where all the lights were out. Back in my flat, I opened the window again and Chopin spoke to me once more. But I was unsure, and wondered if some sunken fathom of my mind was melding the night's murmur into music. I turned back to my writing, and in the desolation of night solitude, wondered what it all meant.

The Great North Road
2014

The car was parked outside the kissing gate on the path to the village churchyard. Nobody was sitting in it but two bundles of flowers rested on the passenger seat. A big one of daffodils and a smaller one of tulips, deep red. And twine. The twine had been intended for the smaller bunch. I stood, deep in thought, on the other side of All Saints Church, a few paces away from its northern gate, the seldom opened Devil's door. There was a tradition, or should I say a superstition, that when a baby was baptised, Satan might fly from the child's body. Since demons couldn't cross a consecrated portal, this door would be left open at a Christening for the evil thing to rush screaming from the church.

I studied a gravestone, though the person named there was no relative of mine:

Frances Woodhams
Who departed this life 20th January 1975, aged 78 years
Sleeping in eternal peace

She leapt into my head, an elderly sparrow of a woman with bright eyes, always neatly turned out in the oldest of clothes. Each Christmas time she would bring us a present, one that often as not turned out to be wildly unsuitable.

Sometimes my mother had forgotten to wrap a gift for her and I would later be despatched to her cottage with something that, as my mother said, 'will do'. Miss Woodhams had a brother, mute and mentally impaired. She looked after him. We said then, with the casual cruelty of children, that he was simple and she was a batty old maid. Now I thought of his learning difficulties and realised that she'd been a heroine. I thought of all the things she would have given up, of lives not led, of all the roles, lover, wife, mother, earner, that she might have had without her brother. The duties of care: those bonds that tied her to the village and to her poverty. And I thought of my parents and wondered what kindness from them, or what past respects they had paid her, that had led to this annual ritual. I had never thought to ask about it whilst they were alive.

One Christmas holiday, it must have been in the late 1960s, I explained to her that I was by myself as Ulla and Harold were in London that day.

'Once I went to London, Young John. I took a coach right down the Great North Road and walked around the London sights.' Could my memory be right, did she really have a faraway, wistful look in her eyes when she said that? Were the seventy miles to the capital so huge a span to her? Or she might have said: 'Once I took the Silk Road and walked in

Isfahan.'

I'd become the hinge on which a world had turned, a witness to a vanished time. The forensics people say that every contact leaves a trace, and I stood wondering if it was true. Were all lives reduced just to ledger entries in the Registry of Births and Deaths? What else? My feet took me in the direction of her old house, not far from the churchyard, but it was long since demolished, and now the graveyard stone might be the only other evidence that she had ever existed. 'Except my head. What if that is the only other place where you leave a trace?'

As I walked back, I paused on the bridge over the brook that runs by the village. Picking up a twig, I threw it into the water, on the upstream side. I crossed over to watch it float along, to the grassy place where the stream made a bend. There the stick was caught up on some debris in the water. At that spot, Young John and a school friend once made a raft. The boys assembled some discarded drums that had once held agricultural chemicals. They bound them together with some planks they'd found, using baler twine taken from a field. After their craft was built, they rafted a couple of miles with the slow current, to the next village. The adventure occupied all the endless summer day.

It had been an upsetting trip. I'd driven up from the

Barbican on the Holloway Road, and knowing there to be works at Archway, had taken the old Great North Road route up Highgate Hill, passing the small statue of Dick Whittington's cat. I wasn't sure if it was charming or ludicrous. Supposedly it was near there that Dick, having decided to return home after failing in London, heard the church bells and turned around to try his luck once more. I'd chuckled at the thought this road would have been the wrong one to take Dick home – he came from Gloucestershire.

I'd been grateful for the reminder the little figure gave me. Two or three times in our careers Becky and I had had opportunities for jobs in the North, but each time problems had arisen. So we'd turned around, Whittington-like, rather relieved to be heading home, scuttling down the M1 motorway back to London. Then I'd asked myself why I thought of it as the Great North Road. Nobody said that anymore. It was the A1, or sometimes the ugly 'A1-M'. And then I wasn't sure why in my childhood it was called 'Great' anyway. It was because it was a long road, I supposed, as I ruminated on it in the car. Or because there used to be a different North Road, the old Roman Ermine Street that set off from the City via Shoreditch. It's a slightly longer route, up through Tottenham, the A10 and crossing the Ouse in the Huntingdon area to join the Great Road at Alconbury Hill. I was headed for a point a few miles north of that hill, where I had not been for many years.

As I'd got beyond the Huntingdon turn-off, the highway altered, the old dual carriageway having been upgraded to motorway. I'd recognised the place names on the signboards, and expected that it would revert back to the old road before many miles had passed, that it would get to seem familiar before I reached the place where the accident happened. But it hadn't been so. At last, I'd realised that this new motorway had paid no heed to the old junction I sought. I'd come off at the next roundabout, saw that the first exit pointed to the old "B" road and took it. I'd found myself driving back down South on a minor way, parallel with the motorway. A little further down the route crossed over the A1, still running parallel with it. I'd told myself that now I was on Ermine Street.

The old crossroads had been superseded by a bridge. Passing over it, I'd stopped at the roadside where there was a metal gate. Beyond it was a track back to the A1. Maybe it was part of the former B road, but if that's what it was, it petered out at the motorway embankment. I got out of the car and tried the gate. It was locked fast. Looking back at the lorries rushing up the motorway, I'd felt confused and dispirited. It seemed as if this new road had been laid over the old one, so the A1 was higher there than it used to be and the alignment seemed to have been altered too, completely obliterating the previous geography. I didn't recognise it at all. The constant hum of vehicles melded in my ears to that sinister chord in E flat. The instruments were ill-tempered, and I had to raise my hands to my head in a vain attempt to block out the off-key sound.

Once more in the car, my thoughts punished me. If I was going to do this, then I should have bloody well done it years ago, before the A1 was upgraded here. I'm too late, too ploddingly slow, as usual. I'd meant to leave the tulips close to the spot where the accident happened. I'd intended to find a suitable piece of road furniture; my mind's eye had seen the small offering tied to the upright of the signpost at the crossroads. It would have been there as a memorial, until the weather or some passing maintenance man removed it, and people would wonder who it was for. They would have been able to appreciate how easy it was for someone to die there, at that dangerous junction. Today, all trace of both sign and junction had disappeared, banished into history as surely as the Roman legions tramping up Ermine Street, or the stagecoach horses trotting along the Great North Road.

I'd been a skeptic in that post Princess Diana change in national sensibilities. It amazed me that Becky, bright, down-to-earth Becky, had put her own peonies onto the massive floral tribute outside Kensington Palace, and saw no point in adding to it with my own. At first I'd been left cold by the hug, the kiss-greeting, the heart on sleeve, the flower shrines that had appeared on the London streets. Those desiccated bunches of blooms with faded ribbons that had attached themselves to lampposts or railings marking a road death or a murder. At first I'd preferred to cling to the old virtues of decorum and reserve. But I'd changed. Over time I'd changed.

As I took the bouquets from the car, I was mulling over two photos, large prints on ancient cardboard. They'd come from a chest in the loft of the Kennington house. Over time the images had flattened out to an almost monochrome grey. I'd put them onto the scanner glass without much hope that it would help me to see what the photographer had intended. I'd experienced a frisson of delight such as must have been known to Daguerre and Fox Talbot as they waited in their dark rooms with chemical-stained fingers. In modern times the wait is just the eye's blink. Without my employing any digital trickery, clear images sprung onto the computer screen.

These prints must have witnessed the turn of two centuries, for what greeted me was a handshake back to the last quarter of the 1800s. One picture showed the village High

Street, much as I remembered it, although with all of the demolitions and developments of recent years, it was very different now. The other was of a country lane, and at first I didn't recognise what I was seeing. Then it hit me. I was looking at the dilapidated thatched cottage where my grandmother was raised, that plot being separated from where I now stood by a large field. The cottage had been there until a few years after the Second World War, demolished when my father had the new house built. Two young women posed shyly in the foreground. Priscilla's older sisters, I thought. And then if you looked closely, two heads were poking over the garden wall. I'd been pretty sure that one was my great grandmother Mrs Arnsby, whose looks I knew from another photo. The other, a cheeky young lad's face - might that be Frank? But why had these two chosen to be fixed in time without their bodies?

Photographs: those strange combination of accident and artifice. Maybe Mrs Arnsby felt that she and her son weren't well enough turned out. Or maybe the photographer wished only to include the two girls as an adornment and the mother and brother were interlopers, whose unbidden curiosity resulted in them being photographed.

At the three headstones that comprised my family's presence in the churchyard, I lifted my eyes to take in the neat pasture, and then around to the sturdy thirteenth-century church with its fine spire. There could hardly be a more English scene than this. Around the world if I produced a photo of this place people would say: 'Oh, that's England.' And here was the gravestone for that German girl, my mother. It struck me with a fresh force how profoundly unlikely her journey had been, pulled out from under the crushing heel of a murderous despotism to this quiet spot. She had died at fifty-nine of cancer, and Hannah and I put her ashes here, her memorial filling up the bottom half of our father's gravestone that had seemed achingly bare when it had been made three years earlier.

I pondered a call I'd taken a few days before. Hannah's voice had been clear and it was hard to believe she was in Auckland. She'd called to say that she would be coming back to the UK. 'No, not the London job, and just as well probably; I'm not sure I could afford to live there now. The Manchester one, I got that. Didn't want to tell you until it was official.'

I was delighted for her, and for me too.

'Brilliant, well done, Hannah! You must have been away ten years or more.' My sister, the wandering star. Me, forever stuck in the London mud.

'And thanks for the photos you emailed me, the old village – pretty amazing.'

There was a pause, perhaps a trifle awkward.

'I don't suppose you've found it, John, the one we talked about?'

'No, I haven't. Surely it must be somewhere, I can't believe that Mum would have thrown it away.'

I was looking at the simple inscription we wrote for our parents' gravestone. Harold had died at the young age of sixty two. At the time I'd been overwhelmed by the feeling that some hex must have been laid down on him. I still felt that sense of unease.

Harold had worked with the earth, with bricks, stone, concrete, those hard materials that, you would think, stand the test of time rather better than soft flowers and flimsy photos. Our house had been a sort of testimonial to his exactitude, his concern with quality and comfort. As a boy I'd helped him build an extension to it. When I was young it was often fun to be the journeyman's assistant, but as the work proceeded through my teens it became a duty, a burden. I guess what kept me going was that I sensed the project was about something else than just providing the family with extra accommodation. But I hope that something of Harold's forethought, his diligence, rubbed off and influenced me in my professional life.

Yet not all stone is hard. Jane's headstone must have been

made from a softer material as fifty years of weather had made the inscription almost illegible. With my fingers I traced her letters, all but obliterated to the eye. Without her name the only message the stone carried was a general statement of the impermanence of human life. I thought then that stone was rarely enough in itself. Words are needed too, like they are for photographs.

When we came to sell our parents' house, Hannah had suggested that we install an inscription that memorialised our father's work in conceiving and building it. I thought then this was a non-starter of an idea, and we didn't do it. There at the graveside I regretted it. My London years had accustomed me to such things and the experience was always enriching. The official royal blue plaques, of course, are legend. There was a Frith Street roundel that had to be my favourite. One night, stumbling out of Ronnie Scott's with jazz and too much wine in my head I'd looked up to see the plaque remembering Mozart's stay in the street and wondered if I was seeing things. For those whose lives were considered less prominent or less notable, some of the London boroughs provide a plaque. And then there are those inscriptions made by individual property owners, those enigmatic statements of historical connection. I used to wonder why some of them were there since words change nothing for the householder, because they must already know what the plaque proclaims. Now I came to understand: in making an alteration in the way the property is seen a change is made for all. Perhaps that's what their originators had wanted: a talisman, something that offered their house future protection from alteration, or even from abolition, through the shifting sands of the housing market.

After placing my flowers on the family graves, I returned to the car, for the first time on this visit gazing over the field towards the back of our old house.

That's odd, I thought. The silhouette looks different. Have they done some major works over there?

I strolled along the tree-lined track back to the lane on which our house stood. My foreboding grew with each step. When I reached the lane I spoke out loud. 'Holy fuck! It's gone, all of it! What is this crap?'

Our distinctive home, with its extension that through my teenage years I had laboured for Harold to build, was no more. Three new houses crowded onto the plot: tacky, formula houses that, without meaning to, shouted out they'd been built by a speculator cashing in on the village's recent status as a dormitory serving the newly fast roads. Two of the houses appeared occupied but the end one still had an 'under offer' board at the front.

Opening the gate I walked around the house into the back garden. Mostly a lawn, with the turf lines still showing, it seemed not much larger than the tiny open space we'd had at the rear of our London town house. I could hear Harold's voice within me: 'What's the point of living in the country if you've not got a garden worthy of the name?'

I peered in through a back window: a kitchen with magnolia walls, fitted units from the builders' merchants, you know what I mean, the sort that look good for a few months and then will start to cause trouble and be ripped out after a year or two. There wasn't anywhere to sit down in the garden, or otherwise I'd have crumpled onto it. What had disappeared was not just where so many memories were located, my family history, but it was Harold's memorial that had gone. Something he did for his family, for himself, when overcome by grief when Jane died.

A flicker of anger started to burn in me. Against the person who had done this, against the accountancy times in which we live. Disgust at the taint of commerce that pervades our lives. Then, as usual, I let the 'pull yourself together, John' voice in my head choke my fury down. It told me that I should look on it as a sort of progress. Didn't Harold sweep away the century-old cottage seen in the photo, and now his work was swept away in its turn? Who needed a garden as large as the one that he'd made? People want practical places to live and evidently these new houses suit some of them. It's just elitism to think of them as 'spiv' houses. Yet I didn't agree with my own inner critic. The old cottage had been uncomfortable and incapable of modernisation, incapable of receiving running water and a ring main. Harold's house had been a huge leap forward into the age of science, but these were backwards houses. They weren't going to last either, because they hadn't been well enough made. The apogee had been passed.

And in that moment I missed Becky, missed her arm, missed her wisdom. I rang her number, expecting just to take comfort from her recorded voice, and was surprised when she answered. A long jumble of words fell from me.

'John, are you saying that it's been pulled down, your old home, that wonderful house your dad made? The bastards, the bloody bastards! Who would do that?'

It was a pattern: Becky was having my anger for me.

'Yeah,' I said.

'Well, aren't you mad about it?'

'I guess so. Just sad really.' Then remembering my inner voice, I said: 'Maybe it's progress.'

'It sounds more like vandalism to me. Are you sure you're not just pushing on regardless?'

'You're probably right.' I said.

'So what are you feeling?'

'I don't know. Numb, I suppose. It's like the house was another parent to me, a sort of birth mother. And now she's gone and that means the end of my link to where I came from. But I know I'll survive it; I mean it's as if I have foster parents to go back to.'

'Go on.'

'Well, it's as if London is my foster mother. I feel at home there.'

'That's a good thought to hold.'

We talked on some more and she said: 'What are you doing about food tonight?'

'Don't know; I'll pop into Marks and get a ready meal.'

'Why not come over and we'll make a meal together? And a glass of wine with it, best not to eat alone after something like this.'

By walking down the lane I could make a circuit to the other side of the church. As I did so I thought of the vagaries of flowers, photos, stones and bricks. They were all deficient. The word trumps them all; words are memory's keys. Once again in the churchyard, I took three daffodils from the abundance I'd left with my parents, and dropped them gently at the foot of Miss Woodhams' stone. Much had happened in the thirty or so years since Ulla and Harold had died. I'd been so busy and had changed everything in my life. I looked back on it as an arc of time spanned by the brilliance of Becky's love, a time in which careers had been built, a child raised to manhood, four houses bought and sold. I was thinking of those years as ones in which London's gravity had held me captive, kept me in orbit to the life I'd made there. But all that time I'd had unfinished business here in the village.

Because in another way it's as if nothing in me has changed, as if I'm still eight years old, rigid, sheltering under the kitchen table the night of the accident. Praying to a God I didn't really believe existed, even then. I stared once more at the church and I thought of the Devil's door. How I'd spent my life pushing my back against it, forcing it shut. When I what I needed was to open it to let the demons out. That was my work now.

And then all I wanted was to be back in the city that had adopted me, back in London. To be sharing a simple home supper with Becky. Twenty minutes later the car was on the A1 once more. I couldn't feel any affection for it, the Great North Road, the ribbon that curved its way from nearby the village to London. The road that had led me from childish days to my adult life, and on which I could rewind my steps, part tourist, part time-traveller. It lurked in my subconscious as a malign presence. There were sinkholes hidden under that skein of tarmac laid over much-quarried ground. Without warning they could open, swallow up a life and drag it under the black waters beneath. Yet in turning to face the Road, acknowledging what it meant to me, I felt the possibility of power. Perhaps I might transmute or transcend the events of my youth and if I could not change my path, at least I could change the way I walked upon it.

I was checking the rear-view mirror when I heard a voice in my head: 'Once I took the Silk Road and walked in Isfahan.'

Vauxhall Slipway
2014

There are times when I feel that I've failed at everything: failed at work, at marriage, at parenthood. That's when I get myself out of my tiny flat, my box in the London air that tastes of engine fumes. It was one of those times when my shoes had walked me to the Thames, to the oozy foreshore left by the receding tides at Vauxhall. There's a slipway there by the side of the secret service building, and you can use it to walk onto the southern shore. That's when I saw them, the mudlarks. Three of them, with their metal detectors and headphones. Each of them was eyes down, in a private world, intent on the study of slime and grit. Even in my low state, I felt superior. What a way to pass the hours, grubbing down there for London's detritus!

A while later, coming back with my coffee in hand, I saw them again. The tide was rising and it would soon submerge their bank of stones and sludge. Two of the detectorists were by the slope, packing their kit into holdalls as they talked about their day. The other one was in a puddle of shallow water, washing a find in the cold Thames water. I hadn't realised before that it was a woman, and as I looked at her she let something fall from her hand, returning it to the Thames.

'Had a good day with it?' I asked as the men walked up to the Albert Embankment.

'Probably only one thing.' He showed me three or four small objects, all the grey-brown colour of the river. The river mud didn't smell foul exactly, but there was an unhealthiness there, a metallic odour and something that reminded me of rotting seaweed. He picked up a small find and shook it, making a rattling sound. 'Know what that is?'

'I've no idea.'

'It's a bell. I won't know how old till I get it home and clean it up. Could be an animal bell, that's fallen off as it wandered along the shore. There's one in the museum, three hundred years old. And I thought I'd show this band to you, Oonagh, seeing as you're not interested in anything else,' he said, holding up a ring.

The woman had come up the slipway now. She was about my age, wiry. Her grey hair was dishevelled and her teeth yellowed, with one missing at the front. Her face took on a hungry aspect at the mention of the ring. 'Give it here, Steve!' The light in her eyes died as she looked at the object he'd placed in her hand. 'Pah, it's nothing, a washer, and you know it. Mean trick!'

After the other two had left, Oonagh rolled a cigarette and lit it. She took a Thermos flask from her rucksack and sipped at her tea.

'Are you an expert in rings then?' I said.

'No … except that I've found a couple of them in my time. But not one I wanted.'

'You're after a particular sort of ring?'

'No. Not a sort of ring. *A* ring.'

I looked at her in some amazement. 'Whose was it, if I might ask?'

'Mine.'

'Oh no! It must have been very valuable.'

'It was a lot to the boy who bought it for me. Neither of us earned much. It was our engagement ring.'

'And you lost it in the river?'

She looked away from my face, no longer wanting to meet my gaze. She shook her head, and I waited. 'No. I threw it away, over Chelsea Bridge. And now I'm trying to find it.'

'Look,' I said, thinking to lessen the self-punishment in her voice, 'we all do things that we might regret, after a row between us or something.'

'I did worse than that. I went with someone else. Thought I didn't need him, or his ring. Broke off with him and broke his heart. My new man was older, richer. Treated me mean, left me. I never wanted big things, just ordinary things. A man, a house, kids.' I was looking at her careworn face, finding that I could imagine it as youthful and fresh. 'But I never got it, the life I should have had. Threw it all over with the ring. But then it came to me. The truth. Time's a whirlpool, so there is a way back. The ring's the key. I must find it ...'

'What happens if you do? Find it, I mean.'

She gave me a stare that I couldn't quite interpret. Truculence, I suppose. 'I know what I know, right! It's got nothing to do with you!' There was defiance in her eyes.

'Sorry, if I've upset you,' I said, taking a step backwards. 'I didn't mean to pry. Only tell me if you want to.'

She came closer again, and spoke low, as if we'd become conspirators. 'They don't know it, but I do. Here. Right here, in the marsh, by the river! The vortex will spin backwards. But you must have the key to do it. To make time unfurl. When I get the ring, I get my second chance. I won't throw it over again, nor him neither! We'll be together again as we were supposed to be. Like it never happened.'

I didn't know what to say and came up with something like: 'Have you been looking for long?'

She had a far away look in her eyes. 'Got my first detector in ninety-nine. What's that? Fifteen years, must be.'

'It's a long time,' I said, appalled. 'Do you look further and further downstream?'

'No. The tides wash to and fro ... it could be anywhere

now, upstream or down, South Bank or North. One day I must find it. Stands to reason.'

'I hope you do,' I said, wanting to end this conversation with someone who I judged to be deranged.

'I'll be back tomorrow at low tide.'

Over the next few days, I completed my task. Climbing up the rickety ladder into the loft of our Kennington house, and removing the contents of the old trunk that I'd taken from my mother's flat after she'd died. It had followed Becky and I through several house moves. It was full of old papers and photographs, and I had thought to ask Jake to help me get it out of the attic, but things were still strained between us. Anyway, there was nowhere in my tiny Barbican place where I could keep that trunk. At each house move I had been going to get around to sorting through it, but there had always been more pressing things to do. So in the end, each time I'd put it off and forgotten about it. Or rather, I thought I'd forgotten about it, but looking back now, maybe I'd always been aware of its faint pulse sounding out in some hidden detector of my mind.

I soon realised that there was so much in each box of papers I took from the chest that I should rummage through it, to scope the work I'd got to do. But it proved impossible not to get drawn down the trails they set. The first letter I pulled out was about music lessons. It was addressed to Mrs Scrivener, written in February 1962, and politely suggested that John should return to his piano tuition. 'He is developing his musical understanding and competence. Moreover, John possesses the gift of perfect pitch, which surely should not go to waste.' The author went on to say that he did not want to intrude on the tragedy and suffering that our whole family must be experiencing, but that he felt he should write because music can 'so often provide solace and a channel to express one's feelings'.

At first I had no memory of playing the piano, and strained to make out the signature. Desmond Poulton, oh yes, a tall balding man of unending patience drawn up from the mud of my memory, taking me through my early music grade exams. I searched for a response from Ulla, but if she sent one, then she never kept a copy. The music lessons must have ended with Jane's death.

I went back to work on the photos, wondering why it had taken me half a lifetime to start to go through them. In my move from Kennington those of them that weren't in albums – most of them – had cascaded from their various envelopes and folders. My mother's and father's family photos had been shuffled, mingled together, Germany and England, Jew and Goy, just as their genes had done in Hannah and me. There were hundreds of prints, and the task of digitising them on my home office scanner was going to take me many months.

I dwelled on the difference between my mother's Mainz photos and the rest. When removed from the albums, written in Ulla's strongly cursive script on each print's reverse were the names of all the people it included. There had been a deliberateness here, a determination to make a record, one that might outlive her, as indeed it did. Many of them were of her school group, a small band of kids whose Jewishness had barred them from the state school system and who were being educated in the Bezirksschule set up in the synagogue. Countryside outings, gymnastics lessons, a couple of Purim events. Only later when I visited the little museum in the Mainz citadel did I understand that I possessed a record of the evaporation of a community. The Jewish vibrancy of Mainz was leaving it, as people managed to get out. Ulla had been one of the last to leave, a few weeks before the outbreak of war. The photos themselves had not stirred much interest from the museum volunteers, and I supposed that they possessed others from that time. What did excite them was the names, the words that made sense of what the eye saw, that supplied identity to image. Faces were joined to the Reich's fastidious logs of the destinations of those young girls: London, Boston, Paris, Shanghai. Theresienstadt, Auschwitz.

Amongst Ulla's albums was a small wallet book with age-brittle cellophane pockets in which photos were placed back to back. I had the choice of forgetting the scanning or destroying the album. Of course, I chose the latter. A piece of paper was in one of those aged pockets folded between the photograph backs and almost invisible until the cellophane was ripped and the photos taken out. It had proved to be a piece of my maternal grandfather's headed business paper. I hadn't seen the like before. Probably this was the only remnant of that once thriving enterprise that had made it through to the twenty-first century. Within the folds of the notepaper was laid a pressed flower. It occurred to me that Ulla had put it there before she stepped onto the kindertransport train to London, to life. Was I the first person to see it for more than seventy years? A small piece of beauty salvaged from the wreck of her childhood, the ruin of her forebears' enlightenment project of integration and equality. She left no clue as to what memories the flower had held for her.

And then more text, in German this time. It was typed with no errors, and this was a carbon copy. I wondered who the top copy had been sent to. It was from someone who styled herself as Aunt Lina. My German's not so good and I thought I must have misunderstood. I ran it through the translator program on my computer, and realised that I had made no mistake.

I arrived in Montreux in late March 1945. A resettlement post has been set up in the Hotel Belmont where I'm revelling in the plentiful hot water and full rations! We've each been given a supply of blue airmail envelopes.

'Our transport from Mainz arrived in Theresienstadt on 28th September 1942. I had been taken from my own home together with Aunt Rosa who had lived with me since 13th August when her house had completely burnt down and she could save nothing but her bare life. Once there we could move about freely ... Rosa and I were much together until her transport in May '43. We get permits for walks; for next week I have permission to visit Zurich. I look forward very much to this and I hope to see Robert Kahn.

I was still puzzled. Robert Kahn was Ulla's father, my German grandfather who'd spent the war years in Switzerland. Who were Lina and Rosa? I only began to understand when I came across a copy of a neat record form, stating that Rosa Kahn had died in May 1943, in Auschwitz. Ulla had never told me, never told Hannah, nor anyone else as far as I knew, that her grandmother was still alive when war broke out. So, it was my great-grandmother, Rosa, who had been killed in that most satanic place.

In the weeks that followed I attempted to come to terms with what Ulla had buried in the silt of years. It was as if she couldn't live with the reality of Rosa's life and death. So she'd hidden it away from us all, and must have tried to scrub it from her own memory. Of course, it was always there, and I shuddered to think of how the fact of Rosa must have called out to Ulla at night. My God! There was a pattern: Jane, too, had lain in the shallow grave of a forced forgetting. Yet Ulla had left just enough for me to grasp a memory of Rosa and drag it up into the daylight. Had she done the same with Jane?

Another week, another box of old photographs. I opened up an album I'd seen before, entitled 'My baby's first year'. There were many small monochrome photos of Jane as a newborn, in her pram, with her parents, with baby toys. I was about to close the album, when I saw that a slit had been made in the back cover. Inside, there was an envelope which contained another, larger, photograph. It was a school portrait of a girl, well looked after, happy, with a note of seriousness in her eyes. It was the one that Jack had sent away for.

Several months later, at just gone six in the morning, my run took me past Bankside. There was a lone figure on the mud, Oonagh, sweeping over the sludge with her electric broom. Then she was digging with her spade before kneeling and using her trowel. In the grip of her madness, she dug with a furious energy. She placed something in a bag before continuing, stooped again. How many thousands of times had the bleep in her headphones raised her hopes, only for them to be dashed by what the ooze yielded back to her? I saw her disappointment. She looked beyond weary as she took up the search once more.

Jake

Kennington Park
2014

I'm there, working on my project. My mum's house in Kennington. Well, my parents' place actually but my father doesn't live there anymore. And I've sort of spilled out of my own room. Vinyl. Much the best way of recording music, but it takes up a lot of space. So I've set up my trusty Mac in the living room, and fire up Pro Tools. Finn had phoned to say he'd turn up at two o'clock. Finlay Galbraith, known as Finn. New Zealand. Couple of years younger than me so twenty-three now. Itinerant. A whizz at all things mechanical, electrical. My best friend.

'Is that Kiwi time or Brit time, Finn?'

'What sort of question is that! I'm totally on Brit time now.'

So I don't take the headphones off noise cancel till two thirty and sure enough it's past three when the doorbell goes.

'Who's Alan B. Shepard? Some sort of local hero?'

'Good afternoon to you too, sir.'

'Oh yeah, hi Jake. It's just that I saw that name on a tree a minute ago.'

I start to laugh.

'Right … name on tree. You smoking again or what?'

'No! Saw it when I was getting off the one-five-nine bus. A nameplate on the road tree. Alan B. Shepard. Come to think of it, it doesn't sound like a Brit name … you guys don't use the middle initial, neither do we. So that makes him American. Why do they need the middle initial?'

'Not sure. But for once it helps.'

'Because?'

'Because … he was an astronaut.'

Finn Wikipedias him on his phone. 'You're right too. How did you know that?'

'Must have done it sometime in my twenty years of schooling. There's a lot of curriculum time freed up when you don't have to study Sheep-Shearing 101 and all that.'

'Sheeit! Prejudice wherever we Kiwis go. The Conchords were so right!'

We're both laughing.

'Jake, any chance of a coffee?'

So I make up a cafétière and we sit sipping it black.

'Don't suppose I could sleep on your sofa for a few days? It's got a bit, you know, strained, in the Brixton house. Kirsty's boyfriend came back from his trip and …'

I give him a knowing look.

'I guess I can square it with the old dear for a few days, but it'll need to be time-limited. Any plans for where next?'

'Yeah, some of us have got our eyes on a place round Whitechapel to occupy before the developers get the builders in.'

Finn, last of the squatters.

'Meant to say, that Oscar guy was round. He's been trying to contact you. Streamed your latest on BuzzCloud and wants you to do something for an exhibition. "Breathing Space", it's called; Art and Public Space, something like that. He's organising a group of artists – students, I guess. They want some sounds to play, something new, original he said.'

'And is there anything new to be done? Hasn't it all been done before and is simply rehashed? Time to be open about it. The only thing left is plagiarism and recycling. Hey, and am I thinking of the same Oscar? Beard, denim, tweed.'

'The same.'

'God, yeah, he's emailed me. What do you make of him, Finn?'

'Umm, I guess "Oscar" and "organising" aren't two words often said together.'

'Exactly. I reckon he's one of those trust fund babies; you know, hanging around the art world, still waiting for one of his old school mates to give him a job.'

'Sounds an interesting little plan though. Maybe check it out.'

'Don't suppose they've any money? To pay anyone?'

Finn grins. 'Hey, see that pig winging it past the window!'

'Have you ever thought, Finn, how everything's fucked up in this city?'

'No, what do you mean?'

'The Boomers have fucked it all up. People like my mum and dad. Or maybe they've just gone along with it. Time was when it was worthwhile studying, getting the degrees, and all that. Now where has it got us? Take you and me. We're not in the middle classes, we're not in the proletariat. Tell you where we are. We're out on the fucking margins. You're working your butt off at Nu-Club, setting up, setting down, but what do they do? Stick you on zero-hours so you get a pittance. When I say I'm working for Dot-Marketing, people are all impressed. What I don't tell them is that it's a weirdo part-time contract outsourced through some tax-dodge cowboys so that when they've taken their cut there's fuck-all left for me. If I couldn't stay here I'd have to be checking out Whitechapel like you.'

Finn takes a glug of coffee. 'Yeah. Though some of it's my choice too. I wanted to hang in London. Maybe I'll get a career when I get back to NZ. And you – you wanted to put the music first – I remember you saying that. You hate the rat race.'

'Whoever said the rat race was for rats got it wrong. It's for mice. Little timid squeaky mice. Like my old pop with his mouse briefcase scurrying off to meetings. And it makes me feel like a teenager.'

'What does?'

'Living with my Ma at my age.'

'This town's mad. The price of getting a roof over your head – insane!'

'Tory government, Tory Mayor, what do people expect?'

'How do they vote, Jake, your Ma and Pa?'

'Not for that lot! Yeah, might be surprising with Dad being so straight-laced civil service and all that. The thing about Dad is though he's repeatedly failed the viva in dealing with stuff in front of his nose, in other ways he's pretty smart. Nobody with half a brain would vote for them!'

'They get in though, don't they?'

'Come on, Finn, Nu-Club on a Friday night, you know like I do that there's plenty of people well short of half a brain in this town.'

We talk on and Finn says:

'Guess I'd better get on and see if all my stuff will still fit into the backpack.'

'You look like an astronaut yourself when you're wearing that thing.'

'Yeah, well, you know us antipodeans. Everest, London, the Moon. It's all the same to us!'

I give him a hug and say:

'See you later, man.'

And I get on with the music. Then one of the turntables on the Vestax jams. Stuck solid. I take it apart and can't see what's wrong. And I'm muttering something like: Why won't you fucking turn, you bastard? You would wait until after Finn has gone. He could've fixed you in no time. All of the ingenuity in it, the vinyl, the turntable, the electronics, all fuckin' useless without motion. It's scrapheap junk. And it's a parable of my life.

I need a walk and go out, slamming the front door. I'm going over familiar ground. Wondering if it could have been different. If I'd had more confidence when I was younger. If it would have been different if my parents hadn't sold up in the suburbs and moved to inner London. Wondering why it had been so strange with my father when I went away to uni. It was like he'd said in his head: 'that's done'. Then took the whiteboard cloth and wiped me away. He can be so kind, but inside there's something cold. Asking myself what it is about me that'd made Caitlin treat me so bad. It must be three years since it ended. I don't suppose there'll ever be another girl for me. One thing I know, women still like a man to have some money in his wallet. And I absolutely don't.

Wondering if it's always going to be like this. Hand-to-mouth. Bumping along the bottom. I try telling myself that there's others who've got it far, far worse than me. It doesn't help. It never does. Try telling the man on a precipice that the other guy is standing on a narrower edge than his.

Walking along my normal street and I realise I've got a companion. A metre behind me is a black Labrador. Elderly. More than a tad overweight. No sign of the owner. Seems to have a definite sense of where it's going. It adjusts itself to my pace, but doesn't do anything else to attach itself to me. We walk to the crossing to Kennington Park, where it sits waiting for the green man. We cross and it plods in through the entrance. In the deepening dusk the park takes on a mysterious air.

I say under my breath: 'If you're my Iroquois spirit guide you're late, ten years late. At least. And why aren't you a bit more youthful, energetic?'

We reach the gate to the dog-walk area. The Labrador stops and looks at me. I open the gate, and it walks in as if this was an entirely routine thing. I get on with my evening walk. A group of crows are pecking over the grass. They look pissed off, as if they've arrived late at a party to find that the food's been eaten and only meagre leftovers remain.

It's a remnant, Kennington Park. It's a bit of freedom left over from when a huge ancient common was carved up. After the Chartists gathered on it, most of the common was taken away. I feel a kinship with it. I started out with so many prospects for my life, and gradually they're being cut from me, and I'll be left with only a remnant. The possible is shrinking. I'm like everyone else. One by one our dreams are thrashed out of us and in the end we let them go – we accept being fenced in.

I stroll around with such thoughts as the evening sky darkens towards night. A park man is ringing his hand-bell. Throwing-out time. It's not the chirpy 'hear ye, hear ye' ring of the town crier I heard once in Croydon town centre. The way he's doing it, it has a doleful, haunting sound. More like a medieval leper's bell. Or an announcement of my incarceration at the Bedlam asylum. It used to be at the other end of Kennington Road. I feel the rhythm of words.

'You're cast out, outcast. Cast out, outcast.'

Ahead of me I see the man open the gate to the dog area, and the black dog walks out. It waits on the path for me and goes by my side to the exit. I decide to take a different way home. The dog turns to retrace its route. A few paces on and I swivel round to look at it. It pauses, looks over its shoulder to gaze at me and I sense more than see that our eyes meet. We each return to our path. The streetlights are coming on.

A few days later and I'm thinking that it's all Finn's doing that I'm wasting my time. I'm in a workshop room in the art college along Kennington Park Road. They're planning an extra-curricular exhibition so there are students from other schools too. St. Martins. Camberwell. Someone from Goldsmiths. There must be some sort of network here. They're mainly female, almost all foreign students. A guy from Poland, a girl from Ghana, another girl in paint-bespattered jeans who tells me she's from Tokyo. A guy called Marco in a red beanie hat, who, when he's asked to say where he's from, says: 'I identify as human'. Oh my God, what a juvenile idiot! There's five others. Not including Oscar. He's saying something facile about art marketing.

My antennae are working overtime. It's not who's in charge exactly, but more who's got the sway. 'It's a man's world', the song goes. And I guess it still is for my parents' generation. And in finance and politics. Not so much in my world though. Sometimes it looks more like a girl's world. And I don't begrudge them it. When they've worked for it. When they've got the brains and they often do. It's just that sometimes you can see the eye flutter. The hair flick. The out-bust. When they're around a man that's got the power. That's when it grates on me. But not now. Sorry, Oscar – it's not you.

And after a while I think I get it. It's the Japanese girl. She's the one who's listened to, who seems to make the points that hit home. She comes over to me.

'I'm wondering if you'll do it?'

'No, Kimi, I won't.'

'Why?'

'Because you've not left me enough time. The music's a part-time thing with me. I have a day job to do sometimes. And everything I produce goes out under creative commons – I don't get anything back from it.'

I'd have guessed she'd have said, 'that's a shame', or something, and would've left it there. But she says:

'I'm fed up with this place. I'm going to walk round the park. Come along too – if you like.'

So we walk to the gate ... me struggling to think of anything to say.

'What's it like living in London when you're from the other side of the world?'

'Actually, I'm Anglo-Japanese. My mum's from here. My parents met when Pa was studying and she went with him to live in Japan. When I was a kid my father's firm moved him to Swindon ... stayed there for years and that's when I first visited London. And it was like … like London attached hooks in my head, and I knew it would always drag me back. I had to live here in this city. It's … it's my drug. So, back in Japan, I made it happen, a school exchange, then bachelors, masters.'

And I'm thinking, that's how your English is so good, no accent.

'But don't you miss Japan?'

'Yes… but I'll never be as completely at home as I am here. I can't believe there's another place on the planet that would fit me as well. I never want to live anywhere else! And my visa will run out and I'll have to go.'

I'm taken aback by the feeling in her voice.

The park is its usual varied self. Six or seven of its green parakeets fly squawking between the trees. I can never tell if they're laughing or quarrelling. Mums with kids in buggies, people with dogs chatting in the dog-walk area, an old guy on a bench, some young guys building muscle. And all colours just getting on with it. I'm not listening now but in the past French, Portuguese, and that language the Somali people speak, have all reached me whilst walking here. Beautiful cheek-by-jowl London.

She breaks into my thoughts as if she was thinking that way too.

'All the effort you could go to travelling around the world to meet different people. Why do it when they all come to you here in London? It's one of the things I love about it, the way it's reached out and brought the nations here. And it's been doing it for so long. I think of it as the 4D city.'

'Not sure I follow,' I say.

'Four dimensions. Pulling people in from all the corners of the world and sending them out again. And it's got a time dimension. You keep running into the past here, the past is present around you. Time is folded over, contorted in London like nowhere else I know. Take this place. At first it seems an ordinary small, town park, a bit neglected really, at least to Japanese eyes, and then you realise that once it held an ancient sacred space.'

'Did it? I didn't know that. It still has a strange aspect sometimes.'

'I'm sad the sacred little hill was flattened when they made the Park. And then I think how brilliant it is that's there's a space for things to grow, to flower here.'

It feels odd, learning stuff about my home city from a foreigner. So as not to seem like a total ignoramus I say:

'Of course, the Chartists had a major rally here, back in eighteen forty-eight.'

Kimi already knows about it.

'Don't you find it odd that there's no memorial to them in the park?'

I'd never thought about it. But I pause for a moment and say:

'Actually, it's outrageous. If this was Paris they'd have monuments everywhere.'

'And it would be called *Parc des Chartistes* perhaps! Though someone told me there's a mention of them on the church over the road there.'

'Didn't know that either.'

Suddenly energised I say: 'Let's look at it.'

Back in the park proper, Kimi asks if I've noticed the memorial there to people who died in the war.

'The war memorial, you mean?'

'No, not the one with soldiers' names on it. The other one.'

We walk over to it, a slender stone remembering Londoners who were underground at that spot, taking cover from an air raid, when a German bomb scored a direct hit on their shelter. Many were killed but it was hushed up at the time – news of so many deaths was considered likely to harm morale. So this memorial is a recent act, a considered remembering. Some words of Maya Angelou's are carved there. I'd never really focussed on them before but this time I read them aloud:

'History, despite its wrenching pain, cannot be unlived, but if faced with courage, need not be lived again.'

'What does it mean to you, Jake?'

'What's passed is past, I guess. And we can do different in future.'

'Maybe we can only do different if we bring the past into our minds, work on it and take the trouble to understand it.'

She impresses me, this Anglo-Japanese girl. In that instant all my thoughts of the nobility of Angelou's sentiment are displaced. Dislodged by a fresh awareness of Kimi's female shape under those old clothes she pulls on to make her art. I fumble towards words of my own. 'Yeah, I suppose. Umm, perhaps I could adapt a piece I started last year, got stuck on and put aside. Maybe it would work. What about having a listen and telling me what you think?'

'Love to. Can I download it?'

'I never put up anything unfinished. No, I'll give you a USB stick, or a CD if you like. For your ears only. Maybe I could find my way out of the rut it got into.'

So we head back to the house and I burn the track onto a CD, smiling at the thought that it's a technology that will soon be as outdated as vinyl. I reckon nobody will care though, nobody will collect it. When I finish I see that she's been looking at my books.

'You like the Americans. Chandler, Roth, Elmore Leonard, and I see a Cormac MacCarthy,' she says, picking it up.

'Yes, I like them, don't know why. Well, actually I do; they're a sort of X-Ray laser beam on us. Borrow it if you want.'

I see she's about to decline, then changes her mind and slips *No Country for Old Men* into her bag.

'Thanks. Look, I've got to run. I'm meeting someone and I'm getting late. Fifty-nine bus into town for me.'

I realise I'm holding a feeling. Disappointment. It's not a new one for me. This time it spurs me to say:

'I promised I'd pick up a loaf of bread. The shop's past the bus stop. I'll come with you.' So we walk along Kennington Road talking of *Norwegian Wood*. She glances back and sees her bus.

'There's one! I best get it. Bye, Jake.' She runs on to the stop. Stepping onto the fifty-nine she beams out a lighthouse smile.

And I'm thinking, was that for me?

I stop at a roadside tree. Maybe part of my brain has remembered what Finn said, because for some reason I look upwards at the trunk. Placed high there's a small metal name plate.

Eugene A. Cernan, it says.

Leake Street
2014

I'm in bed, though not asleep yet, when my phone rings. It doesn't bring up a name, but I answer anyway.

'Jake. Hi. Do you have a step-ladder at your place?'

'What? Who is this?'

'Marco. Finn told me that you've a garden shed and there might be one in it. I'm going to need a step-ladder.'

'Do you know what time it is? And yes, as it happens my parents do keep one there.'

'Good. One of those lightweight aluminium ones?'

'Yes. What's all this about, Marco?'

'Right. I need you to bring it with you to Leake Street tomorrow.'

'I'm not going to Leake Street. I'm going to work.'

'Tell 'em you're sick.'

'Marco, I'm not going to throw a sickie! I need the money! And no way will I be wasting my time helping you make graffiti in Leake Street or anywhere else.'

'I don't do graffiti! I do art!'

So follows five minutes of acrimonious interchange, which somehow ends up with my agreeing to take the ladder down to him the day after tomorrow – it would be a better day after all, he says – and to pick it up again when he's finished.

'Ten o'clock,' he says.

'Right. And I'm not hanging around waiting if you're not there.'

'I'll be there.'

'And I don't see why you're so insistent that I bring the ladder. You could come here and get it yourself.'

'You need to be involved, Jake.'

'Why?'

'Because you do.'

'I'm surprised that you've even got time to redecorate Leake Street. I thought you said that you've still got to make a start on your work for the exhibition. Not even having a clue about what to do.'

'That's changed. This *is* my work for it.' Marco is just impossible.

I get through the day on automatic pilot. I'm worrying at a problem in my music. There's a place where I need an echo, but I can't get it quite right. Anyway, and it's become normal to me, my mind is in orbit around Kimi. I'd arranged to see her straight after work in a bar the students like. She's there already when I arrive and she's deep in conversation with Marco. They're at a table and have spread a rough plan of the exhibition hall on it.

'Hi, you guys. Can I get you anything?'

Kimi declines but Marco wants me to get him a shot.

She comes over to me whilst I'm at the bar, shoving the plan into her folder. 'At last! Marco's getting his work together for the show.'

'I know.'

'I'm thinking about how to organise the space. Look, I'm sorry, but I've got to rush off.'

'Oh no! That's a shame. I was hoping to talk with you. About how it's all going.' It's a half-lie. I want to talk with her, but not about the work.

'It's OK, don't worry. It'll go well if everyone actually produces. Everything going alright with the music?'

'I guess.'

'Sorry that I've got to go. I always seem to be in a hurry these days. But something's come up at my place.'

'Right. I mean is everyone OK? Significant other OK?' There's a slight pause and she looks at me from the side of her face and I can't gauge what she's thinking. 'Jake, are you trying to find out if I've got a boyfriend?'

'Maybe. Or girlfriend. Sort of. Yeah.'

She shakes her head and I think she's going to say "No." But she smiles. 'You'll have to ask around'. Then she's gone. I'd already asked a couple of people. They didn't know. So I end up spending ten minutes drinking with taciturn Marco. About the last person I'd have chosen.

'See you tomorrow,' he says, without offering to buy me a drink.

The next day, muttering against Marco under my breath, I haul the stepladder down Kennington Road towards Waterloo Station. Leake Street is a poorly lit road in a Victorian brick tunnel under the massive hulk of the railway terminus. It's where the street artists do their stuff, and they pretty much seem to own it. There must be some dispensation or agreement that they can do more or less as they please. I've walked it a few times either as a short cut, or, in an idle afternoon, to view the changing chaos of the art. You might see the odd flattened cardboard box down there, even a grotty blanket roll, but for some reason the street doesn't appeal much to the homeless, even though no cars are allowed. It can feel a tad spooky, but nothing bad has happened to me when I've been on Leake Street[4].

I pass a guy working with his cans, the smell sweet and toxic in my nostrils. He comes over to my side of the road to better view his picture. Pulling his respirator to his collar, he asks me what I think. So I rest the stepladder and look. He's

4. Author's note: There has been some changes to Leake Street since Jake was there. The side arches have been opened up and eateries have moved in. The street lighting has been improved, so the nights are less worrying than they used to be.

painted a rectangular frame. On one side he's overpainting a lurid cartoon character and on the other a series of what I take to be practice tags. It's a landscape, a tumble down house on a rural road. There's a tree, and fields. Not bad, if you go for that chocolate-box look. 'Yeah, keep going, it's good down here to open a window onto the countryside.'

He looks disappointed, as if I don't quite get it. 'Hmm, more a window in time. It's this street before the station was here.'

'The street was here before the station?' I'd never stopped to think about how Leake Street came to be, but surely it had been built as part of Waterloo as a way to get from one side of the station to the other without having to cross the tracks. Or as access for the stores and stables that must have been there, in a maze of arched galleries on either side of the street. Once, I caught a glimpse of them when a side door was open.

'Yep. Just a normal street with houses, gardens and a factory later on. Then the railway comes. The company never wanted to build their terminus here, they wanted to go across the river but they couldn't get permission. So there's no grand design to it really. At first just a bridge to carry the track across, then another bridge and so on. In fifty years you go from this –' he points at his work '– to this.' He indicates our filthy brick tunnel with its collection of grimy litter trapped here by the eerie eddies of wind. In that moment I feel the street's fall. It went from light to perpetual night. It's gone to squalor. I almost like it, like the extreme ugliness. It draws and fascinates my eyes.

The only other presences on the street are two figures silhouetted at the northern end. One of them turns out to be Marco. The other one is Finn.

'Hey Finn, didn't think I'd see you here.'

He cups his palm under his chin in that way he has when he's uncertain of something. 'Yeah, Marco's roped me in!'

'Hi Jake,' says Marco, hardly casting a glance in my direction. He's staring at a section of the tunnel on the other side. 'You've got the ladder. Good.'

What the other artist told me is still playing on my mind. 'The guy over there said that the street was here first, before the railway. Just a normal street and then bit by bit it got walled in as the station was built above it. It got entombed, like, like Pharaoh's servants were in the pyramids. You know, when he died, and they were supposed to be buried with him. To help him in the afterlife.' Finn's intrigued, and we chat for a minute about it. He says that we're part of the street's afterlife. Marco doesn't seem to be listening.

'Perfect. This'll do it.' Marco's chosen a slice of wall near the end of the tunnel, so it receives a small amount of grey daylight. There's a painting of a man playing a piano. He seems to be naked, except for a comic bowler hat. That work already has some tag scribble over it, but it seems a shame to me to extinguish it altogether. From one of the two hold-alls Marco's brought with him, he produces a tripod and camera. After five minutes of adjusting the set up, he says to Finn, 'Go for it.'

Finn uses a marker pen to trace where the tripod legs stand, and whilst Marco packs it away, takes a cordless drill from his rucksack. He drives a brass screw into the centre of each circle he's made. 'You should be able to find those again. Right, time I left you to it.'

'Just one more thing,' says Marco, and plucks a respirator from the other hold-all. It's not a simple house decorator's one like the guy at the other end of the street had, but something that looks more like a gas mask, with filters on both sides of the face. 'Jake, I need you to model this for me.' Protesting, but curious, I put it on, and stand in front of the wall, but he's still not content. 'Hey Finn, can you just pull the mask a bit away from Jake's face so that the elastic is taut? No, not like that, turn so that you're both sideways on to me. Bit more. OK. Hold that.' He fetches a pad and pencil and begins to sketch.

The muscles in my neck are beginning to ache. 'Fuck this,

Marco, how much longer?'

'More or less done,' he says, but it's another couple of minutes before he snaps the pad shut. 'Bye.' We've finished being useful to him and he wants us gone now.

'That was well strange,' I say to Finn as we head off to the other side of the river.

'Yeah, he's something of a one-off. I don't know if he's an artist or a … wanker.'

'He's certainly the second of those, but maybe he's both. And he's going to photograph his work as he paints it?'

'I don't think so! Didn't he explain it to you? He's going to come back and photograph it twice a day, as it gets painted over.'

'What! Why?'

Finn shrugs.

'I'll ask him myself this afternoon,' I say. 'I've got to go back to pick up that stepladder.'

'Sorry about that, Jake, I realise I've landed you in it. Marco's like a force of nature when he wants something.'

'No problem. Anyway, I'll be interested to see what he's done.'

In fact, I don't see Marco again that day. Because when I get back at the agreed time, neither he nor the stepladder is there. And I'm saying something under my breath, something foul, like, 'you fucker, Marco, where the hell are you?', when I catch sight of his street art. Holy crap! It's a man, painted with a surprising element of detail, and although his face is partly obscured, it's obviously me. He's in the clothes I'm still wearing and holding a mixer and cables, looking surprised as a respirator is pulled away from his face. But it's not Finn who's doing it, it's a girl. She's dressed in faded jeans and wears a green beret. There's nothing sexual about the way she's been painted, but I find it hard to stop looking at her image. It takes half a second before I'm gawping in shock. I wonder if I've made a mistake and take a step back. But no, there can't be any doubt. The girl is Kimi.

In the next minute I go through a storm of feelings. At first I'm puzzled about why we two should be in his picture. I'm furious that he didn't ask me first. I wonder if he'd asked Kimi and if she said it was OK, then what would that mean? But I'd take a bet that he hadn't asked her either. Then I'm embarrassed. Marco's linked the two of us together – her hands, the respirator, the band, my head – and held us up to the world. There's an intimacy between the Leake Street me and the Leake Street Kimi. But it's not there in real life. My God! I've just realised how much I wish it was. I've been outed. I let a fresh wave of fury sweep over me. How dare Marco mess with my life!

I see a couple of things I'd not noticed at first. There's a place where he ran out of paint, or of energy, because you can still see part of the piano from the picture underneath. Or maybe he just liked it like that. At the bottom of his work, Marco's made a small shape, it's a cartouche such as you find within Egyptian hieroglyphs, and inside it, he's written 'De. Composer'.

I walk along Leake Street, still cursing Marco, but this time my anger is mixed with a grudge of respect. The guy could, at least, paint. There's a couple of artists working further along the tunnel, one of them stepping off a ladder he's been using. It looks like the one I'd brought down this morning.

'Is that yours?' I ask.

'No, I was asked to keep an eye on it until the owner came round.'

'Red beanie, working down there,' I say, pointing. He nods. 'I'm the owner then.'

I stop for a moment at the bucolic offering, now finished. The artist has painted the frame so it looks like it's in a gallery. The paint has trickled downwards. He's put a nameplate on it: '*Here, before nightfall*'. I'm in a bad mood and it seems trite to me now.

Other thoughts come to me as I trudge up Kennington

Road. A painting like Marco had done, well, it had to be planned, sketched out time and again beforehand. The cartouche was likely the only thing in the picture that wasn't in some blueprint he had hidden in his folder, a childish joke he'd thought of whilst he overheard my conversation with Finn. There's a deviousness to him that I'd not suspected. Then I feel foolish because I must be his dupe. That stepladder business – had it been a ruse to get me to Leake Street, so that he could get a fix on a last detail of my features? A fix on how I move, a fix of my character?

Once home, I phone Finn. He's at work so can't speak for long.

'You won't believe what that little shit did!'

'His art?'

'He's put me into it … with Kimi.'

'Is that bad? Must be, I guess, for you to be so pissed off with it.'

'Just go and see, and tell me what you think.'

'Will do, tomorrow some time.'

The next day goes by, trying to concentrate on my music. However hard I try, I can't stop Kimi coming into my head. I walk around the park wondering how long it will be before the street's artists supplant Marco's images of us. Finn calls round in the afternoon. I put the coffee on.

'Did you see it?'

'Yeah. I'm surprised he could even produce something … something that looks like painting. If you know what I mean.'

'You get why I'm mad with him?'

He cups his chin. 'Hmm. Mind if ask you something?'

'Go ahead.'

'Are you and Kimi … ?'

'No, but … you know, I'm so … I would so much …' I can't find the words. In the small silence that follows, Finn must have understood.

'Jake, bruv, ask her out. Let her know how you feel. Hear what she says.'

'Yeah, but what would she see in me? I'm struggling, failing and failing again.'

Finn looks a bit shocked. He shakes his head. 'If she's got any sense, she'll be thrilled,' he says. Good old Finn.

The next days slip by: work, music, and trying to spend time alone with Kimi. And always it's tomorrow that I'll be asking her out. I wake in the small hours and lie there, wondering about the two of us. Thinking about our painted avatars in Leake Street, wanting to know if they're still there, pristine, wondering if they've been maimed or altogether done away with.

Perhaps it's a good thing that I don't see Marco for a

week. I've calmed down a tad.

'Your work, I hate it.'

'All of it? Or any particular piece?'

'Don't be cute with me, Marco. You know I mean the Leake Street one.'

'Oh … you mean my take on "Breathing Spaces". I heard.'

'Why didn't you ask me first?'

'Would you have agreed?'

'No.'

'That's what I'd thought. Can't see why you're worried. It'll be overpainted soon enough.'

'Not soon enough for me, Marco.'

'Get some paint and do it yourself. Hey, let me know when, and I'll come and take photos. The subject extinguishing his own image! Great, a sort of suicide! Or maybe it's Kimi you want to kill off?' I react to that without meaning to. 'Ha. Thought so! She's safe from you, isn't she, Jake?'

'What's the point of working on something just to snap photos of it being covered over?'

Marco rolls his eyes. 'We all get overpainted, don't we? And we're all overpaintings, or do you think you're the one and only that's been laid down on a blank piece of board?'

I turn away in exasperation. Though come to think of it,

what he says isn't a million miles away from things I say about music.

Two weeks later and I wake with my heart pounding and a bad voice growling in my head. I'd done something wrong and as punishment they'd amplified London's gravity so I fell and couldn't get up again. I was fixed, spreadeagled on the road. Men came with bricks and walled it over. I was trapped, entombed, forever.

I know I won't sleep again. I have to get up, get out. Pulling on some clothes, I shove an old torch into my pocket. I have a plan, but I'm not sure I'm bold enough to see it through. Yet my feet take me under the yellow lights to Leake Street. It's deserted and it feels dangerous, as if I'm being watched. But I don't give in to fears and switch on my torch instead. Fifty paces in, and someone is following me in the shadows: I can hear his footsteps. I pick up speed, but the stalker does that too. I stop, and after a fraction of a second the other footsteps stop as well. I want to run, but continue a steady walk. Halting suddenly again, I swing around with the torch. I don't see anyone. The footsteps have stopped again though. With relief I realise that I'm being stupid. I've been haunted by the echoes of my own footfall.

At the other end of the tunnel, I seek out Marco's picture, but I can't find it. I'm thinking I must have mistook the location when my beam lights up the head of a brass screw sunk into the road. This is the site, but the wall opposite is quite different now. Marco's art has been obliterated by a huge flowing word, "Zynebots", in silver and black. What is that: a band, a computer game or something else? I've no idea. I cross the street to look more closely, unearthing a spot where the previous work shows through in spaces between the letters. It's a piece of the piano. In the crook of the "S", I find a remnant of Marco's art. Kimi's face is still looking out, as if she too, is searching for the place where, once, I had been.

Little Compton Street

2014

I'm in Soho. In one of the record shops on my regular circuit, I'm there with the vinyl collectors, the nostalgia geeks, the music archaeologists. A few years past we were seen as misfits, now they say we're trending. Who cares? But in fact Soho's not what it was for records. Many of the little stores have been forced under. It's losing its edginess, and soon it'll be as conventional as the rest of the West End. You need to go to record fairs now to pick up unusual vinyl, or to buy online. Or maybe you'll strike lucky in a charity shop. Still, I've got a couple of records because I think they were a tad under-priced. I mean I'll play them when I get home, but I don't suppose they'll be useful for my music. Should be able to make a few quid reselling them on eBay.

People have the wrong idea about music. About how the new stuff comes to be. That it bursts like a genie from a bottle into the mind of some guy with the creative juice. Or flows to him like a dream. Or emerges unprompted from a jamming session. Not so. Everything's been done before, really. Composers, creatives, artists – whatever you like to call us – all we do is reorder the building blocks, turn them round, try them in a different colour. Somehow it can still sound fresh.

And somehow the ear, or perhaps I mean the brain, picks up what's underneath, picks up on the lives those building blocks have led before, before they were turned around and repainted. I want it to be a bit more obvious, that it's been 'previously owned', so I often use samples, a phrase, a beat, or just a single note. They've all been played before.

A couple of weeks ago Kimi asked me about it. 'Isn't it only a few experts who will recognise where it's come from though, Jake?'

'Sure. Only the cognoscenti understand the former lives the music has led. But I think, or at least I hope, the hearer picks something up subliminally. Feels rather than knows that in the new there's a connection with the past.'

She looked as if she was going to ask another question, but stopped herself. I wanted to kiss her. Didn't do anything about it. Wish I had.

'I do like your music, Jake.'

A text comes pinging in. Finn.

'where r u?'

'sister ray'

'b there in 2'

'Hey Jake, thought I'd find you in the Berwick Street Exchange.'

'Was there, but they were playing old Dylan tracks, and

there's a limit to how much of the likes of "Subterranean Homesick Blues" I can stand.'

He laughs and says: 'right with you on that one!'

We browse together for ten minutes or so, without finding anything either of us feel we have to buy.

I say, 'Reckon I've finished up here. Shall we go get a coffee?'

'Yeah, great. I've found a café a few yards away.'

I'm always wary of Finn's 'few yards'. He's a Kiwi and his feel for distance is different from mine. I put that in the back of my mind as we cross Broadwick Street and make our way along Old Compton Street, passing some seemingly very acceptable cafés.

'It's just the other side of Charing Cross Road.'

The traffic has been slowed to a standstill by the works on the CrossRail underground railway up the street, and we thread our way through. Most of the traffic island on which we end up consists of a grating. Something beneath it catches my eye.

'Wait a minute Finn. What's that down there, behind those cables?'

'Hmm, looks like a street sign.' He slips off his backpack and rummages in it for a moment.

'In a job like mine it pays always to have a torch handy.'

In its beam we read the words: Little Compton Street.

'What is this?' he says. 'A street beneath a street? London's so weird.'

'Charing Cross Road must have been laid over another street. It's archeology, Finn. One stratum on top of another. Like Troy …'

We walk on.

'It's hardly Greek or Roman down there though.'

'No. Victorian maybe. Think of those people walking along Little Compton Street, my ancestors – could be. Rushing around doing their stuff. Hustling after that job, that deal, that girl. Thinking it's all a first. That it's never been done before, never mind all the past centuries. Or centuries to come. And today we like to think that we're originals when we're just a turn of the same wheel.'

'Like your ancestors have been buying vinyl in Soho and peering down street grates!'

'OK, OK! Perhaps last century Scriveners bought vinyl, and before them, sheet music. Why not?'

'Yeah, but do you actually know that?'

'Course not. I'm only supposing.'

'It's your father's lot who were the Londoners? So what's he passed on to you?'

'Nothing. Well, not much. I know that he was raised in the

country and came to London after uni. His dad was a Londoner though. That's about it. And in any case that family history deal gets really boring after about twenty seconds. To me anyway. What about your dad, what did you get from him?'

'Family records, stories sure. Photo albums going way back to when my father's lot got to NZ at the end of the nineteenth century. As immigrants to a strange land I suppose their impulse was to record stuff. To document who they were, where they'd come from.'

We reach Finn's café. We go in and ask for our Americanos.

Finn says to the barista: 'Is Amy in today?'

'She's not due in for a few minutes yet.'

I get the picture now.

'Just someone who came into the Club,' he says. 'How are you getting on with Kimi?'

'Nowheresville. She's working twenty-four/seven on the exhibition and stuff.'

'If you ask me, she likes you.'

'Yeah, well, I didn't ask.'

Finn pulls an iPad out of his pack. 'Let's do some searches on Little Compton Street.'

He passes it over to me. The street was obliterated by the

construction of Charing Cross Road at the end of the nineteenth century. 'But look, I don't think we were peering down into another street. I think we were looking into the top of a utility tunnel.' He shows me photos of the tunnels taken by urban explorers. They're full of cables and pipes for fresh water and foul. Street signs have been placed down there, Piccadilly Circus, Cranbourn Street, Little Compton Street. 'They were probably put there to let the utility workers know where they were. And in the meanwhile the street layout above has changed. It looks like a real street sign down there for Little Compton Street though. Which is a puzzle.'

'Brilliant stuff, Finn. A subterranean memory of a street. And this looks interesting. Says here that there was a pub on Little Compton Street where Verlaine and Rimbaud went drinking.'

'Know of them, never read them,' he says. 'Do you think they were there sloshing down the pints?'

'Those two? Nah, they'd be getting smashed on absinthe!'

I'm trying to put together into words something that's occurred to me. I mean there's a way in which I'm not surprised that the streets are laid not on solid ground but on hollows. The tarmac covers catacombs. We've casually pushed them out of our conscious minds.

'Do you think, that we're aware of all this stuff buried

under our feet? I mean subconsciously. That it gives off something that Londoners pick up?'

He looks at me for a few moments. 'Could be. Londoners have a way of being. Must come from somewhere.'

'What's our way of being?'

'Like you don't talk much in public. Like there's a depressive way of being in this city.'

'Is that fair, Finn? London's a big party town.'

'Sometimes I think that's the other side of the same coin. I see it at the Club. Ridiculous drinking; people popping handfuls of party pills. Running away from yourselves. Getting unconscious. And sudden flare ups into violence.'

'Verlaine and Rimbaud would still feel at home then! And I can't say you're wrong. But who knows where that stuff comes from?' And I'm thinking of the streets. How the brain picks up deep resonances. Layer on layer of lives, each one holding a pattern informed by what went before, and subtly ordering the shape of lives that come after.

'Want to show you something,' says Finn. He pushes away one of those cardboard coaster things and places his iPad on the table. 'Downloaded an app that tracks your movements but forgot to turn it off. So it's been tracking me for a couple of weeks.'

I see a map of London and dotted lines that show where

315

he's been.

'Look at how they cluster. My trips from Whitechapel to work. Out to yours. There's our vinyl hunting in Soho!'

'What's interesting is how little of London you visit.'

'Exactly. Like I think I'm staying in London, but I'm only ever sampling a small part of it. And where can you go to really see all of London, the full extent of it?'

I was quiet for a minute because I'd never thought about it before. From the Heath you get a good view, though even there it's really just a view of central London. Once I was up on the hill where the Ally Pally stands. You can see more. Or on the Downs near Purley, where we lived when I was a kid, there were one or two places where you could glimpse it through the houses. But all those are just partial views. London's too big to take in.

'What's the tallest building now?' I said. 'The Shard? Maybe if you went to the top of it?'

Finn puts the map onto satellite view and we zoom high over his footsteps, as though we were birds.

A girl's voice says: 'Hello, you. Following me around then?' She's a Kiwi or an Aussie perhaps.

'Ah, Amy, I was just passing with my friend Jake here and we thought we'd stop by.'

'Hi Amy,' I say. 'Look, you guys, I best split. Got to get

on with the music.'

'Jake, perhaps I could stay over at yours tomorrow night? We've got an early start on Saturday.'

'Sure thing. See you then. Cheers, Finn. Cheers, Amy.' As I leave they have their mobile phones out, swapping numbers.

I'm pissed off as I step out. With Finn. Why is it so easy for him, and so hard for me? I stop walking when I see myself in a shop window. Fuck it, I'm looking at the person I'm angry with. What stops me going for what I want? And that's the cue for the voice in my head. A snarl from the usually placid Labrador that's been prodded in its old war wound. Kimi likes you! What's the use of like? Does she lust? For you? Not a fucking chance. Then he moves onto familiar ground. London's full of gorgeous girls, sexy girls and you've not got one have you Jake? Wasted years pining over Caitlin, who had the good sense to brush you off like she would shit stuck on her shoe. That's how it works. How I step down into the dungeon. How I'm lowered into the oubliette. Sometimes the voice gets deeper, more sinister – the growl of a night Doberman.

You're a failure. That's how people talk of you. Jake the loser. Nobody wants your piss-awful music. You're a live-with-mum boy. At age twenty-fucking-five. Without a proper job. You're a dead-beat, deadwood, dead-end. Drop dead.

Drop dead! DROP DEAD!

But I know more about it now. How it works. I know that being outdoors and walking helps me. That thinking on good things can kick the dog away. So I make myself remember what the students said on the piece I've remade for them. I remember the times when I've hit a wall on a music project, and yet found my way through. I think of my friends ... of Finn. That he's a great friend to have. Piss off, black dog! Then it's as if I find my own utility tunnel upwards. And now I need to reach up and push away the grating to climb out onto the surface.

It'd been dry this week and the town's getting dusty. I'm thinking of a book of photos in the Kennington house. It's of old London and there used to be drinking fountains and horse troughs in the streets. Now they'd been taken away. If you haven't got a place of your own or cash to buy bottled water might you die of thirst in the London desert? I once read that people who have lived for generations in Earth's arid places, they don't fear dying of thirst. They know where water is always to be found. What they do fear is drowning. The sand bakes hard, so when there's a storm the ground behaves like rock, like flagstones on the pavement. The dips and gullies turn into furious torrents that flow unchecked. I'm thinking of it: you're merrily picking berries in the valley, and there's been not a drop of rain. A downpour from miles away snuffs you out. Raging water thunders into the canyons. Half an hour later the water's gone, leaving your drowned, broken body. Probably with most of your clothes ripped off through the sheer force of the surge.

Down by St. Martin's-in-the-Fields a homeless man puts out his paper mug. I search in my pockets for change, and realise I've spent most of it on the coffee. I drop all I have into his cup. It's less than fifty pence. He seems pleased.

'Thanks, mate, you're a gent.'

'I have a question.' He looks at me with suspicion, as if I've just turned a gift into a trade. 'Where can you find fresh water, I mean drinking water?'

He nods in the direction of St. James's Park. 'Park toilet block. Or any Royal Park.'

'Thanks,' I say.

I walk home. I tell myself it's because I want to. But it's also that I can't really afford the fare. The fifteen in my wallet has to last me a few days until my money from the sometimes day job comes through. That begging man might have as much as me. But there the similarity ends. The Scriveners have a well on their land. They have to work to pump it, but it produces a steady flow. Not a river full. But enough. So that's the difference between us. I still have access to a well. His people didn't have one. Or they did but it ran dry. Or maybe he drank it dry. It makes no difference – I'm no better than him. It's all in the turn of the wheel, what causes us to move in different cities. Whilst walking the same London streets. Yes, I'm the beneficiary of class. I can stay in Mum's house for a few pounds put into the kitty each month. And there's a savings account with five thousand in it, a gift from Grannie. She told me to keep it for something special. Lately I've been thinking about it.

Back in the house I try to get on with my music project. But it's as stuck as ever. My desk is crammed full with electronics, cables getting in my way. I'm fed up with the thing, and decide to modify it. In the garden shed there's a couple of small wooden boxes, which, on their sides, will serve as shelves. All I need to do is to screw them together and then fix the whole thing to the desk. They even have slatted bottoms with gaps wide enough for cables to pass through. I grab Dad's toolbox – shiny and neatly organised – and look round for the electric drill. It's nowhere to be seen and I reckon that he must have taken it to his flat. There's an old hand drill that I've noticed before though I've never seen him use it. Dad has always liked gizmos, and thrown out old stuff, so I wonder what he's doing with this thing.

It's satisfying to use, the old drill with its wooden handles. It slows me down, in a good way. I find an ancient countersink drill bit and ease the screws just under the surface of the wood. I'm pleased with my customised music desk. In the tool case I see two metal pipe clasps and screw them to the end of one of the boxes. The hand drill is perfectly stowed. I guess I've appropriated it.

The woodworking has given me a little distance from my music, enough to realise that something in me is dammed up. It comes to me that the same thing is what's stopping me getting close to Kimi. Finn had told me to let her know how I feel. So I try to give voice to what I feel about her. It sounds something like: you're the most amazing girl I've ever met. It sounds something like: I can't stop thinking about you. It sounds something like: I want you. In my life. In. My. Bed.

And then the idea seeps into my mind. Or the conscious bit of my mind, since when I become aware of it, I feel it's familiar to me. How I could make a change to what I do. What the special thing is that I could buy with Grannie's gift.

Early next morning the weather breaks. It rains from one of those slate grey London skies. There's no breeze. The cloud is homogenous, seems to go on for ever in space. And in time too: there's no prospect of it ever ending. It rains all day, yet I have to get out the house and do one of my usual walks. Now it's hard rain, the sort with large raindrops that splash up from the pavement so that even in my hoodie I get wet both from head down and feet up. So much rain that you wonder where it can go. The roof gutters can't send the downpour away fast enough and water splashes over the sides down onto gardens and patios, but somehow the drains cope. Somehow the sewers have not been overcome. The ground's sodden and can absorb no more. The trails in Kennington Park made by impatient Londoners who won't do other than walk direct from gate to gate, they've turned to slurry.

In the evening Finn arrives, burdened by cases of electrics borrowed from Nu-Club, and soaked through. He checks his luggage to make sure the equipment hasn't got wet.

'Dry as a bone. Not like me! Tried sheltering under a Moon Tree for a minute. Big mistake.'

'Moon Tree? You're talking antipodean, Finn!'

'I'll tell you when I've dried out. Got a towel?'

Later, I rustle up a pasta for him and Mum. She puts candles on the table and breaks out a bottle of red. In the flickering light we talk of the exhibition. And Finn asks about my mother's side of the family. All the time the water pounds down outside our window.

That night it rains on the deserted city. It rains for ten

thousand years. The deluge returns acids from the fumes London has exhaled over centuries. Drop by drop it washes the town away. Dissolves it. Melts it down like wax. Water percolates through the buried layers of the cities of previous ages. In the utility tunnels, the gigantic Victorian sewers, the underground railways, in all those manmade caverns, rainwater leaches through. It makes subterranean lakes and waterfalls. A glistening cave-scape takes shape. The rain holds the memory of the city it has erased; the stalactites and stalagmites that form create a transmuted, miniature London. It emerges from the pools as Venice does from its lagoon.

There, in my row boat, I hold up a lantern and gaze out. The shimmering glow shows me an immense stalactite like the Shard, a vast stalagmite that's a replica of the Houses of Parliament. There's Big Ben! I know that I must locate my own home. I see the first house I can remember, an inner London terrace. Pulling hard on the oars, I find the suburban house of my childhood. The moisture on it shines. At last, and with relief, I come to the Kennington house. Then I'm overwhelmed by sadness at the realisation that I just live there, that it's not home. Home is something I still have to find.

Water drips onto the lake. The plunk, plink, plink of the drops sounds like music. And then it is music – my music. It sounds entrancing, beautiful to me. And I'm sad again because there's no one with me to listen to it.

John

The Dark Arch
2014

My mind flows towards the dark spaces, towards those places where clear waters carry the taint of death. Can you understand then that I suspected I'd find something like it? And if the Dark Arch, and the drowned men under it had never existed, I'd have found something else, found other bodies. It would be their story I'd be telling. But, as things are, it's young Mr Whitehead who splutters back to life for a brief moment.

I stood by the boating pond in Finsbury Park. I was early for my appointment with Benjamin. The park was noisy, full of the shouts, screams and laughter of children. A service truck clattered its way along the road for a minute, overwhelming the woeful bark of a small dog tied to a fence whilst its owner snatched a cup of tea in the park café.

Trying to see myself, I leaned over to peer into the greasy water of that dark pond. The ripples and detritus blurred the image. I wondered what others saw when they looked at me. They'd say, 'he's never had to labour for a living', with his smart casual clothes and manicured fingernails. And their guess would make my age older than I really am. Yes, probably so because I felt older than my sixty years. In that moment, in my heart, I was an old man. I was wearied, tired like I am after an uphill run.

Concentrating on the reflection in the pond, I passed through it so that I hardly saw it. I turned the small black wheel, the one that I took from Granddad's hearing aid. It's been inside my head for more than fifty years. I twisted it to just above the point where it would click and switch off, fading down the sounds of that summer's day. Then I could travel through my brain's whirr to be entirely on my own, as if I was passing through a waterfall into the secret cave of thoughts. It was something I'd been able to do since I was eight years old, that night when the world fell in on me. The night that Young John died. The night that a second John started to take over.

I had another tuning wheel, my fader, that lay behind the black one. I always thought of it as grey; it turned down feelings, took the edge off emotions, dulled pain, twisted off joy. That's how my second version, the responsible, dutiful John, had lived out the years: with the bright lights turned down. At that moment I wanted to take John Two, grab him by the throat, hold his head under that slick, sick pond surface until his office-soft hands lost their grip and his civil service legs stopped thrashing.

John version two was an impostor.

'Just fucking die!' I must have said it aloud, because I was aware of someone stopping to look at me. It was a mother who'd been passing by pushing her baby buggy. I released the black and grey wheels, and turned my head to the park. As I straightened my back, I wondered if there'd been something in my stance that had made her think for a moment that I was about to vault the low fence and throw myself into the water. I mumbled an apology back at her, and, evidently relieved, she turned back to her walk.

Minutes had passed at the pond side. Glancing at my watch, I resumed my slow steps until I reached the unremarkable brook near the park's Endymion Gate. It ran steadily onward between its neatly shuttered banks, banners of green weed waving gently in the flow. It was completely man-made, but in that moment I preferred it to many a rural rivulet. The water was so different from the pond's. It was clear as glass. And there was something else about this New River: it was both old and young.

The appointment began. Window looking out over the park; two reasonably comfy armchairs, water jug and glasses. I settled myself into the seat. Opposite me Benjamin did the same.

327

'What have you brought today?' he asked.

'After Jane, I guess that my mother had no space to think about what was going on for me. It's as if she spent a lot of energy denying that Jane had ever existed. The thing about Jane was ... was that I always thought she looked out for me.'

'Your sister, also your guardian angel from what you've told me.'

'Yes. I suppose so.'

'Did you not go to the funeral John?'

'No, I was sent away and didn't even know there'd been a funeral until many years afterwards. When I got home everything had changed. My parents were altered. Harold was quite badly injured – full of metal pins and pints of other people's blood. Yet, I think now that Ulla was damaged even more. All of the childhood photographs had been put away, along with anything that reminded my parents of Jane. But that was my childhood too, shut away.'

'Did they talk about her, or perhaps celebrate her birthday?'

'Good God, no! I don't remember anything like that. Granddad Jack lived with us at that time, so the family went down by one and nobody spoke about it. That's how they managed, how they coped with the pain, I guess ...' It was excruciating to talk about it. It felt as if I was cracking open a carapace, like a crab shedding its skin.

'It seems that you are telling me that your sister didn't so much die, as get erased. Does that sound right to you?'

'Yes. They pressed the fucking button. Delete. We've touched on it before. After that, I changed. Ulla and Harold were in pain, and I suppose I started to take that into account in how I managed myself. I sort of kept myself in check, felt that I should take care of them. So I morphed, became someone else. The river I'd been gliding down became impossible, impassable, and I dammed it up instead... All this stuff, this old stuff of mine. I guess it's what was responsible for my... glitch.'

Benjamin raised an eyebrow.

'OK. My crashing out, my crashing into the buffers.'

I was keeping something back from him. I wasn't ready to disclose it. Instead, I said, 'I'm thinking that one event, the traffic accident, caused two deaths.'

'Go on.'

'Well, Jane died at once. But what I have to face is that Young John began to fade away that night. He died too.'

There was a long pause before he responded. 'Young John. Well, perhaps you're resurrecting him.'

Another week, another session with Benjamin. 'I'm

thinking of my family, my family of origin,' I said, picking up on his manner of speech. 'They were bright, resourceful people, Harold and Ulla, caring ones too. Yet for all the luck they had in getting through the war years, misfortune overcame them in the end. Where does ill-chance come from, Benjamin?'

'Hmm, I don't know the answer to that question! Do you think they tried to stop the ill-fortune coming on to you and Hannah?

'Yes, of course. Maybe that's why they worked so hard to erase all trace of Jane. To delete the past. I'm not sure that it worked, even for them.'

'And has it worked for you?'

'At first maybe it did in a brutal sort of way. But no, because there's a shadow in my head. It'll always be there I guess. You would say that Young John found himself in a different play and had to write himself a new script. I might put it like this: the disorderly bubbling flow that was Young John wasn't possible anymore, so he dammed himself up and let the waters pool. If waters don't flow they become stagnant, the toxins build up ...'

Benjamin thought for a moment. 'And would you say that now you're doing something else? Because it seems to me that you're digging a new channel, finding a new route.'

'I hope I am. But I carry things my parents passed onto me. Without meaning too, I suppose.'

'It seems to me you're saying there's a way in which your parents passed on a taint of misfortune to you.'

'Yes.'

'And have you, are you, passing it on, to Jake?'

I was dismayed. That such a question could even exist, that it could only have one answer, and that it had never before occurred to me to ask it. 'I must do, have done. Isn't that what you're saying?

'Tell me what *you're* saying.'

'The water in the pools of my life wasn't as pure as I always told myself. It contained some dark taint. And how could that darkness not affect my marriage and parenting? If I'm swimming in water that has a tinge of poison in it, the next generation is fated to imbibe it too, isn't it? I mean, how can it not be transferred on?'

'That's one question I *do* know the answer to,' Benjamin said.

An hour flew past. I changed my route back home as I wanted to follow the New River. Through the park it was fenced off, and as it was too shallow for swimming, maybe the fence was there to prevent drowning. That's one activity you don't need deep water for. The river was a mongrel, a hybrid. It took water from the Chadwell and Amwell springs twenty miles north, mingled it with river water from the Lea, and sent it on to London. At that moment I felt a kinship with it.

The men who engineered the New River grew up in Tudor times. As I walked I pictured them in their knee britches and ruffs. It took a few years to build before it opened in 1613. They didn't have the technology to take the River as the crow flies. So it followed the contours, using the landscape and winding forty miles down into London. Chadwell spring is roughly twenty feet higher than the destination at New River Head, so the drop could be no more than five inches in every mile. It was an extraordinary combination of geography, skill and hard work that brought the River into the city.

An idea came to me and as I walked back to the Tube station I called Tony on my mobile.

Do you think of this wonder of its Age, the New River, as a boon for all future ages? Let me tell you that it didn't always flow pure. Time was when it led to the Dark Arch. For some it became a portal to the Styx and to the Underworld. For them, the New River flowed towards hidden, sinister things. And my mind, too, flows towards the Dark Arch.

I closed the door to Benjamin's consulting room and moved to shake off my backpack. For a moment the strap caught on my jacket sleeve. I felt nervous. This was the session: I'd decided to tell him. As I sat down, Benjamin's intelligent eyes were on me.

'What have you brought today, John?'

'Apart from my crooked head, this,' I said. Reaching into my backpack I gave him an A5 envelope. 'You once told me that we do have the power to take underground things up to the surface.'

The copy photograph was a little too snug within its paper sarcophagus, and it seemed to take an age for him to extract it. He knew at once whose face was shown there.

'What are your feelings now you've found it? What did you feel when you saw her face again after so many years?'

'It's strange. I felt confirmed. That Hannah and I hadn't imagined it. I was right: Ulla wouldn't have destroyed Jane's portrait. I'm sad that this image survives and Jane doesn't. But when you say "after so many many years" ...' My words ran into the swamp. 'It doesn't matter,' I said.

'What came into your mind just now?'

'It's not important.'

He gave me a skeptical look.

'OK, then. It isn't so long really since I saw my dead sister. I saw her last year. She was in her school uniform.' And I told him of what happened on Exhibition Road. It was slow. I was a stone, and each word was a drop of blood. But in the end I'd told of all my visions, my sounds.

Benjamin asked me about details, and about my feelings when they were in train. He stroked his chin whilst he thought about it for a while, but didn't seem very surprised. 'I have a feeling that this was the event that prompted you to seek help. Am I right?'

I nodded my agreement. 'It's madness, isn't it?' I said, 'I'm having episodes of insanity. Maybe they'll be others and I'll end up in an asylum, or under a liquid cosh of some concoction of drugs to keep me quiet.'

Benjamin chuckled. 'I've come to know you a little through our sessions together. Would you agree?'

'Of course.'

'It's not exactly my field, but there are reasons apart from schizophrenia why people have auditory or visual hallucinations. And, sorry to disappoint you, they're not exactly uncommon. As far as I can see, you're not the slightest bit psychotic, so I think we can safely rule that out as a cause. We maybe in the realm of the neurological sciences here, rather than in the psychological ones.'

The clock in the consulting room seemed to have speeded up: It couldn't be that my minutes were all ticked away. Benjamin had written out details of some books he wanted me to look at. Just as I was about to leave my chair, I heard vehicles outside sounding their horns. There must have been a traffic hold-up in the street. The clangour was faint, as if the problem was a little way away. There was something I recognised in the minor chord that came to my ears. Benjamin seemed not to have heard it.

Afterwards I walked over to the park café. Tony was there with his latte. I'd suggested that he and I use the morning to walk some of the way along the New River. I got my coffee and sat down at the table with him.

'Thanks for coming along Tony.'

'Oh, I'm looking forward to the jaunt,' he said. 'It's not a stretch I've been down for a long while. Good session?'

'Making progress. He's a wise bird. Do you have regular sessions with him still?'

'Yes, I do. I'll be normal one day and not need therapy!'

'I hope that normal never happens for you!' I said.

Then I rushed onto another topic because, as Tony had once told me, 'my stuff is my stuff'. 'Look, this is where I want to go.' I pulled my blue book from my backpack, and opened it up at some notes I'd made.

'I tell you something,' said Tony, 'in a town as wet as London, and all those small streams flowing into the Thames, it's strange that people had to dig out a whole new river just to get a cup or two of drinking water!'

'Too true. I reckon the River Fleet alone could have kept them in water until the nineteenth century. It started all pure and clean on Hampstead Heath. But it hadn't been looked after. None of the rivers had been. They'd been filled with countless gallons of piss and shit, the puss from God knows how many suppurations ...'

'Thanks for putting those images into my head John! Sure, the Fleet became an open sewer, and I do know what a sewer is! They could still drink the spa water though ... Hey, did you find out why they stopped using the spas?'

'I did. Pollution. In the nineteenth century most of them got poisoned by noxious chemicals from all the manufacturing going on in London.'

'What is it about people?' he said. 'Why can't we manage our own presence here?'

'I suppose why people loved the New River, loved the idea of it, was that it showed that we could manage ourselves if we put our minds to it. We didn't need to elbow out the otter and vole in favour of the rat ...'

I handed him a couple of photocopied articles.

'I think I know a lot of this New River info, John. But what's this? The Dark Arch? Never heard of it.'

'Nobody has. The memory's faded, but it used to be down near where the Essex Road is now, and I wanted to see if there's any trace of it left.'

Tony was looking at an illustration I'd photocopied. 'So this is the New River flowing through it?'

'Yep. It was built to protect the River. Mostly from the dumping of rubbish, and well, you can imagine, the cool of the water would be attractive in summer as a kind of Lido. So the New River Company bricked over the River where the problem was greatest. See there – the Arch was four hundred yards long. Behaviour must have become a bigger problem as London grew.'

'The chumps! They could have had wardens and saved on the building costs.'

'I think they did. From my reading up on it, even four hundred years ago in the River's early days, they understood that it had to be minded. So they had staff whose job it was to patrol it to keep polluters at bay. And, you know, Londoners being Londoners, there were plenty of attempts to draw off the water without permission, so they needed to keep that in check. The problems got too much on that stretch, and that's why they built the Arch.'

'Hmm. They sold the water, I suppose? I guess their reputation would have been crucial. For purity of their product ...'

'Their water was probably safe to drink. Unlike what most Londoners had on offer.'

'It was best to drink beer instead, back in the day.'

'Tony, maybe it still is!'

I was hoping he'd chuckle, but instead he was examining a folded sheet of paper that had found its way into the articles I'd given him. 'You've got something else here. Let's have a look.'

'Oh that,' I said. I hadn't meant to show it to him. I'd said to myself that he might be upset, given how he'd been when talking of the mannequin in the water. Though to be more honest with myself, my interest in it showed more about me than I cared to reveal. 'You solve one problem and create another,' I said. Dark spaces beckon the adventurous, or the foolhardy. Young men would dare each other to swim the full length of the Dark Arch.

Tony read what *The Times* had reported in the summer of 1817:

"A genteel young man of the name of Whitehead was drowned in the New River, a short distance from Islington ...

With a companion he had ventured to swim the length of the Dark Arch. When about midway, he was heard suddenly to cry out and make a struggle in the water ... his companion became alarmed and turned back to the shore ... and called out for help ...

Some people, who were making hay near the spot, hastened to the assistance of Mr Whitehead, and waited on the opposite end of the arch to that which he entered, in the hope of his making his appearance, instead of which they observed the body of a man floating on the water, with all his clothes on. On dragging it on shore, they found that the person must have been some days in the water. They looked in vain for Mr Whitehead, who had sunk to rise no more ... His body was found three hours later ...

The deceased was considered an expert swimmer and has been known to swim nearly a mile at a time. His being drowned is supposed to be owing to his having come suddenly in contact with the dead body already mentioned ...which had so horrified him as to deprive him of his faculties."

'Bloody hell, you don't want to go there, do you? I thought that underground car park was bad enough! Hope at least you've got us a canoe!'

'No, no! Might be good if we could. But I don't suppose it's possible any more.'

Tony broke the silence with which we had started our walk. 'It's puny now though, isn't it? The New River. And here and there, it's disappeared.'

'What do you know about pipe-making?' I asked.

'Nothing at all.'

'Me neither. But it must be hard to make big pipes. Because if they'd known how, it would have saved them the bother of building a river. It must have been worked out in the nineteenth century, because that's when they started putting sections of the river into underground pipes.'

On Green Lanes, the New River went subterranean and there was nothing for us to see. But it did surface again, or at least a part of it did, further down. At Canonbury the remnant reappeared, nourishing a small linear park. This narrow space held a whole ecosystem, plants, insects, birds, so different from the pared down life in the Barbican pond. Down by the Essex Road, search as we might, we couldn't find any trace that the Dark Arch had ever been.

'I'm not sad that it's gone,' Tony told me. 'That I don't have to peer into it, or wade into it with you!' Then in a more serious tone he said, 'And the corpses have gone too. Remember them, John, and then let poor Whitehead rest, and the other guy too!'

Yet the Dark Arch was still in my mind, as near to me in that moment as the New River was to us, falling under our feet into London. I took a breath to clear my head.

'Let's get lunch,' I said, as we walked along Essex Road.

I went underwater that night, even though I was high in the Barbican, six stories up in Mountjoy House.

I'm gliding a few feet above the Great North Road. The tarmac is translucent grey like thick ice. Here the road hides deep waters. And under it there's a man's face with hands clawing upwards, desperate to escape his entrapment by the ice-road. I recognise the features. They're my own. I'm swimming, swimming hard in the Dark Arch, I must get back to the light. I find myself entangled by Jane's weightless body still in her green school uniform. Her face is pale in death. I free myself only to come against the inertia of another body. It's Harold, still in his working suit. He seems asleep there in that dark place. It comes to me that I must leave, or be drowned myself.

I was wet with sweat when I awoke. I wanted Harold to have woken up as well, to be with me then, and not be thirty-five years in the ground. There was no sleeping for me after

I'd written down my dream. That's how I came to be on the Pentonville Road, a sole night walker amidst the dark city. It was still wound down, even if it was preparing to rise from its fitful, insomniac doze. I crossed into Claremont Square. Walking round the raised green at its centre, I peered through the edging fence and the saplings planted there. It's a hidden reservoir, dug out by the New River Company in the early eighteenth century. It's still used to smooth out the peaks and troughs of water demand. I was listening, damping down the hum of the sparse traffic and the faint voices from a drunks' argument a few streets away. I was almost sure it was my imagination, but was that a murmur, a gurgle? As the replenishing streams flowed inward, the whole system was in a slow rhythm, like a tide.

Without needing to consult my map, I left the Square along Amwell Street, named for that clear Hertfordshire spring that has bathed London for four hundred years. Waters that people had willed, laboured, to make flow, and with mindfulness lasting centuries, had kept healthy. A few minutes later I'd walked down to the site near Rosebery Avenue where the New River had ended in a circular pool. It was from there that elm tree-trunk pipes once took the quenching water down into the City. I'd arrived at New River Head. It's not needed any more for purifying the drinking water. The job's done now by modern plants outside the central zone.

New River Head has reversed its function. Not putting water in, but pumping it out. I couldn't hear them, but the pumps were working there, keeping ancient memories at bay. We've tried to delete it, but it hasn't gone away, that old London of marsh and mire, of brackish mudbanks, of slow brooks that meander through the flood plain to pay tribute to the Thames. That's how it was when the Romans came here, coined the name Londinium, and set it all in motion. Different Londons followed them: the streams were put underground, and the Thames walled in. During the years of industrial London, a myriad of thirsty factories pumped up the ground water. Then the smokestacks came down and the town had to find out how to earn its living in other ways. And the waters began to rise again. Yes, the swamps want to come back, back into the Tube tunnels, back into the deep basements of the City's office blocks, to flood up over tarmac and paving stone. So the water company has to pump, to pump night and day to stop the memory of those previous Londons from surging back.

Changing my direction, I moved towards the crossroads with the Farringdon Road. I felt it all settling in my mind, falling into place. Falling was the word, because gravity and topography was what it was all about. Today one hardly notices it, but here one is slightly high: the City lies lower. It's not chance, it's analysis and careful intervention. I never understood it before. The New River is so near the old river. The old Fleet river whose life course took such a wrong turn, whose flow is so different from what nature had set out. Those elm-wood conduit pipes must have been roughly parallel with it, as if the new was intended to make good the failure of the old.

'If I'm swimming in water that has a tinge of poison in it, the next generation is fated to imbibe it too, isn't it? I mean how can it not be transferred on?'

'That's one question I *do* know the answer to,' Benjamin said.

'What then?'

'In self-awareness you become strong. You can deal with it, your body can process it. You have to drink those poison drops yourself.'

A few short yards down Farringdon Road, in an unremarkable side alley, I stood by a street grating outside the silent and dark Coach and Horses pub. I'd expected to have to kneel, and to place my ear close to the grate to hear it. But I didn't even have to stoop. There was a waterfall beneath my feet. The roaring waters called up at me as imprisoned deep in its brick sewer rushed the mistreated Fleet. I emptied my head and listened for a few minutes. I heard piano notes amongst the river's surge. As I tried to make out the melody, human voices rose up too; the timbre of Jane's voice calling for me; Young John's questions; a German inflection in Ulla's voice; Harold weeping; Becky's laughter; Jake's angry words.

However much I do, wherever I sail, my past course will always be there. It's buried, but not forgotten, not now. My eyes welled up. A single tear fell through the grate towards the sunken Fleet.

Jake

Waterloo Bridge
2014

Finn and I walk through drizzle to the church hall by the Park. Most of the students are there already, setting up. 'Right, here's where I change up a gear,' he says and moves into action, arranging cables, lights and speakers. Kimi is directing the exhibitors to places she has pencilled on the plan she carries folded in the pocket of her jeans. I think her face lights up for a fraction of a second when she sees me. But no, it must be wishful thinking: she frowns and moves on at once to intercede in a developing dispute about who goes where. All I really want to do is look at her, but I wrench my eyes away and feign a passion for the artworks.

I catch sight of Marco's red beanie heading for the door. Next to me is his exhibit, a wide computer screen displaying photographs of what happened in Leake Street. I watch as the naked man at the piano morphs into Kimi and me. We stay together a while before my face and body are replaced by a boy on a bike. All too soon that morphs into the Zynebots text and Kimi also has all but disappeared. It's back to the beginning now, and I watch as it loops again and again, calling the two of us into our brief existence and obliterating us until the next reincarnation. I focus on the corner of the piano that is a constant presence, then on Kimi's face, part of it still there until the sequence moves to the beginning once more. As I stand away from the screen, I catch Kimi's eye. The warm, breathing Kimi, that is. She's been watching me from across the room. I can see she's anxious and move towards her when one of the students speaks to her and they both rush to the other end of the hall.

Finn powers up a music box and my composition starts to run. In a flunk, I move over to him. 'It sounds shit, Finn. Is that the best you can do?'

'Keep calm! I can only work with what I have. It's not like I could remove a whole sound system from the Club! It'll be better when I've had a chance to sound check and adjust.'

After ten minutes, it does sound better. I mean, not exactly good, but passable. I realise we'd not talked about when to play it. 'Let's not run it on a loop because Oscar said it needed to be eight minutes, forty-five long, and that's exactly what it is, and all it is. Play it too often and we'll all be sick of it by the end of the afternoon.' So we work out a simple schedule.

There's nothing for me to do. I wander past artists frenetically assembling their pieces. I'm drawn to a triptych called "After Poussin". In the centre panel, the park, my park, has become an oasis. The trees are palms. Four figures cluster around the memorial to the people who died underground in the bomb shelter in the Second World War. The other two panels show desert scenes. In one, dunes have covered up most of the surrounding buildings, although the top halves of tower blocks remain, seemingly deserted. In the opposite canvas, the sand hasn't come up so high, but towers have been broken and blackened as if by war. Or by fire. I peer down at the attribution. The artist is Kimi.

'Hi everyone. Hope you're ready for us. We can't open the doors until this is done.' Oscar has come in with a small group. From their luggage two men produce a lighting rig, stills cameras and a video camera on a tripod. One of them opens a laptop. It's a part of the exhibition I never really believed would happen. In the world for everyone who doesn't get here today, the art show won't happen in this small hall, but in a park-like virtual space. These guys have the software skills to make that happen. I see now why Kimi and the others were so keen to defer to Oscar, to keep him in the tent. My music bursts out. We hadn't agreed to play it now, but Finn must think he needs to check it through again. A woman has come into the hall with Oscar's group. She doesn't have a handbag, but carries a brightly coloured folder. Clutching it as she stands a little apart from Oscar, she seems to be taking everything in. She stays near the door until the music completes. I notice her speaking with Oscar and then she walks up to me. I'd thought she was about the same age as him, but I see now she's a few years older, in her thirties.

'You're Jake?'

'Yes.'

'First time you've written a score?'

I'd never thought of my work as a score, exactly. I'm flattered. Then agitated because I'm feeling I can't control my creation anymore. 'I guess so.'

'It's of interest. Let me have your card.'

I've never had a business card, and I'm kicking myself for not getting one done for this show. Not wishing to seem so unprofessional, I say: 'I seem to have left them at home today.'

'Have mine.' She reaches into her folder, produces a card and hands it to me. It's stylish with the font in indigo. All it says is: Harrison. Producer and Director. Plus her contact details, of course. 'Call me next week. Thursday would be good.' I see her take a slow circuit of the hall to peer at the art, and leave.

In the afternoon, as I walk across Kennington Park, I reckon that it's been a success. The exhibition. Enough people, good response. They weren't all faking it. I'm pleased with how my music went. I stop at the memorial with Maya Angelou's words on it. Walking out past the other memorial carved with the names of the soldiers who died in the two World Wars it comes to me that the names of those who died in the shelter are still underground. The remembering needs effort, as does the hushing up. Because we mostly don't face history. I don't. Don't know very much of it. Oh, I suppose I know a bit of the bigger picture, wars and governments and that sort of thing. Nothing really of the family history. What were the lives like of those past generations of Scriveners who lived here in London? Why should I expend the energy to dig up what they did? Haven't I got to get on with my own life? Or maybe I'm dooming myself to live their lives again.

The elation from the exhibition has worn off and I'm despondent. Kimi had been too busy for me at the exhibition. She'd been giving off 'don't bother me' rays. Finn said she liked me, and maybe that was it. She doesn't want more, does't want even to have the trouble of fending me off. Was it even worthwhile my meeting up with her and the rest of the students for the celebratory drink?

Wandering back to the house, I find myself back at Eugene A. Cernan, looking up at the tree named for the last human being to walk on the Moon. I puzzle over why his name is there on the trunk. Last night I forgot to ask Finn to explain what a Moon Tree was, and he'd forgotten to tell me. Maybe it's just shorthand for a tree named for an astronaut. I look up into its branches, remembering that I was near here when Kimi gave me – what? A magnificent smile? Had I imagined that too?

Someone is standing near me, looking up into the branches. From the corner of my eye I can see it's an old man and I look at him from the side of my eye. He's dressed in a neat but elderly suit and a shirt and tie. His sandals and white socks look out of place. I'm trying not to make eye contact as I sense that he wants to strike up a conversation. My tactics fail.

'How old do you think it is?'

His voice has a high pitch, like old men's voices sometimes do. The question, and his suddenly piercing stare, take me aback. I don't want to get involved with a stranger who might not have all his marbles. There's an uncomfortable pause.

'What? The tree? No idea, er … it's tall … a hundred years?'

'Maybe. People say that the nameplate's supposed to remind us that it flew to the Moon. And Apollo finished in seventy-two, don't you know.'

He points to the line of road trees. 'Yes, people say that

it's here where they fell to rest.'

'What, these trees went to the Moon? It doesn't make sense!' I can't keep a note of ridicule out of my voice.

It's his turn to sound a note of scorn. 'People think the trees were taken into space as seeds, of course. But the real reason for the nameplate has been forgotten. And I was talking about London. How old do you think it is?'

I can't work out if he's mad or wise. 'I'm not sure. The Romans were here … two thousand years?'

'More even than that. But near enough. Too much has happened for past times to be held in mind … most things lie unremembered.' There's another awkward pause between us. 'It's been forgotten … most people don't look … won't see. Things are forgotten here … London town. Well, I must press on.' He turns around as if to get on with the journey he'd first intended. After a few paces he stops for a moment. Turning back, he takes a step towards me again.

'Ah, I'd nearly gone and forgotten what I meant to tell you.'

'Oh – and what's that?'

'Faint heart ne'er won fair lady. Good day, young man.'

I don't speak. Don't know what to say.

He turns away again and I watch him walk up the road in the direction of the War Museum. How did he know what I'd been thinking? Telepathy? It's rubbish. My face, my posture must give out cues. And I'm appalled at the thought that I'm an open book that can be read by this passer-by. Can I be read by anyone? God, I hope not, but then, even Marco had found me out.

Back with a coffee in my room I tap out some notes in my diary. I like simple explanations, in which case the astronaut nameplates would be like memoir, a recording, however modulated and altered, of real events. Thinking like that, I come down on the side of there being a real link with the Apollo moonshots. How likely is it that someone would go to the trouble of getting the nameplates made and hammered onto the trees, if it was all a fiction? And then my view of it swings right around. Isn't fiction all around us in the stories, plays and movies that fill up our consciousness? Creating the Moon Tree myth would have been a lot less work than writing a novel.

Come evening time and I'm forty-five minutes late when I walk through the pub door. I receive a cheer as a greeting. Finn is there with the students. They're all a couple of drinks in. They must have agreed earlier that I should be a source of amusement.

'How did you manage to persuade us all to contribute to

your music video? You've got a nerve, Jake!'

'When you're famous remember us little artists who painted the scenery for you!'

It's joshing, of course, and I'm OK about it. I lead the conversation on to listing the ten best music videos of all time. There's a contest about who can think of the oldest music video, and we go back to the time of the Beatles, someone mentions Dylan in *Don't Look Back*. The one where he has the placards singing *Subterranean Homesick Blues*, and Allen Ginsberg pops into shot.

'Yeah, backstreet NYC,' somebody says.

Well, no, I think.

Kimi says, 'Wouldn't it have been great to have been around then, when it was all new? I want to go to all those places where they made those early music films.'

She has a nostalgia for her parents' time of youth. I've noticed it before. Not something I share. There seems no prospect of detaching her from the group, so I inhale. I have to speak to her then and there.

'What are you doing tomorrow, Kimi?'

'Finishing up an assignment, I'm up against the deadline on it.'

'All day?'

'Umm, yeah. Why?'

'Because I thought we two might meet up.' A couple of the other girls exchange an 'I told you so' glance.

'Monday's better. Agreed to meet a friend at Regents College for a morning coffee. You?'

'First thing in the morning I'm in Barnsbury checking out a piano.'

'Not a keyboard, a piano?'

'Yeah. I've got an idea about changing how I do my music. We could meet up after.'

'Wait a minute. Jake with an acoustic, analogue piano? Made from wood and wire?'

'Yes.'

'Why change?'

'Because ... because sometimes I feel that my work's going round in circles. Like... like it's got trapped in *Groundhog Day*. Maybe the feel of wood and wire, as you said, is a way out.'

'Jake. Jake, you're a surprising guy sometimes. I'll text you Monday if it'll work out.'

And I have to be content with that.

Sunday. A drag. I'm home alone. Everyone seems to have coupled up. Finn is with Amy. I try to get on with the music and tinker for an hour on it. It hasn't worked: I erase what

I've done. Picking up the hand drill, I think that it feels natural in my hand, as if it's always belonged to me. I want to use it again so I rummage in the shed for some wood and make up a speaker stand. It's a rough thing that I end up with, yet I'm proud of it.

Later in the day I feel the need to get out of the house and walk down to the riverside at Blackfriars. Low tide. The muddy banks have become a field for treasure hunters. On the north side of the river the office towers of the City gleam in the morning sun. They remind me of the flamboyant tombstones you see in a nineteenth-century graveyard. Highgate. Or Paris' Père Lachaise where I once went looking for Jim Morrison's grave. Each memorial impressive, in its way. But together they seem ugly, vacuous. They negate one another.

I'm intrigued by the pattern of the water under the Jubilee footbridge. There's a downstream flow; and a submerged force that calls the water back. I guess that's the turn of the tide. Together they drain momentum away and circular eddies move under the pillars. I walk onto the bridge and stand on the edging, leaning out to get a better view. A passing woman gets the wrong idea: 'You alright there?'

'I'm fine. Wanted to get a better view of the water.' It sounds lame to my ears. We're both embarrassed now and she smiles and walks on.

I sit on the steps near the memorial to the Blitz firefighters. I'm thinking about Dad. About me. Like I've got two streams of manhood from him. There's the civil servant bit. Victorian in a way. That Protestant Ethic, full of 'shoulds' and 'oughts'. I can't respect it, even though it's in me too. Then there's – what could I call it? – a more artistic flow. He's all but blotted it out, but it's there. In me they meet and circle around.

Monday. I'm standing outside a barrister's house on Hemingford Road. The piano's in a terraced house that must be worth, what? One and a half, two million quid. I've decided against the Upright that was on offer there. It needs work to put it right. There's another one in Kentish Town. It's a bit of a schlep but I decide to walk it. I check my phone. Must be the hundredth time this morning. When I get to the Brinsmead apartment block off Grafton Road, I don't get an answer on the door intercom and call the mobile number I have. Should have done that before. The woman says that she's already accepted an offer. She tells me about the piano in case the sale falls through, but actually it doesn't sound OK either. A wasted journey.

I'd been wondering if I might do better at a piano showroom. Spend more money, get something nearer what I need. There's one down near the Marylebone Road. The app on my phone shows me a walking route. So I turn onto the Prince of Wales Road and come out at Chalk Farm tube. I walk over the pedestrianised railway bridge into Regents Park Road towards Primrose Hill.

I have an odd feeling that I've been this way before, except that I haven't. Not as a conscious being anyway. Perhaps as a kid? Shit. This is déjà vu. It's unsettling, like a dissonance held soft and long. I decide to walk up the hill to escape the strange sensation. That doesn't work. It's still with me as I look out over the bowl that holds central London. I get to thinking. Round here used to be a favourite of 'creatives' before the houses got so dear that only stars and bankers can afford them. Maybe I've seen a film or a music video of this place.

'And the view is so nice.' I say it aloud. In my head I can hear a song from my childhood days. The next instant her text comes in.

'in hub café in regents p. u?'

'near i think'

'find me here?'

'most def! 30 mins'

In the crowded café it takes me a few moments to spot her. I wasn't expecting her to be with another girl. She looks

Japanese too. The friend's looking at me with interest, and I realise they've been talking about me. That's why Kimi didn't wave as soon as I walked in. She introduces her friend but the name doesn't stick in my head. I'm confused by her presence, crestfallen that she's there at all. We three talk politely for a few minutes when the friend speaks to me. 'Must get back to college now. No need to worry, Jake. You'll have Kimi all to yourself!' She kisses Kimi on the lips and says something in Japanese. Kimi looks embarrassed and pleased. Her friend departs laughing.

It's all a little tense. Neither of us knows what we're doing.

'How was the piano? Did you buy it?'

'No. Not what I was after. It needs too much work to get it right and I'd have ended up spending as much money on it as I would to get a better piano.'

'So what will you do?'

'I was on my way to check out a showroom.'

'I've got an hour or two. Want me to come with you?'

'That'd be great.'

'Let's do it now.'

So in Albany Street we stop off at Marksons and after an hour I've bought a second-hand Upright. They're the place to buy a Bechstein really, but I end up getting a Yamaha. Kimi asks me to play something on it for her before I finally decide. I remember her nostalgia and the Beatles' 'Fool on the Hill' comes to me. Perhaps part of my brain is still up on Primrose Hill. She smiles at me, haggles with Mr Markson on the price and organises the delivery. At the door she says, 'and you've still got twelve hundred pounds or so left. Any plans for spending that?'

I do. Two hundred for taking her out on a date. A thousand contingency. If I need to get to Tokyo. Since I can't exactly tell her, I say: 'Oh shoot. I never asked my mother if it would be OK to have a piano in the living room!' Then I go for it. 'Kimi, I want you to come out with me.'

'I'd like that.'

'Tomorrow?'

'Sure. Tomorrow.'

That was easier than I'd thought.

At night I trudge back to North London. The dunes have come south of the Falloden Way. I slog through them past the skeletons of buildings in the Finchley Road. Sand fills up the ground floor rooms of houses. I tramp along a cutting that once must have held a great railway line heading north. The rails are buried deep beneath the sand. At Chalk Farm I step out and walk to Primrose Hill. The London below me is a small settlement, the Thames a stream. The parks are brown and withered. I do away with gravity and leap from the Hill. I fly, fly over London. To the South, Riddlesdown and beyond are desert, shifting dunes have replaced the rolling green. The people and their houses have gone.

From up here I can see streets I know, neglected, lined by the desiccated bones of trees. Except there is one row of trees still green and lush – the Moon Trees lining the street near my mother's house. I can see lines in the dry parks and gardens – the presence of ancient roads and buildings are showing through. An older London is reappearing. Even in the drought the city's memories have not been completely erased.

There are the tracks made by Finn, the ones he showed me on the app, but now on the ground itself. And my own like dark grooves on a vinyl record. Now I see fainter grooves: they are the footfalls of my forebears. The city holds a remembrance of them too. I see how the separate trails of each generation have criss-crossed, intermingled with each other. In some places they cross my own meanderings, in others they lead to where I yet have to go.

In daylight I catch the dream before it fades. And I tap into my journal: *I've had a vision of London. I've seen it north and south; east and west. Seen its future. With all of the wells drunk dry. Maybe this is the way it all ends. With no tears left to moisten the sands?*

And then I write: *Or is it my own desert future that I've seen?*

We'd agreed to meet in a bar near Waterloo Station.

'Why there?' she'd asked.

'Because,' I'd said, 'I have plans.'

As I walk down Kennington Road, a half-moon is in the sky, even though the summer's daylight is far from done. I'm early at the bar. I sit there looking at my phone as the time moves past the hour. She's five minutes late, then ten. I decide I'm going to play it cool. I won't call until she's thirty minutes late. Time seems to have slowed down, each minute that passes makes me believe that she's changed her mind and decided not to join me. Oh wow! There she is, fixating my gaze. She's wearing a bright green frock and a green beret, like the one Marco had given her for his Leake Street painting.

'Kimi, you look amazing, I mean even more amazing than usual. Is it a special occasion?'

'Of course it's a special occasion. It's our first date, Mr Fool-on-the-Hill.'

'What about yesterday, doesn't that count?'

'No! That was only a meeting and … a little shopping.'

We decide not to have drinks after all and walk up to Waterloo Bridge. I can't find a way of being natural.

'By far the best view from any of the Thames bridges, don't you think?' We stride on, side-by-side but not touching.

'I like the view, yes. You can see so much of London. And there's a good light here.'

'To me, it's lighter in another way. I seem to weigh a little less, not being so … so dragged down by the heaviness of London.' Kimi is listening to me and I feel self-conscious. Somewhere in my head I locate a useless piece of information, learnt from my father, I suppose. I speak it because in that moment I can't trust my own words. 'There was a bridge here before, and it had to be pulled down. People used to call this new one the ladies' bridge, because women built it in the Second World War.' Shit! I sound like a tour guide.

'And will our date consist of you providing me with fascinating information about Waterloo Bridge?'

No, I'm about to say, turning to face her. She's very close by, much closer to me than I'd anticipated. Without thinking, I put my hand under her chin, stoop and kiss her. And she throws her arms around me in a whole body hug. She's kissing me back. Hard. There's a longing in that slight form.

'I've been willing you to do that!' she says.

I stand there for a few seconds taking her in. Hardly able to believe what's just happened. 'Yeah, I guess I've been slow, sort of … stuck.'

'Maybe this can unstick you,' and she kisses me again. 'Now I'm beginning to feel like I'm on a date. So what are we going to do, Jake?'

'I'm going to show you the place where one of the first music videos was shot, that one with Dylan and those placards …'

'But don't we have to go to New York for that?'

'No, we don't. Because the film was made over there! And then I've booked us a table at a restaurant I've heard about. Let's see about going on somewhere after that.'

'This really is beginning to feel like a date.'

She threads her arm through mine as we walk on across the Thames. Across the ladies' bridge, the lovers' bridge, the bridge of song. Walking over the water towards the Savoy Steps, I can hear the music coalesce in my head, music that's never before been heard by anyone, anywhere. Because I haven't laid the tracks down. Yet.

Treadgold Street
2017

'Jake, I might have something for you. We should meet up. My house next Tuesday, two o'clock. That OK for you?'

'Oh, hi Harrison. I'll check', I say, putting my phone down for a moment as I bring up my calendar on my computer screen. 'I can do it.'

'Good. See you then.'

I've only been to her house once before, and that time I came away with an agreement that I would create some music for a production she was involved in. She probably has another one coming up. That's the likely reason she'd want to see me face-to-face. She's one of those people who tends to rely on the phone or on what she calls 'the inter-web'. For a nanosecond I feel elated. Then it kicks in, the sinking feeling. Because this time will be different. Her place is right close to London's newest monument. The one that wasn't meant to be a memorial at all. I don't want to go near it. It's all too horrible, too grim.

I've seen the clock on my phone, and I'm going to be late. Shit. I tap up an Uber. There's one three minutes away. I'm meeting my father in a café near his place in the Barbican. The two of us had a big falling out a few years back, and though we've buried the hatchet, there's still a wariness between us. Guess that's why he suggested coffee rather than lunch.

So, five minutes later, I squeeze past the canvases by our front door and climb into a dented Prius. It's driven by a man from Romania. He's pissed off with something: me, London, the world, I don't know. My phone's in my hand again. WhatsApp has pinged me. Harrison.

'Forgot. Read Hallucinations by O. Sacks.'

WTF? Harrison, terse as usual.

The driver makes an angry hoot at a car that's being a bit pushy in the traffic. 'Who's going to drive you around in all this for these pounds?' he says.

'What mate?'

'When I go off away, somewhere …'

Poor feller. I expect he crash-landed into London from a bad place, looking for the streets paved with gold. And what he's got from it is this car, and me in it. I hate this, this contrast. Because, and I hardly dare think it, but right now, I'm exhilarated by my life.

'Yeah, you're right.'

I'm five minutes late. Dad's already there, of course. He's still one of those must-be-on-time people. He's bagged the corner with the leather sofas. He stands and we exchange a clumsy hug.

'Americano as usual?' he says. 'I'll get myself another.' He comes back with a couple of vanilla slices as well. Once settled, we go through the usual how-are-you-fine routine.

'How's Kimi?'

'OK, very OK.' I steer us away from her. Long habit, but I'm bursting to say something this time. I don't. I'm sworn to say nothing until these first twelve weeks are past.

'In fact,' I say, 'I might be getting some more paid work. Music work.'

'That sounds good. Who from?'

'Remember I told you about Harrison? She liked what I did last year.'

'So she should. It was excellent, Jake.'

Though he says it, and I feel a rush of pleasure at his affirmation, deep down I feel something different. That even now, I'm a disappointment to him. Maybe he holds that wish that I get a 'proper job', like an accountant or something. I suppose that's why I keep things between us top layer, in the treble. We don't go in for any of the basso profundis stuff. Ha! Not even baritone between us. Unsatisfactory, this lack of intimacy, but that's not to say we don't care.

'Dad, have you ever heard of a novel called

369

Hallucinations? By Sacks?'

He looks surprised and I notice that he's gone pale, and I wonder if he's OK. Before I can question him, he goes on. 'If it's the one I know, then it's not a novel, Jake. It's a book of medical case histories. He deals with several different kinds, auditory, visual, déjà vu, *jamais vu*, that sort of thing … Why do you want to know?'

'I should think that someone in Harrison's circle has the idea of doing something with it. You know, for the stage or an indy film.'

'How could that be done? It seems a hard ask.' He starts on his pastry, eating it leaf by leaf. He's flipped it over so that he gets to the icing last..

'Jake, you know I said I was doing some work on our family's history? I've found some notes from your great-grandfather and grandparents. I've written them up. Thought you might like a copy.' He delves into his backpack, a practical, urban one. That's new. Before he retired, he carried an ugly briefcase. A bundle of A4 is on the coffee table and inside I'm sighing: more junk for our tiny flat. Out of politeness, I flick through it. Doesn't exactly look a captivating read. Great-grandpa worked in a piano factory, apparently.

'It ends long time past, in the nineteen-eighties.'

He looks defensive, or is it shyness? 'I'm thinking of, well, I'm writing, some stuff of my own. To get it more up to date.'

The weekend finds me up at Camden Town tube station. The sky is the grey of gunmetal. And now I'm the one who's on time and it's Finn who's late. Though neither of us have lived up this way, we've got old haunts here. He's only ten minutes late, and I joke that he's practically a time-obsessed Brit now. Bear hugs. We make our way up to Camden Lock through the usual crowd of jaunty tourists. They're enthusing about the simulacrum of London they can see in the shops: let's get a union jack t-shirt, a plastic police helmet, a Gandalf tattoo.

'They've sort of bounced into London,' Finn says, 'and they'll bounce out in a week or two thinking they've touched ground, but they haven't. They've just been on a trampoline they brought with them!'

'I prefer the way you did it,' I say. 'Staying years and digging in. Becoming a Londoner, one of us. I wish you weren't leaving, Finn.' That's the cloud over us both. Finn's going back to NZ next week. For good.

'You know, Amy's been back in Auckland a couple months now. Feels longer.'

'How's things over there, how's her mum?'

'The chemo has gone well, but she's not out of the woods yet. Amy's found us a flat. Looks better than I'm used to, though maybe that's not saying much! Hope we'll be able to afford it. Oh well.'

'It must be a weight off Amy's mind, being able to keep an eye on things.'

'Sure. And I'll be able to check out my old dears. How did coffee with your father go?'

'Quite good really. He gave me these notes he'd written up on our family history, going right back a hundred years. I don't think I'll get round to reading them any time soon. Maybe never! Who needs it? There's enough going on for me right now!'

We'd heard about the fire. Nobody was hurt and it was contained, wasn't it? We don't think about it until we get to the corner of Camden Lock. That smell of old burn, of wet smoke, still lingering in the air. What does it remind me of? Tar, or maybe asphalt, burning plastic? I can't place it, but to me it's something unnatural, devilish. Then we see our destination, fenced off and quarantined from the hubbub. 'Camden Lock Vinyl' definitely not open for business as usual. Shattered windows in the small shop upstairs where Finn had tried out a guitar.

'Why does shitty luck always fall on the little guys?' he

says. 'They run those places for the love rather than the money. In a way that makes them the big guys, doesn't it? We rely on them.'

'They must have lost their stock of records. Hope they manage to reopen again.'

In a low mood, we try a record stall on the Jamestown Road market but it's meant for the tourists and not for us.

Finn is shaking his head. 'The zeitgeist's all changed, Jake. A few years ago we were part of a balloon having the oxygen pumped in. Fun it was too. Now the air's being let out, bit by bit. We're the wrinkles on a deflating balloon, that's us. Maybe it is the time for me to go, after all.'

We decide to walk down by the Canal as it flows through Camden Lock. We're walking in the direction of Little Venice when some spots of rain cause us to put our hoods up. We're ambling, just talking easy as we often do. Without warning, the canal water is boiling as the downpour hits it. We jog back, laughing, to the Lock and shelter for a couple of minutes under a market awning.

Finn rubs some water off his face with his hands. 'Should have known to have brought something waterproof. You're never far from a soaking in this town! These were my best trainers too.' He's looking down to his shoes all stained with mud. Somewhere on the way back we went through a soggy patch.

I'm watching a couple of morose record hunters looking at the burnt-out store. 'Fire and Rain,' I say, 'those guys are very welcome to London!'

We head for the World's End pub on the corner near the tube. It's not a favourite of ours, but it's there. It's a cavernous place when no gig is on. Like now, it's completely devoid of atmosphere. I get the drinks. We sit at a table underneath an old pub sign that's hung there. It's bears a picture of a head with a red hat. I squint up at the writing: The Mother Red Cap. According to the notices in the side entrance, that was the pub's name once.

A shiver runs down my back. The old crone above our heads is spooking me. It's a feeling I'd had before, if I can but work out when.

'Do you reckon that's the original sign?' Finn says, 'it looks so pristine. Maybe they've had it repainted.'

Marco's words come back to me: 'we all get overpainted, don't we? And we're all overpaintings ...' I shiver again remembering Leake Street at night, when I felt spooked by my own steps.

'Hey, Finn, Let's move to that corner there, I don't like this table.' So we pick up our drinks and settle the other side of the pub, away from the Mother Red Cap. I tell him about

Harrison's call.

'You're getting known, and it's not before time. Enjoy it man, you've grafted for it.'

It's wonderful that Finn is so upbeat about how things are going better for me. It's not just that the deal's not done yet, but something stops me from being jubilant. 'Other people graft, Finn, but luck doesn't come up for them. Or it burns them. Burns their stock, if it doesn't actually burn their bodies or those of their loved ones. They don't bounce in. They seem to crash through the crust of this town, and get pulled into a deadly place. Finn, don't you ever feel London's got a vicious beast hidden away underneath? That the little guys get fed to it every now and then? It could be me, it could be you. So I always think: why them and not me?'

'Luck of the draw, I guess,' he says.

'Wish I knew where luck comes from, like I wish I knew how it is that I got dealt the musical card. The one that means I can make music. It's just turned up in me, you know. My parents don't do it.'

Finn is looking at me with amusement. 'You told me the family stories your Pa gave you would stay right at the bottom of your reading list. That you'd likely never get round to looking at them. Maybe you should bump that reading up the order, give it some priority.'

Tuesday afternoon comes round all too soon. I arrive at Harrison's terraced house in Treadgold Street. Yet part of my brain is still walking the short distance from Latimer Road station. I hadn't wanted to stare at it, but I couldn't stop myself. And now the very blackness of that tall block[5] has left an after-image on my retina, like a bright light would do. So it's in Harrison's front room with us, even though the windows are in the wrong direction to actually see it from there. Her manner is subdued too. I manage to mumble something about the nightmare nearby, how bad it must have been. She looks at me with her face in shutters-down mode. I've made a misstep: she doesn't want't to talk about the trauma. At least, not with me.

'It was murder, Jake. It still is. Enough said.'

We move on at once to talk about the work. A couple of hours later and I'm stepping out of her place. Despite everything, I'm happy. We've made a deal and for now I'll be able to drop one of the mind-screwing jobs out of my rag-bag of a portfolio. Instead, I'll be working on the music. The next moment my spirits crash as I take it in again, the atrocity

[5] Author's note: In June 2017, a fire consumed a block of social housing apartments, Grenfell Tower. Seventy-two people died. The blaze was spread by cheap, but highly inflammable, decorative cladding that the tower's owners had affixed to the building's exterior.

down the street. I walk past Grenfell Road, this time behaving as the locals do. Not looking up. Averting my gaze from the dark tower, as if I fear that it's home to an evil eye. Wishing I could close my nostrils and seal out the unmistakable smell of burn, four weeks on and still lingering in the air. A policeman, about my own age, lifts up the police tape and walks from the crime scene. His bearing is bolt upright, as if he's a soldier. He wears his face like a mask. I see him stop in mid-stride, exhale, and shut his eyes for two or three seconds.

At first, on the train home, what's on my mind, isn't the music or the deal. Not even on the notices curling in the shop windows, those pleas for information about people who were loved: an old man, our mum, my sister, these beautiful children. It's on the anger, as palpable in the air as the reek of lives burnt up. Unlooked for, music for 'Hallucinations' appears in my brain. I'll base it around a chord in E flat minor. I get to feel I've always known those sounds: dark, baleful, menacing. They've been there forever, under my skin. Or do I mean under the city's skin? Because I can hear where it's cracked open. What comes to my ears from underground is an ancient groan. A growl. It's music that's been waiting a long, long time for me to tune my head, and to write it down.

I fancy that I still have the smell of old burning about me. Has it followed me here? Or is that London's zeitgeist now, the smell of destruction in the air? The feeling comes, and it still is with me: I'd walked through deep shadow, past the place where London's underneath had opened up and an ugly truth had been revealed. They were dragged down, those people, though I can't begin to comprehend why it was them who were marked out to take the fall.

Then the uneasy contrast: I was grabbing another piece of sunlight, climbing up my rung on Treadgold Street.

Acknowledgements

This novel could not have been written and published without the generous support of many people. In particular, the author wishes to thank:

Jonathan Bayer, Ethan C Bontly, Eric Carlier, Lynda Haddock, Alan Johnson, Sylvanie Joyeux, Hilda Kean, Stephen Kramer, Charley Lanning, Paula Lanning, Helen Lentell, Gill Lucas, Joy Lucas, Sean Maher, Maria Mercurio, Jean Owen, Michelle Stokes, Anthony Stone and Seyran Turkmen-Bontly.

I am grateful for the help of many others in reading and offering a critique of drafts of the manuscript. These include Brigitta Ansdell-Evans, Ted Aves, Judith Banbury-Silk, Kerry Beckett, Henry Bewley, Carsten ten Brink, Donna Hillyer, Shirley Hughes, Brenda Kirsch, Gill Lucas, Jean Owen, Nicky Rowland, Blanche Sears and Henry Tegner.

Huge thanks go to my tutor, Mike Walker, and to other creative writers at Morley College, for their wisdom and encouragement.

Finally, most of the book was written at the London Library. I so appreciate the help I received from staff there in researching material for this work.